OATH IN ASHES

A MAFIOSA PRINCESS COMPANION NOVEL

LIZA MALLOY

This book is dedicated to everyone who has struggled to shake a label. Only you can decide who you are. Write your own life story, and keep 'em guessing with those plot twists.

CHAPTER 1

Catalina

The distant ringing of my phone dragged me out of sleep like the tide. I neared the shore of wakefulness, then the sea of dreamland would welcome me back just as the waves tugged again. When I finally pried my eyes open, I was so groggy that I nearly forgot how to answer my phone. Just as I went to click the button, the call ended.

I groaned and tugged my pillow over my head. I could've sworn I'd set my phone to Do Not Disturb the night before, right as I'd chased an Ambien with a couple of Melatonin tablets. I was not normally a junkie—didn't even take medicine most days—but the insomnia of late was killing me.

Judging from the pounding in my head, it was perhaps quite literally killing me.

I lifted the pillow to confirm that I had in fact silenced my phone. That meant the caller was either my parents, whom I'd set an exception for, or that the caller had dialed my number repeatedly in quick succession, thereby evading the curse of Do Not Disturb. But before I could check which, my phone rang again.

The call came from an unknown number, but since I was already wide awake and annoyed, I answered.

"There you are, my little sleepy head. I thought you'd never wake up," the caller greeted me, his syrupy sweet voice making my stomach churn.

"How did you get this number?" I asked, pushing to stand. Rationally, I knew his words alone couldn't hurt me, but I felt powerless lying in bed while talking to him.

"Chica, don't you worry your pretty little head," he said, cackling as if he'd just told a joke. "You'll get it later," he added.

Huh? "This isn't cute, Carlos. We broke up. Stop calling me." I prided myself on keeping my voice firm and level, despite feeling like I was about to collapse. "I'm hanging up now."

"If we can't talk on the phone, I'll just have to come see you again," he said, before I could disconnect.

I cringed. "You don't even know where I live now."

"Don't I?" he replied.

I didn't answer because we both knew he didn't. Not this time.

After the breakup, Carlos had made it abundantly clear that he wasn't the type to take "no" as an answer. He'd called incessantly, dropped by my apartment at all hours, and left creepy notes in my mailbox. The final straw was when I came home from work to find two dead rats sprawled out at my front door.

I'd gone to the cops, hoping to get a restraining order, but apparently, I had no evidence that any of that was Carlos. The security cameras inside the lobby of my apartment building never caught him delivering any of the letters, and no cameras caught him on the day of the rat incident, either. Besides, the officers insisted Carlos's notes were flattering, if misguided, and that no threats had been made.

Part of me wanted to push for some legal protection regardless, but then I'd realized it was pointless. Carlos was not the type of guy to follow the rules. He wouldn't listen to a piece of legal paper telling him "no" any more than he'd listen to me. So, I did the next best thing.

I immediately moved in with my friend, Lexi. After that, the notes stopped. But, so did my sleep. In the ten days since I'd moved, my longest stretch of sleep was probably ninety minutes. In between vivid nightmares so detailed that I could've sworn they were real, I'd wake and relive the actual nightmare that had been my relationship with Carlos. And then I'd spend a decent chunk of time rethinking all of my life choices and panicking about what I'd screw up next.

"I could visit you at work instead," Carlos continued.

"Don't call me again," I repeated, channeling all of my inner strength to stand up to the bully.

"Maybe I'll visit your sister instead," he said.

My breath caught in my throat.

"Although she's not as pretty of a sleeper as you are."

"Stop it! This isn't funny Carlos. You don't even know where I am now, so—"

His sardonic laughter interrupted my rant. "I guess you haven't found the present I left you yet, huh?"

My heart thudded at the implication of his words. I fought the urge to sprint straight to the front door, to confirm if he was bluffing or not. I currently wore nothing but a flimsy tee shirt and panties, so I at least needed shorts or a bath robe to venture into the hall.

"I thought we needed another picture of just the two of us, but then I also wanted a little souvenir. I tried to just cut a little lock, but you keep your room so dark that I took more than I needed for my bracelet."

"What are you talking about?" I said, thoroughly confused by his off-kilter rant.

"I'm just trying to apologize, okay? And my cousin Bella will fix it for you. My treat. Just call her and set up the appointment and then how about I pick you up around eight pm?"

"Why would I ever agree to go out with you?"

My phone chimed with a text right as he answered.

"Because nobody else will ever love you the way I do," he said. "Or maybe because you don't want to share me with your sister, which is what's gonna happen if you ever talk with the cops again. Anyway, look at the picture. It'll jog your memory of how good we look together. I gotta run now but I'll see you at eight o'clock tonight."

He hung up right as I flicked on the bathroom light. I was just going to grab a bathrobe, but the moment I caught a glimpse of my reflection, I stopped dead in my tracks. On the right side of my head, my hair jutted out over the top of my ear. If I hadn't known better, I could've sworn someone had crudely chopped a hunk out of the side.

I reached up to touch the strands, trying to control my breathing. The jagged tips were definitely freshly cut, but that didn't make sense. I'd heard of sleepwalking with Ambien, but if I'd given myself a haircut, why would Carlos have made all those comments about it?

Right as I glanced down to the counter, where a pair of metal kitchen shears rest beside a tuft of my hair, my phone buzzed again, reminding me of the unread message. Dread flooded my core as I waited for the image to fill the screen.

The blurry photograph was of me and Carlos. He was grinning widely, but my expression was blank and my eyes were closed. Actually, I appeared to be asleep in the photo. Then, I looked closer. The right side of my hair had been chopped in the photo too.

A chill ran down my spine. Carlos had been in my bedroom, and I hadn't even woken up.

I dropped my phone and screamed until my throat went raw.

Angelo

I sipped my Campari then moved on to the next clue on the crossword. "Four down," I read aloud. "Fate or destiny, starts with K."

I began to write "karma" without waiting for input from my mother, who was seated beside me. She tsked loudly, causing me to pause. Then, I noted that the clue called for a word of six letters, not five.

"Try kismet," she suggested. "That's when—"

"I know what kismet means," I interrupted, my tone perhaps sharper than necessary given the context.

My brother Matteo chuckled from across the room, and I shot him daggers with my eyes.

This was what my life had evolved into as of late. As if my situation wasn't pathetic enough, what with my last girlfriend having died shortly before I was supposed to propose, now I spent my weekends doing crossword puzzles with my mother.

"Is dad coming or not?" I snapped. "I'm hungry."

"Clearly. You seem cranky," my mom said.

I blew out a sigh and checked my watch. We were supposed to have a family dinner at seven pm. It was already a quarter till eight and my father had yet to make an appearance.

Not that I had anything better to do than wait.

"You know what might perk you up?" Mom asked.

"More crossword puzzles?" my brother suggested.

"I think you're getting bored," she said, ignoring Matteo.

I didn't disagree. I'd come to Italy with my parents and brother less than a week ago, and already, I'd run out of things to do. From the moment our flight had landed in Rome, it had been abundantly clear that the only reason I'd been invited along on this trip was because my family was worried to leave me in the U.S. with only my younger sister available to babysit me.

My brother was taking over a few business prospects from

our dad, and my mom planned to catch up with countless relatives. But I was just along for the ride. As the technical heir to the family business, I needed to maintain some oversight on all aspects of our holdings, but certainly not the level of detail that this trip entailed. Besides, all of the businesses I managed on a day-to-day basis were based back in the States, in Bridgeport, Connecticut.

"It's time you start dating," my mom continued.

I snapped out of my daydream and peered up at my mother. Matteo perched on the edge of his seat, watching us both as if ready to break up a fight if need be.

"I'm not trying to be insensitive. We all understand you've gone through something traumatic, but you're not going to move on if you don't try. I'm not asking you to settle down right away. Just go on a date. Something casual."

I caught my brother's eye as he bit back a laugh. He was well aware of the "casual" activities in which I'd been partaking over the last few months. Not so much dates as hookups, but whatever. Sex was much easier to handle than relationships.

"Ma, I appreciate the concern, but I am done dating. For good."

She started to frown, but just then our dad burst into the room. His scowl alerted me that his mood was probably about as chipper as my own. "Who are you dating?" he asked.

"No one. He said he's done dating," Matteo clarified.

Dad shrugged and poured himself a drink. "Not a bad decision, in this line of work." He sat beside our mother, who didn't seem put off by the comment, even though she was married to someone involved in the exact line of work I was taking over.

Mom warmed all the food and began serving us all. "Was that a work call?" she asked Dad.

He shook his head, which meant that he'd discuss details in front of her. "No, an old friend of mine is having some issues with his daughter. Apparently she fell in with the wrong crowd and now her old boyfriend is stalking her.

I cringed. Had my mom not been present, I would've inquired why they didn't just kill the guy. No, I wasn't a total psychopath, but honestly my tolerance for dirtbags was pretty low at the moment.

Dad forked a bite of pasta into his mouth before continuing. "Cops can't help much, and apparently the guy is sort of an up-and-coming player in the Mexican drug cartel out of Jersey, so—"

"What's his name?" Matteo interrupted.

"Carlos Ortiz."

Matteo shrugged, not recognizing him, but something about the name pinged my memory. I chewed for a moment, and then it came to me.

"I know him. His guys screwed something up at the ports with one of their clumsy drug deals and it delayed one of my customer's legit shipments. We lost like fifty grand over that deal."

My dad gazed at me as if trying to decide if he could do anything with that information. A moment later, he resumed eating.

"So why call you? Did he want a favor or something?" Mom asked.

"Oh, right. Well, his daughter is the same age as Giada. He was thinking maybe the two of them could be friends and that would somehow keep her safe just by virtue of our strong reputation."

"I can't imagine that would help anything to just be a friend of ours," Mom said.

"That's what I told him," Dad agreed. He gazed out the window while chewing, then shook his head. "It's a pity because I'd love to help him out. Jorge is an old friend and his wife and two daughters have always been sweet. Once upon a time, Jorge probably could've taken care of this sort of problem himself, but he was diagnosed with Parkinson's a few years back. Poor guy walks with a cane now and he's selling off his old business holdings."

Dad's phone pinged, and it was a text image. He zoomed in on what appeared to be a family photograph and smiled. "That's his oldest, Catalina Lucia. You probably met her when she was younger," he said, showing the picture to our mother.

She shrugged, and then Matteo and I both glimpsed the photo. Dad had zoomed in on a pretty brunette. She was petite, with long brown hair and bronze skin. Matteo wiggled his eyebrows at me.

"What if one of us dated her?" Matteo suggested. "That couldn't hurt, right?"

I stomped his foot so hard under the table that I wouldn't have been shocked if I'd broken a toe. But mischievous Matteo barely even flinched.

"Well, it sounds like her ex-boyfriend is pretty determined. I think she'd need to move in to make much of a difference, and even then—"

"Yeah, seems like a bad plan," I interrupted. "So, tomorrow, are we—"

"Now hang on," Matteo jumped in. "I think this is kismet!" He paused and smirked at his use of the word. "Mom was literally just musing about how it's time Angelo get back into the dating game. And Angelo here is always complaining about how you're slowly leeching the business away to Luca."

"I am not!" I shouted, although I quite literally bitched about that nearly every day. In my defense, I was right. Ever since our sister Giada had married Luca, heir to the notorious Marino family business, Dad had been gradually shrinking my piece of the inheritance pie. I didn't disagree that we needed to stay on good terms with the Marinos, or that it was a bad idea for us to work together. But I drew the line whenever Dad seemed to think he needed to reward his son-in-law with a portion of the business that I was supposed to take over.

My dad held up his hand like a referee, but Matteo kept going.

"It's like I always tell you. Once you're married, Dad will take you more serious," he said.

"Married?" I roared. "First you want me to date some stranger, now I'm getting married? Are you two hearing this?" I turned to our parents, for once expecting immediate support from them.

Instead, my parents both appeared deep in thought. Then, they exchanged a glance with each other.

"You have got to be kidding me," I said, dropping my napkin over my plate and scooting away from the table. "This is the most absurd idea I've ever heard. Send me the ex-boyfriend's address and I'll take care of this the old fashioned way."

I stormed off to my room, which felt horribly inadequate for making a dramatic exit. At thirty one years of age, I owned my own house, back in the U.S. But when the family traveled to Rome, we generally stayed together, in a villa that had been in our family for generations. Usually, that arrangement felt practical, but tonight, it just made me feel childish.

I'd barely had an hour alone when there was a soft knock on my door. I didn't respond, but my father let himself into the room a moment later. He sat on the foot of the bed, adjacent to the sofa where I sat, reading the same page of a book over and over.

"I'd like you to listen before you make up your mind," he began.

I gazed up but said nothing.

"Your brother made some fair points, but no one is forcing you into anything. Your mother likes the idea because she feels you're in a rut with your personal life. You tell her you don't want to date, and we both understand why, but this seems to avoid all of those pitfalls. And if we agree to some relatively short period of time, like twelve months, then you may be out of your rut by the time the arrangement ends."

I grimaced at his word choice, but remained silent.

"As for the other part your brother said, well I don't trust Luca more than you. But the fact that he's settled down does mean he's stable in a way that you aren't. And I don't want to patronize you, but there's just something different about the way you focus on business once you've got a family to consider, too."

"Even if it's a fake family?"

My dad shrugged. "I don't know. Maybe? But either way, your mom is convinced you couldn't possibly be more miserable than you are now. And it would be helping an old friend and making a huge difference for the family business you're so eager to take over."

"How so?"

"I haven't discussed the details, but I figure if we save Jorge's daughter, we don't have to enter the bidding war for his shipping contracts. He just gives us that part of his business as a thank you."

"How much is that worth?" I asked. "Like, in dollars," I clarified, lest he thought I was asking about the stain it would leave on my soul.

"I'd have to look into it. I'd planned to offer at least a few hundred thousand as a starting bid, but I hadn't researched how much higher I'd go."

I rubbed my fingers against my temple. Having my father in my debt to the tune of half a million dollars wouldn't be bad. Nor would getting my mother off my back. But at the cost of my sanity? No thanks.

"Her name is Catalina Lucia Alvarado. She's originally from California, but she's been living in New York since graduating high school. She's a librarian." My dad stood and started towards my door. "Just look into her and tell me what you think tomorrow. If you're not on board, we won't even propose the idea to Jorge."

I said nothing as he left the room.

CHAPTER 2

Angelo

I wanted to dismiss the idea as ridiculous and never think of it again. But my brain had other plans. I lay awake thinking about it all, listing in my head over and over all the reasons it was a terrible idea. Yet before I even fell asleep, I caught myself countering several of my own points.

My life was already miserable and why make it worse? Well, maybe it couldn't actually get any worse.

I was a mess romantically and had no business dating? Hmm…this arrangement would take me out of the dating game for a full year, giving me the time I needed to fix my head without any romantic distractions.

I needed to focus all of my attention on my work, since that was the only area of my life that wasn't a dumpster fire? Well, this deal would help my dad and improve our business.

I finally quit arguing with myself and turned to the computer. I did a quick internet search on the girl. There were more Catalina Alvarado's than I would've expected, but a link to each of her social media pages popped up beside the picture Dad had shown me. The girl appeared to post her every move on Instagram, but at least she'd had the sense to set her account to private. I clicked to follow her through my fake account that I'd set up for strictly stalking purposes, then proceeded with my research on other sites.

The internet revealed her old high school and college info and a handful of other random tidbits. There were also dozens of photos of her at various public events over the past couple of years. Catalina was a fervent advocate for public libraries too, it seemed that her branch employed Catalina as the public image of the library whenever possible. I suspected that was because her face—and the rest of her—was definitely easy on the eyes.

Catalina looked nothing like most women I'd dated in the past, and was nearly the polar opposite of Julia, but I couldn't deny she was attractive. Her green eyes seemed almost too big for her face, particularly when paired with the cute button nose. Her full lips curved into a bow, and something about the smile, combined with the twinkle in her eyes, convinced me that Catalina was a force to be reckoned with despite her small frame.

My phone buzzed, telling me my request to follow her had been approved.

I scowled.

I'd hoped she'd accept the request, but also wished she was wise enough not to. If the girl truly had a scary stalker, she needed to be careful. What was the point of setting the account to private if she was going to grant access to random strangers anyway? For all she knew, her psycho ex had set up this fake account, not me.

I scrolled down the page, overwhelmed with the quantity of photos. She literally documented every day of her life, sometimes twice. Most of the pictures were of Catalina, either alone or with others, but she also photographed places she went and, occasionally, foods she ate. I may have lingered a tad longer on the bikini pictures than her others, but she was undeniably sexy no matter the outfit.

I wasted nearly two hours on her page before silencing my phone and attempting to resume my efforts to sleep, but by then, I was doomed. All I could see when I closed my eyes was the image of those hauntingly beautiful emerald eyes, seemingly beckoning to me to rescue her.

I eventually fell asleep, but woke more exhausted than I'd been the night before. I dressed and went to find my father, relieved that he hadn't yet left for the day.

I selected a ridiculously small teacup—the only type of hot beverage dishes we had in this villa—and filled it to the brim with coffee, adding just enough milk so I could down the first cup like a shot without burning myself. Then I poured myself a second cup and sat across from my father.

"I looked into the girl," I said. "And I have some concerns."

My dad looked up, both intrigued and surprised.

"First, what makes you think she'd agree to this, even if her dad does?" From what I gathered about Catalina, she wasn't accustomed to doing what she was told. She appeared to live a very independent life.

"My impression from her father that she is very scared at the moment. Her ex has a lot of connections, he's made threats against her family, and he broke into her house while she was sleeping and cut her hair. The police can't help, and if she moves back home, she loses all her friends and her job. I think she's at the point where she knows she doesn't have any other options." He shrugged. "But if not, then you'd just have to handle it like any other problem. You seem to have good control over your men, so I don't anticipate you being bested by a girl."

I considered that, then moved on to my second concern. "Marrying her off won't do any good if no one believes that it's real. But if she needs a fast solution, how would we possibly convince anyone it was real? Everyone knows I'm single."

Now my dad smiled. "Your mom was talking about that last night. We could tell people you two were childhood friends and have kept in touch over the years. You've been talking a lot lately and she's really helped you through everything since… your false arrest."

I cringed at his terminology. Even though no official charges had even been filed, I would never feel my arrest was "false" when I had, in fact, intentionally shot and killed my girlfriend. Just because the law yielded a convenient loophole didn't change my actual guilt.

"You haven't been yourself lately. I don't think it's too much to ask people to believe she talked you into a last minute leap of faith," Dad continued. "And as for this girl, well, it seems like she's impulsive by nature and an elopement is well in line with her character."

I agreed with his assessment of Catalina, but took issue with part of his plan. "She'd never actually elope. She documents everything on social media. She would never get married without at least her family present, maybe a couple of friends. And she'd take hundreds of photos."

My dad cringed at the notion of posting on social media. I shared his sentiment. The idea of broadcasting my entire life to the world, particularly in my line of business, repulsed me. And if I were to marry Catalina, she'd have to stop sharing so much. But I'd have to implement that rule later, if we actually wanted people to believe the arrangement.

Still, my dad said nothing, letting the silence stretch between us.

"Fine, I'll sign on for one year if Jorge agrees to give us the business you want in exchange." I stood and refilled my coffee cup a third time, then sauntered out of the room. I walked past my mother who, judging from the shocked look on her face, had heard the entire conversation.

Then, I marched straight out the door. I needed some fresh air.

Catalina

I tied my fluffy pink bathrobe over my pajama pants and plopped onto my bed, half expecting to still see the pictures of One Direction that had covered my ceiling the last time I'd lived at home.

It was weird being back home, even if virtually nothing—other than the posters—had changed since my childhood. The bedding was still pink, as were the pillows on the chaise lounge beside the bed. The curtains were white, but with pink floral accents. Even the bathroom rug was pink.

Aside from the excess of pink, the room was fairly sophisticated. High-end furnishings filled the space, and an abundance of natural light poured through the many windows. My framed high school and college diplomas hung evenly above the desk, and limited edition Fernando Botero prints filled the wall above the bed. The only part of the room that clearly hadn't been approved by a designer was the side opposite from the window, where boxes containing the remnants of my most recent former life were stacked well beyond five feet high.

I had not unpacked anything yet. Actually, I hadn't decided if I was ever going to unpack anything. I couldn't just hibernate in my childhood home forever. Maybe I would stick around and help my mom for a bit, but the prospect didn't thrill me. Nor did the other option, moving far away and never returning.

I had some friends out in L.A., and the idea of year-round sunshine didn't totally repulse me, but my dad said Carlos had too many contacts there. If I wanted to distance myself, it would have to be someplace Carlos would never go, like one of the

Dakotas, or Canada. And even if I did move, I'd still have to stay off the radar, going into my own sort of unofficial witness protection program. At least until Carlos moved on. As stubborn as he was, that could take years.

A knock on my door interrupted my thoughts. I could tell by the force of the knock—or lack thereof—that it was my mom, so I didn't bother to move from my cozy perch in the bed.

"Come in," I called.

An uneven shuffle of footsteps ensued, so I turned, seeing both my mom and my dad entering the room. My dad now walked with a cane, but only in private. In public he still strived to maintain the healthy, strong persona that he'd cultivated in his younger days, before his Parkinson's diagnosis.

The change in his appearance had not yet transformed my perception of him though. Even when he appeared weak, I remained acutely aware of the power he yielded over my life, and an inkling of fear rolled through my belly each time he approached.

"Do you have a minute?" he asked, sitting down at my desk chair.

I blinked, trying to decipher if he was joking. I was a grown ass woman, hiding out in my childhood bedroom, unable to return to my own apartment or job or even see my friends. What exactly did he think was occupying my time?

"Yeah," I finally said, scooting to sit at the end of the bed.

My mom sat beside me, flashing that artificial smile that moms always use when they're about to share bad news and don't want their kids to throw a tantrum.

"We have good news," she said, her words a stark contrast to her pained expression.

I quirked a brow.

"We found a solution to your, uh, little problem," my dad said.

"Our problem," my mom corrected, shooting him a pointed

stare as if his terminology had somehow singlehandedly destroyed our family unity.

"I'm not moving to Canada," I blurted out.

"No. I found a way to keep you safe without you having to move far away," Dad said.

I gazed around the room, wondering if their big surprise solution involved me living as a prisoner nestled within my childhood bedroom.

"You can keep your same friends, your same job even," my dad continued.

"Same apartment?"

He shook his head, but that really wasn't a dealbreaker. My apartment wasn't great. Nothing in New York was, even with a rich daddy paying.

"You'll stay in a house in the suburbs," my mom chimed in.

"Okay. How exactly is this going to keep me safe? Is the plan just to murder Carlos and hope his buddies take the hint?"

"Catalina Lucia! We do not joke about such things in this family," my mom scolded.

My dad's more measured expression made me think he'd considered that option and dismissed it, but I wasn't about to judge.

"Do you remember my friend Marco Conti?" he asked. "From the club?" He paused. "Taller man, dark hair. Italian?"

I shook my head, not having the energy to tell my dad that all old, white guys looked the same to me.

My dad frowned. "He has two sons and a daughter. I'm sure you used to spend time with Giada when you were little."

I shrugged.

"Just tell her," my mom urged.

"Mr. Conti has a successful shipping business and tons of contacts in the business world. He also has some…less savory connections. No one messes with the Contis."

"Okay. What does that have to do with me?"

"If you're associated with the Conti family, no one will touch you, either."

"Pretty sure that's not how that works. If it did, I'd think your name would be good enough."

My father forced out a sigh so low that it resembled a growl. "They have a different culture and different rules, Catalina. If you marry one of the Conti boys, their entire family and every single man who works for them will be tasked with defending you. Most likely, their reputation will be enough to keep Carlos away, but even if he did try anything, the Conti's associates would keep you safe."

"What reputation?" I asked, still struggling to remember who these people even were. Then, I focused on a different word my dad had spoken. "Wait, marry? You want me to marry someone?"

It's possible my voice got a little loud, as my mother cocked her head to the side and said, "Oh sweetheart, don't be so dramatic."

I opened and closed my mouth several times without deciding on something to say. Finally, I went with the truth. "I appreciate your willingness to try to think outside the box and help me out here, but I got myself into this mess. I will figure out a way to get out of it. Even if it involves Canada."

Now my mother rolled her eyes, like I'd threatened to move to the moon and not a few hundred miles north. "Don't be ridiculous, Catalina. You love your life here. And besides, we don't even know that moving would keep you safe. Carlos could find you anywhere. Hiding isn't the answer. This plan will work, and it's not even forever. After a couple years, Carlos will have moved on and if you're not happy with the Conti boy, you can separate. But you might not even want to. The statistics on these arranged marriages are pretty astounding."

I tuned out as my mom yammered on about the low divorce rate amongst arranged marriages. I tried to piece together the insanity of my current predicament. I pulled out my phone and ran a quick google search of Marco Conti. The first few hits were articles about his business and all the charitable stuff he was involved in. I clicked on a couple and saw photos of him, one picture of his wife, but nothing about the rest of the family. Finally, I scrolled down and saw an article about the Conti's youngest child.

A professional portrait caught my eye first. There was a young couple, dressed in their wedding attire, and then what I assumed were their families standing beside them. The caption identified the couple as Giada Conti and Luca Marino. I didn't bother to look at the Marinos, but I did zone in on the two young men beside Giada, identified as Matteo and Angelo. Those had to be her brothers.

I glanced back to the top of the article and nearly choked on my gum reading the headline. It said: "Local business leaders and suspected crime syndicates join forces to celebrate the nuptials of their children."

I turned the phone to my father. "Is this who you're talking about? You want to marry me off to the son of a mob boss?" I rose to my feet, too appalled to sit any longer. "The Italian mafia. Really, Dad?"

He maintained his composure. "Mr. Conti has never been convicted of a single crime. Those mafia comments are just slurs people use when Italians are successful in business."

"Right. And you think I'll be safe because Carlos would never hurt me as long as I'm part of a totally legitimate, non-violent family?"

Now, he scowled. "I said you'd be safe because Carlos would know their reputation. Just because I know Marco would never hurt a fly doesn't mean Carlos does. I'm sure he believes them to be true gangsters, and he'll keep his distance."

I rolled my eyes. This was next level crazy. "Jesus," I mumbled.

"Catalina Lucia!" my mom scolded, making the sign of the cross.

"I'm not marrying a mob boss. Thanks, but no thanks," I said, dropping back to my seat to signal the conversation was over.

"It's not up for debate," my dad said. "The deal is done. They've already agreed. We will leave for Italy on Tuesday. You'll be wed on Saturday."

I felt my jaw drop. "That's less than a week from now. I'm not… You can't…" I tried to slow my breathing, but just kept panting. "Do you even know which guy you're forcing me on?"

My father's frown deepened.

I thrusted the phone to him again. "Which one am I supposed to marry, Matteo or Angelo?"

He took the phone from my hand and enlarged the photo before squinting at it.

"Oh my God. You don't even know? Did you just call all your friends and see who would take me?"

"Of course not. This wasn't even my idea. I called Marco for help and he suggested it. It's um… Well, Angelo is the oldest and he is taking over all the business stuff, so…" he paused and scrolled through the article. "Matteo is the one who's your age."

"So it's Matteo?"

He nodded. I opened my mouth to protest further, but my father turned to my mom and asked her to leave us alone for a minute. That was never good. My mom stood and smiled at me before leaving.

"Just keep an open mind, sweetie," she said, pulling the door shut tight behind her.

The pool of dread spread from my core, sending shivers down my arms.

My dad didn't wait long enough for me to speak before jumping into his own lecture. "Actions have consequences, Catalina. I realize this isn't your first choice, but you don't seem to understand the gravity of the mess you've gotten yourself into here. Carlos could kill you. He could go after your mom or sister, too. Is that what you want?"

I shook my head.

"It's only one year. You have to admit you haven't done a good job of choosing your own romantic partners, so I believe this forced pause will be good for you. The Contis will keep you safe."

"Look Dad, I get it. I screwed up. And I'm sorry. But I'm not going to marry some stranger just to—"

"You don't have a choice, Catalina. The deal is done. You will go through with it and you will behave. I'm not going to be around forever, and I can't be worrying about you causing problems on top of everything else. Let your mom focus on Valeria for once. Let me concentrate on my health. It won't kill you to put the family first for a change."

Okay, *ouch*.

"Does Matteo know about this deal?"

"Yes. He agreed to it already."

I wasn't sure what to do with that piece of information, but I supposed it was good. Still, he couldn't know much about me.

"What if he hates me?" I asked.

My dad shrugged as if that were a likely possibility. "His father has always described him as an easygoing, laid back guy. I think you'll be fine, but if not, that's okay. Matteo doesn't have to like you to keep you safe. He works and travels a lot. You can lead your own separate lives."

I rubbed my temples, trying to massage away the impending stress headache.

"There is one thing, though. For this plan to work, people have to believe the marriage is real. You cannot tell a soul that you're just marrying him for protection. Not even your closest friends."

"Kristi and Madison will never believe that I just happened upon some random guy and married him the next day. Neither will Lexi."

"I think they will. You're not exactly known for making well-reasoned romantic decisions. Besides, you and the Conti boy are old family friends. Tell your friends you grew up together, had a fling a few years back, and have kept in touch since. Anyone who knows you will believe you jumped headfirst into some whirlwind romance."

I suspected it would take me hours to unpack all the insults from that part of his lecture. "Does Valeria know the truth?"

He dismissed the question with a single shake of his head. "No, and I think it's best if she doesn't. I don't want your sister worrying. She'll accompany us to Italy and your performance at the rehearsal and wedding will be so authentic that she won't question a thing."

He braced himself on the cane and ambled out of my room without another word.

I reached for my laptop and typed Matteo Conti into the search engine. An hour later, I had exhausted the internet sources and knew virtually nothing about my future husband. He was the second in line to inherit the Conti "empire," he spent a lot of time in Rome, and he'd been shot a few years before.

Yeah.

Shot. Like, with a gun.

On the plus side, Matteo looked a lot less scary than his brother. Everything I read suggested that Matteo was smart and nice and not really cut out for a life of crime. Angelo, on the other hand, popped up as a suspect in a whole slew of heinous crimes. Multiple articles used words like "menacing" and "cold" to describe his personality and business dealings. And while I didn't see any sign that he'd ever *been* shot, his last girlfriend actually died in a shooting.

Yikes.

Of course, my toxic trait was letting myself overlook the whole mafia thing long enough to drool over a few photos. Matteo cleaned up well, and the man looked good in a suit. And in one picture, which looked to be from his sister's wedding reception, he'd removed his suit jacket and I could truly appreciate the way his toned arms filled out his dress shirt. The guy had muscles. And he was tall, with thick, dark hair, and deep brown eyes. If he weren't a criminal overlord, he'd probably be my type.

Actually, the criminal thing probably made him more my type.

Well, no matter.

I was about to click out of the photo and sneak downstairs for some food when my eyes happened upon the photo's caption. I frowned, leaning closer to the screen. According to the article, the photo I'd been ogling was Angelo, not Matteo.

I clicked through a few other photos and realized my mistake. Both men had dark hair and olive skin, but Angelo was several inches taller than his brother. He also appeared to have several more pounds of muscle, but that attribute was offset by the fact that he was clearly a total sociopath.

My phone buzzed, alerting me to a message in the group chat with Kristi and Madison.

"We miss u! Planning trip to visit ASAP. Beach day?" Kristi had written.

I smiled at their attempts to cheer me up, but now felt even more lonely. If I had to lie to my best friends, I'd never survive. I stared at the message for a moment, then replied as truthfully as I could.

"Love & miss u both 2. Workin on plan 2 move back but in the meantime, the fam is headed to Italy for last min vacay."

"Good 4 u," Madison replied. "U deserve 2 relax."

I chewed my bottom lip. Something told me this vacation would not be relaxing.

CHAPTER 3

Catalina

$\mathcal{L}$ess than a week later, I found myself sitting in an ornately decorated hotel room in the center of Rome. My parents and Valeria had gone out to lunch, leaving me alone to meet my betrothed. I paced until I heard a single knock at the door. Peering out the peephole, I saw a man in trousers and a button-down with his hands tucked in his pockets. He'd angled away from the door, so I saw only profile, but he the dark hair matched what I was expecting.

I opened the door a crack, then frowned when the man turned to me.

"Angelo," I breathed, so quiet I didn't think he heard.

A flicker of concern crossed his face, but then he extended his hand. "Angelo Conti," he said, his voice deeper than I'd imagined.

"Catalina," I replied, limply accepting his hand. "But my friends call me Lina."

He quirked a brow then brushed past me into the room, helping himself to a sparkling water from the mini-fridge before sitting in an upholstered accent chair.

I shut the door, then sat on the couch adjacent to him. "I'm sorry," I said. "My dad told me it would be Matteo."

This tidbit seemed to amuse him. "Sorry to disappoint," he said. "Although, if I understand your needs correctly, Matteo would not have been the right person for the job."

A more polite person would've assured him that it was not a disappointment, but I wasn't really sure what I felt. Angelo was different in person than he'd seemed online. He was simultaneously more intimidating but also more, well, appealing. The tenor of his voice sounded sensual, and even though his tone was cold, something in his expression wasn't.

"You're beautiful," Angelo said, snapping me out of my thoughts. His brows furrowed as if this information somehow irritated or surprised him. He paused, but I couldn't think of a response before he continued.

"You look pretty in your pictures, but they don't do you justice."

"And that bothers you?" I finally asked.

He tipped his head to the side. "I only wonder what you plan to gain from this."

I suppressed an eye roll, perfectly aware of how much the men had already discussed the terms of the arrangement. "I think you know."

"You didn't ask for this; your father did. So I'd like to hear. What are your demands?"

"My demands," I repeated, questioning.

Angelo blew out a sigh. "Your expectations," he clarified. "What do you want from me?"

I tried to hide my surprise at the question. I gazed to the window, noting the clouds had shifted, revealing a perfectly blue sky. I longed to breathe the fresh air from the park surrounding the stuffy building in which we sat. Ever since I'd entered, I'd felt claustrophobic, almost as though I were suffocating.

The entire time I considered his question, I assumed I'd reply tritely that I had no expectations whatsoever. But when I opened my mouth to speak, something entirely different emerged.

"I want you to be faithful, to uphold all of the marital vows, as long as we're married."

Angelo choked on his own laugh. "No one would believe I could tolerate monogamy that long."

I didn't bother to mask my disgust at his response.

"A compromise," Angelo proposed after a moment. "I'll be discrete. And you'll never know any different than if I agreed to your terms." He paused, apparently for me to consider his counter.

I waited a few breaths, then nodded my agreement. "What are your demands?" I asked.

He smiled in response, but in a way that reminded me of a cartoon cat who'd just caught the mouse. "If I have to play the part of a real spouse, so do you. In every possible way." Angelo's gaze locked on me, his nearly black eyes drawing me in. Then, he abruptly turned, breaking the spell.

"Wait, what does that mean?" I asked, but he was already gone.

⁂

Angelo

I had planned to stay longer, to actually attempt to get to know Catalina that afternoon, but I couldn't. From the moment I'd entered the room, an uneasy tingling filled my veins. I felt drawn to her in a way I shouldn't.

If this plan stood any chance of success, I needed to stay focused. I couldn't let myself get distracted by her obvious good looks, or the way her chest heaved when she was nervous, or those breathy exhales she used instead of fully speaking her mind. I couldn't dwell on the softness of her skin, her sweet smell, or her captivating eyes.

I couldn't let myself fall for the girl I was supposed to protect.

I was not going to ruin another life because I couldn't keep my head in the game.

My driver, Stefano, took me straight to a nearby osteria. I texted my brother to meet me at the familiar wine bar, then ordered a stiff drink while I waited.

Matteo sauntered in right as I started my second drink, looking like he didn't have a care in the world. When he saw me, he laughed.

"Ouch. Didn't go well?" he guessed.

I shrugged. "More like didn't go at all. I learned her name, and that was about it. Oh, and she thought she was marrying you."

"Me?" a bemused grin passed his face. "But what would that help?"

"I don't know."

"Wait, so why'd you have to cut the meeting short?"

I figured Matteo was asking what came up to interrupt us, but the way he phrased it was more accurate. I had been the one to cut it short. But I didn't know how to explain why.

I certainly couldn't tell my little brother I was afraid. I didn't even know what exactly scared me so much. I wasn't scared of Catalina, per se. Maybe frightened by the notion of being married, but nothing about the beautiful, timid woman I'd left in the hotel suite had been intimidating. Obviously, I was afraid of hurting her, and terrified of repeating the past.

But was that all?

"I panicked," I finally said. "She seemed scared of me, and she was just so fragile." And gorgeous, breathtakingly so. "I could tell she's feisty, but she was also shy. I just, I don't know how to do this."

"Marriage? Yeah, not sure anyone does. But you've got the experts coming right now," he replied, nodding to the door.

I followed his gaze and saw my baby sister and her husband brush through the door.

"You invited them?" I asked through gritted teeth.

"I invited her. He just tagged along."

I cringed. Up until recently, Giada and I had not shared the best relationship. In the last six months, that had all changed. She'd convinced me to start flipping houses with her, and her first major design project was actually a house for me. I loved every detail of that damn house, and Giada had proven to be a better business partner than I would've imagined, so I had no complaints there.

My history with her husband Luca was even more complex. Growing up, Luca and I had been friends. But as he was the heir to the Marino empire and I stood to rule the Conti family business, we began to appreciate the nuances of that "friendship" once we hit puberty. Luca dated my sister in high school and broke her heart, then came back when she was in college and did it all over again.

Up until the time they married, I hadn't fully believed that Luca truly loved my sister and wasn't just using her to try to usurp me and my ambitions.

But now, I couldn't deny it. Even after two years of marriage, Luca still stared at his wife with that nauseating puppy dog look in his eyes. He couldn't keep his hands to himself, and he revolved his entire world around Giada's wishes. My sister wasn't any better. I'd probably never seen another couple that seemed so in sync or so in love.

Naturally, that annoyed the shit out of me.

Luca smiled politely and extended a hand to greet us, but I couldn't hear a word he said as Giada rounded the table and punched me on the arm.

"Married? You're getting married?" my sister shouted.

I opened my mouth to answer, but she continued her rant.

"I talked to you four days ago. Four. Do you remember that?" Giada held up her phone as proof. "We went over all the landscaping plans for your house, and I told you about the progress on my basement designs with Alessio. Then, I asked if there was anything new with you. Do you remember what you said?"

I shook my head, still biting back a smile over the look of annoyance on Luca's face when Giada mentioned Alessio. The guy was Luca's best friend and second-in-command. He had also recently moved in with them, at Giada's request. They all got along gangbusters, but apparently Giada had a low tolerance for the smell of Alessio's faux meat entrees. Leave it to Luca to befriend the only mobster in the world who wouldn't hurt a cow.

"You said no, nothing new with you." Giada continued. "You could have mentioned then that you were getting married. Or that you had a fiancée. Or that you had a girlfriend. I swear I've never even heard of this woman before today!"

Luca pulled his wife close, whispered in her ear—hopefully a reminder to keep her volume down—then kissed her head. A moment later she sat in the chair he pulled out for her then went to the counter to order drinks for the two of them.

"You knew her when we were kids. We all used to hang out," I said.

Giada shot me daggers.

"Okay, yeah, not the point. So, I don't know. We've stayed in touch over the years and we had a fling a while back, and then the last few months we've just been talking a lot more. She's really been there for me, and—"

"So why haven't you ever mentioned her?"

I flung my hands in the air. "Because I like her, okay? And I don't want to risk fucking it up by talking about it or making it more than it is. I think we can all agree I've had shitty luck in the romance department, so I just didn't want to make a big deal out of it."

"But it is a big deal. You're getting married."

"That actually wasn't my idea," I admitted.

"It wasn't?" Matteo butted in, looking genuinely surprised despite knowing the entire story.

I shook my head. "No. I mean, her last relationship ended badly. Not exactly like mine, but…not much better. And she's just more impulsive. She was kind of like, let's just give it a try, what's the worst that can happen?"

"Umm, is that rhetorical, or do you want a list?" my sister asked.

Matteo scowled at her.

"Okay, I'm sure history won't repeat itself, but, I mean, marriage is a big deal," Giada said.

"If It's a complete disaster, we'll divorce," I said. "I'm not like you. I don't believe in the whole eternal damnation thing, and if I did, I'm pretty sure my fate is sealed whether or not I commit the cardinal sin of divorce."

"Divorce is not a cardinal sin," Giada said. "But you can't go into marriage expecting it to fail."

"I don't expect anything. I'm just trying to reassure you that I'm not trapped. You seem worried is all." I paused. "I think you'll really like her. Just don't interrogate her, okay? She's shy."

Giada frowned. "You're saying a shy girl talked you into a rush wedding?"

I shot her a look. "That's exactly how you're *not* supposed to act around her. And no, she's not shy once she gets to know you, but she's just starting to freak out about having to meet all of you at the wedding instead of just eloping like we originally planned. And her family didn't react as well as she'd hoped. Just don't scare her off, okay?"

Giada exchanged a glance with Matteo that told me they'd absolutely be discussing this behind my back later. But then they both nodded.

"So what do you need me to get ready for the big day?" Giada asked, pulling a notebook and pen from her oversized purse.

Catalina

I had locked the door behind Angelo, then watched through the peephole until he disappeared down the hall. Then, I'd moved to the window, waiting with bated breath until he appeared on the street below. He'd strode out confidently, hands back in his pockets, never once casting a glance back at the room. He'd climbed into the back of a black town car that appeared to have been waiting just for him.

Once alone, I'd dropped into the chair he'd just vacated, only to discover that a hint of masculine aftershave remained on the fabric. Why would such a scary guy smell so good? Was this God's way of fucking with me? Like, the adult version of how kidnappers all drove ice cream trucks?

I was so totally screwed. I had finally learned my lesson after the mess with Carlos, but here I was, jumping straight into another mess, with the exact same man. I could not fall for another controlling, bossy monster.

My only defense had been my certainty that my new fiancé would disgust me. And while I had many feelings about the man I'd just met, disgust was not one of them.

Nearly two hours passed before I heard my parents return. I waited until Valeria showed off her shopping haul and made her way to the shower before going to confront my dad.

"You said it was Matteo," I said, bursting into the room. I realized my tone was that of a petulant child, but couldn't taper the current of emotions swirling in my brain enough to control my voice.

My dad gazed up from the papers in his hand, his brows furrowing. "What?"

I drew in a steadying breath. "You told me I would marry Matteo Conti. But I just met the man you're selling me to and it's Angelo."

My dad rolled his eyes. "No one is selling you. Believe me, we're basically paying him to take you."

"Not the point," I interrupted, opting to ignore the hurt sparked by that statement. "Angelo and Matteo are very different people."

"You don't know that. You just met him."

I jutted my hip to the side, planting my fists at my waist. "Tell me I'm wrong then," I challenged. "Tell me the gossip has it backwards, that Matteo is the monster and Angelo is the puppy. Tell me you personally know my betrothed and he's not the sociopath the world seems to think he is."

A flicker of hurt crossed my dad's face. "Mija, a puppy won't keep you safe. Angelo's reputation is exactly what will ensure your protection, long after this marriage ends. And I may not know Angelo well, but I do know his family. They're good people."

"They're criminals."

His jaw hardened. "I give you my word that Angelo will not harm you. Okay? You just need to get through the next year. Once Carlos backs off, you can separate from Angelo and get your life back on track. Hopefully this experience will teach you once and for all that your actions have consequences, that you can't just—"

I groaned loudly and stormed out of the room. I didn't need another lecture. I had too many other things to tackle before strolling down the aisle to my execution.

CHAPTER 4

Catalina

In lieu of a traditional wedding rehearsal, Angelo and I were scheduled to meet with the priest the next day. My mother came with me to the church, where we sat through an entire mass—in Italian—during which my supposed fiancé didn't so much as glance at me once. The sanctuary was surprisingly crowded for a Friday, so we were forced to sit close. Angelo's thigh touched my own, which I supposed could help our story that this was a real relationship, but the contact was clearly unintentional on his part.

I found myself watching Angelo as much as I could without rousing his suspicion. He definitely had a nice profile. He looked serious, but professional. Everything about Angelo oozed control, from his perfectly coiffed hair to his neatly trimmed beard. Even the small freckle near his left ear seemed to have been intentionally placed. His dark lashes blocked my view of his eyes, and his only movement was the steady rise and fall of his chest as he inhaled and exhaled through his nose.

No one would look at this man and question his authority.

The man seated beside me was undeniably powerful. He surely commanded every room he walked into, never once questioning his own dominance. I doubted anyone had ever told him no, or at least survived to talk about it. And given my penchant for resisting authority figures, I had reason to be concerned. Crossing Angelo Conti could be downright dangerous.

I tried to decipher some clues about Angelo, but his behavior divulged nothing I didn't already know. Well, except for his smell. My internet stalking obviously hadn't informed me at all about his scent, but now that I was seated beside him, I found myself distracted, trying to guess his fragrance. The scent was full-bodied and masculine, but with some exotic floral undertone that kept the woodsy fragrance from becoming too heavy.

I supposed that was reassuring, that I liked the way the guy smelled. Well, unless it was some sort of intentional pheromone-trick on his part, to reel me in.

After mass, when the priest met with us to discuss the wedding ceremony, I understood nothing. Angelo translated, but only sparingly. I suspected he repeated about twenty percent of the details the priest offered. The priest asked several questions, but Angelo answered them all without my input. Finally, the priest signaled the end of the meeting by standing. He shook Angelo's hand, then mine, then my mother's, before gesturing for us to exit the small office.

My mom stepped out first, and I started after her. Before I reached the doorway, a hand clamped down on my shoulder I stiffened and nearly tripped over my own foot before realizing it was just my fiancé. He lowered his head down to my ear as we walked.

"Could we have a word alone?" he whispered.

I nodded, then gestured to my mother that I'd catch up in a minute.

"Oh take your time, you two," she gushed, way too excited for my taste.

Angelo showed me down a deserted, dimly-lit hallway. I followed hesitantly, trying to ignore the way the stone walls reminded me of a medieval dungeon. The hallway was narrow, and when Angelo turned to face me, his body filled most of the space ahead of me. I could've squeezed by, but barely, and definitely not without touching him.

The man was at least a foot taller than me, and probably double my weight. He was noticeably bigger than his pictures made him look, but I suspected everything he'd added to his figure since the photographs was solid muscle. I'd be aroused, if I wasn't so intimidated by him.

"Look, this isn't going to work if it isn't believable," Angelo said. "You're the one who needs people to think this is real, so you could at least put a little effort into it."

I opened my mouth, but wasn't sure what to say.

"You can't jump when I touch you. There will be photos tomorrow, and we need to look natural in them. We'll need to take photos on the honeymoon, too. You can post them on your social media or whatever."

"Honeymoon?"

He blew out a sigh, looking about as annoyed as if we were discussing an upcoming root canal. "No one told you?"

I shook my head. They probably assumed Angelo had, during our extensive meeting the day before. I hadn't admitted to my family that he'd bailed on me after less than five minutes.

"We're taking a two week honeymoon after the wedding." he explained.

"Where?"

"Capri," he said, sliding his phone out of his pocket to read a text. "It's like an hour from Naples by boat. Pretty island. Private villa. Your dad paid."

"My family is flying home Tuesday," I said, still confused.

"Yes. Typically the bride's family doesn't join the couple on the honeymoon."

My stomach swirled at the thought of being alone in a foreign country with this brute of a man. "Right," I said. "Um, about the ceremony. I didn't understand—"

"We'll do it just like the American way. Your sister and mine will walk down the aisle. Your dad will walk you down the aisle. We'll say the vows, exchange rings, and walk out together. Easy. I'll translate when you need to speak."

That seemed simple enough.

"My sister doesn't know the truth," he added. "Neither does her husband, Luca. Only my parents and Matteo do. So stick with the story." His expectant stare told me he wanted to confirm I knew the supposed story, so I prepared a recap.

"We met a few years ago and realized our dads knew each other. We hit it off, kept in touch, and then met up again a few months back and decided we had nothing to lose?"

He nodded. "Some of our family's work associates will be there tomorrow, but they won't ask questions. It's just my sister who will be nosy. All you have to do is act natural. Just pretend you like me while people are present." He reached for his phone again, frowning as he read this message. "I have to go."

I scooted to the side to let him pass, then paused. "Wait, should I like, have your number or something?"

Angelo turned to face me, an odd expression on his face. For a moment, I thought he was going to give me his number, or respond in some other normal way. Instead, he just shook his head.

"Just enjoy your last day of freedom, okay kitten?"

"Kitten?" I mumbled aloud.

Angelo

I spent the night before the wedding at dinner with my family, plus Luca. My uncle Vinny and his son Eddie, who happened to be my best friend, also joined us, having flown in earlier in the day. Eddie worked closely with me, and was an official part of the business family as well as literal family, so I'd already filled him in on the reality of the situation. I'd sworn him to secrecy, but even as I elaborated that night over drinks, I realized I still wasn't giving him the full truth, but a combination platter of the story we'd invented and the actual truth.

My subconscious need to make him believe the relationship wasn't wholly fake unsettled me. Why did it matter if Eddie thought there was at least some degree of familiarity underlying my arranged marriage? I couldn't shake the thought that I was trying to lay the groundwork for some subsequent, real relationship with Catalina.

The notion was ridiculous, though. Every time I was alone with this woman, fear radiated off her in waves. No matter how attractive I might find her, she viewed me as the beast, squirreling her away to my creepy dungeon where I could keep her all to myself. She obviously believed I was incapable of independently finding a woman willing to settle down with me.

Actually, her perception wasn't entirely wrong.

It didn't help that I'd overheard her arguing with her mother before Mass that day. They'd gone inside the restroom together and I was waiting in the hallway just outside. I'd planned to escort them to our seats, as that seemed the polite and gentlemanly thing to do. But I hadn't factored in the paper-thin walls of the old building.

I'd heard Catalina chastise her mother for "selling" her to a man they barely knew. Her mother's response, if any, had been inaudible, but then Catalina had asked if this was truly the way her mom had envisioned her oldest daughter's wedding. I could've sworn I heard tears then, as the woman confirmed that it of course wasn't, but it was far better than the alternative.

"I'd rather plan your wedding to a stranger than plan your funeral," she had said. "Carlos was in your bedroom at night, with a weapon, Lina. You have no other choice. If this keeps you safe, it's worth whatever cost."

"Whatever cost," Catalina had repeated. "Interesting choice of words, because you understand what is expected, when a couple is married? You get what you're asking me to do? With a complete stranger?"

The sound of running water had prevented me from hearing the rest of the conversation, but I wasn't sure it mattered. Catalina was terrified of me, and I'd callously commented on her wifely duties the day before.

Could I be a bigger dick? Probably not, but I was determined not to think about it anyway.

Eddie, Matteo, and I spent the rest of the night drinking and trying to forget the reason we were all gathered together.

CHAPTER 5

Angelo

As I took my place at the front of the sanctuary the next day, I regretted the second shot of whiskey I'd downed while getting ready. The first one had relaxed me, but the second left me parched and unsettled. I was far from drunk, but not sober enough to talk myself out of going through with this ridiculous charade.

Sure, my love life was terrible. My luck with women was quite possibly the worst of any man alive, so the notion that some insane stunt like this would somehow work for me was absurd. The best I could hope for was to assuage a tiny bit of my guilt. I'd ruined one woman's life, so if I could save this one, well, maybe I'd have a shot at salvation.

Probably not.

The music changed, and my sister appeared at the base of the aisle. She beamed brightly at me, then turned just to my left, where Luca sat. The way those two eye-fucked each other as she made her way up the aisle was nearly enough to make me gag. I was glad Giada was happy, but I still couldn't stomach the way she and Luca were constantly all over each other, even now that they were married.

I turned away from Luca to see Valeria starting down the aisle. She was considerably younger than Catalina, and sauntered with that oblivious confidence only a teenager could muster. I smiled politely at her, my future sister-in-law, and her cheeks blushed beet red. I turned my gaze to the rest of the audience as Valeria finished her walk.

Aside from my parents, Catalina's parents, and the Marino family, there were only about a dozen guests. All of them were family or business associates of ours who actually lived in Italy. Aside from Eddie, we hadn't invited any of our East Coast family or friends. The story was that we wanted to elope, and the small ceremony was a compromise for my mom.

An abrupt change in the music signaled for the congregation to stand. I shifted side to side, my hands clutched nervously in front of my waist. I held my breath till she appeared. I told myself it was too late now, that I was doing the right thing by sticking around and seeing this through, but I knew that was a lie.

I wouldn't be able to save this girl any more than I could save the last one.

The only reason I was even trying was because she was hot.

Actually, hot was an understatement. The woman inching towards me, decked from head to toe in the purest white, was beyond gorgeous. She looked like a fucking angel.

Everything about her was delicate and perfect, almost like she was some hand-crafted doll. Her long hair was swept up on top of her head, showcasing her graceful neck and shoulders. If this were a real marriage, I'd kiss her decolletage till my lips went numb. As it was, I'd probably have to get my fill just staring from afar.

Catalina's eyes were on the ground ahead of her as she walked. I wasn't sure if she was scared to make eye contact or just afraid of tripping, but it didn't matter. She'd have to look me in the eye soon enough.

Her gown was simple, but gorgeous, and it fit her like a glove. I wondered how she'd managed to find something so perfect on such short notice.

I felt as if time had slowed, like the walk shouldn't be taking them so long. I licked my lips nervously, then started forward, meeting Catalina and her father before they reached the altar. The man had Parkinson's, but he'd forgone the cane for the occasion, even though he clearly struggled without it. Saving him a few steps seemed like a simple act of kindness, but it also assuaged by impatience.

"I'll take it from here," I said to him, offering what I hoped was a reassuring smile. Jorge kissed his daughter on the cheek, then transferred her hand to my arm. I gazed at the spot where our bodies touched, noting how small her fingers looked against my forearm. She clutched my arm so tightly I half expected her to pierce a hole in my suit jacket.

I walked her the last few feet to the altar, then tilted my head to whisper in her ear. "Breathe," I commanded. Then, I lifted her hand from my arm, clutching it in my hand as we turned to face the priest.

Her eyelids fluttered, but Catalina said nothing as the priest greeted us both. I debated translating, but decided there was nothing Catalina needed to hear. After his spiel about the sanctity of marriage, the Father instructed us face each other. I turned to Catalina, and she followed suit. I reached for her other hand, and after a moment, she placed it in mine.

The priest spoke our vows in Italian, so I translated quietly. Surely, Catalina knew the gist of it, but she deserved to hear it all, just in case she came to her senses and wanted to back out. Instead, she repeated her lines on cue. As she spoke, her voice was soft, but unbroken.

Her hand trembled as I placed the ring on it, so I squeezed it gently, letting my fingers loiter atop of hers until she gazed up. Our eyes met, and the priest continued. All that remained was the kiss. I'd spent an inordinate amount of time the previous night stressing about this final ruse. I'd ultimately decided that, while a long, passionate kiss might do more to convince the onlookers of the validity of the marriage, something short and sweet would be less likely to backfire.

The moment the priest said I could kiss my bride, I caught her gaze. I didn't dare translate that part, but didn't want to catch her off guard, either. I stepped closer, placed on hand on the small of her back, and cupped her chin with my other hand. Catalina tilted her head to meet me, and I breached the distance between us. Our lips brushed gently at first, and a jolt shot through me.

I deepened the kiss, my heart racing with every moment of contact. I barely noticed the cheers from our families, instead focused on her tangy, sweet perfume, and the softness of every part of her body touching mine. I pulled back the moment I felt my desire start to go south.

Catalina stared at me, lips parted, stunned.

I plastered an artificially wide smile to my face, hoping she'd snap out of it and follow suit. A moment later, she dropped the deer in headlights expression and smiled.

I squeezed her hand as we hurried back down the aisle and out of the church.

Catalina

As we exited the sanctuary, Angelo clutched my hand so tightly that I couldn't have run if I wanted to.

And I really wanted to.

No, actually, I didn't just want it. I *needed* to run.

Like, what the fuck was that kiss? Who could manage to

extend a ceremonial wedding peck on the lips for a full thirty seconds? God, maybe it was longer. I lost track of time when my nipples started to harden. Clearly my body was just as confused as my brain.

We turned the corner and made our way down the back hallway, where we were supposed to wait in a small room for a few minutes until all of our guests had exited and lined up on the steps outside the church. Angelo pushed open the door to the room, stepping to the side for me to enter first.

The moment I did, Angelo dropped my hand. He stared at me, silently. I gazed back, trying not to focus on the lips that had just delivered the best kiss of my entire life—all without even slipping me the tongue.

After a minute, Angelo turned away, gesturing to a table bearing trays with small sandwiches and crudites. There had been similar offerings in the room where my sister and I had dressed, but I hadn't had an appetite then, either.

"Eat something," Angelo said. He poured a glass of water for himself, then leaned casually against the table as he sipped.

"I'm not hungry."

He raised his gaze to meet mine. "Your hands were shaking during the ceremony and you look like you're about to pass out. The last thing I need is an unconscious bride, so stop acting like a child and eat something."

My posture stiffened. Angelo's condescending tone made me feel exactly like a child. But I didn't have the energy or strength to argue, and we probably only had a couple minutes anyway. I reached for a cucumber and cream cheese sandwich, downing the finger food in two bites. Then I grabbed a skewer of grapes, plucking them off one at a time.

"Better?" I asked.

Angelo pushed off the wall and stepped so close that I nearly thought he'd kiss me again. I sucked in a breath, but instead, he lifted a finger to my lip and wiped off a dab of cream cheese. But before the mortification over my messy eating fully sunk in, Angelo licked his finger clean. A jolt of desire shot straight to my core. I silently pleaded with my body to stop sending me mixed messages, and instead poured myself a glass of water.

I turned back to Angelo just as he downed a large swig from a fancy silver flask. He caught me eying him and angled the flask in my direction.

"Might help your nerves," he said.

I shook my head, even though he was right. I wasn't entirely sure what to make of the knowledge that my husband was the type of guy who smuggled booze into a church.

Angelo swallowed another sip, then stashed the flask into the inside pocket of his suit jacket. He glanced at his phone, then nodded to the door.

"I bet they're ready for us," he said.

I nodded, grabbed my bouquet, and started to the door.

"Smile," he said. "It's the happiest day of your life."

I nearly choked on my confusion, but Angelo's hand already pressed into the small of my back, nudging me out into the hall.

He squeezed my hand as we climbed down the steps exiting the church. The attendees blew bubbles at us, and as we reached the black town car waiting to drive us to the reception, Angelo lifted my hand to his lips, kissing it gently. The driver opened the car door for us, and Angelo played the part of the perfect gentleman, helping tuck my dress around me before walking around to the other side to sit.

Just before the driver shut the door, Valeria scurried up and handed my purse to me.

"Thank you," I gushed, relief flooding me. The tiny white clutch held only my phone, lipstick, and a mirrored pressed powder compact, but I felt naked without it.

Angelo settled into his seat, wrapping an arm around my shoulders. I thought he'd scoot away once the car left the church, but he didn't. He did, however, begin speaking with the driver. I couldn't decipher a single word of their conversation since it was in Italian, but I could tell from their casual tones that they knew each other.

"Friend of yours?" I asked, feeling left out.

Instead of answering, Angelo said my name along with something in Italian to the driver. Then he turned to me. "This is Stefano. He always drives me when I'm here."

The man's warm eyes met mine in the rearview mirror. "Piacere, signorina," he said.

"Nice to meet you," I replied.

The men resumed their conversation as if I wasn't there, so I reapplied lipstick using the mirror from my compact, then pulled my phone from my purse. I had a dozen or so emails, all spam, but I scrolled through each one before deleting.

I toggled over to my messages, hovering over one in the group chat with Kristi and Madison asking how Italy was. I needed to reply, but I wasn't sure what to say. Once I told them about Angelo, I would be trapped in the lie.

"You should send a picture," Angelo said, his deep voice interrupting my thoughts. "Then post it to social media."

He was right. The whole point marrying him was moot if Carlos didn't find out about it or if he thought the marriage was a sham. I toyed with snapping a photo of the picturesque architecture through the window, but Angelo slid my phone from my hand. He angled it out and above us, ready to take a selfie.

"Kiss my cheek," he said, adding, "And look happy."

I leaned in, then hesitated. "I just put on more lipstick."

He cast a glance at me, then looked back to the camera. "It's fine. Just do it."

I clenched my abs and pressed my lips to his cheek. The tantalizingly fresh scent of his aftershave hit me instantly, and I shut my eyes, lingering for a moment so he could snap the photo.

"Smile," he said.

I tried, but that was hard to do with my lips on his cheek, so after a moment I turned to the camera. He snapped a few more pictures then set the phone in my lap, finally pulling back his arm. He tugged a handkerchief from his pocket and dabbed gently at the bold red lipstick stain on his cheek, but he dropped his hand before removing all trace.

"Here, you still have—" I began, reaching for the cloth.

"Leave it," he said, catching my hand midair and returning it to my lap. "Looks more realistic this way."

I nodded, and clicked to look at the photos he'd snapped. I looked stiff and terrified in the first, but by the second one, I appeared relaxed. If I didn't know better, I'd say I looked like a girl in love. In reality, I was probably just drunk off the scent of that delicious aftershave.

Angelo wasn't exactly beaming in the photos, but he'd managed to look both semi-serious and happy at the same time. I wondered if he ever actually smiled for real.

I hearted my three favorites, angling my phone towards Angelo. He nodded his approval and I clicked to send the pictures to Kristi and Madison. Then, I wrote,

> Been busy in Italy. Did a thing today.

It was still early morning on the East Coast, but Kristi replied within seconds.

> WTF? Who is that?

A moment later, from Madison:

> Are you wearing a WEDDING dress?

Kristi:

> Did you seriously run off and marry some Italian
> hunk?

Angelo breathed a laugh, so I knew he was reading over my shoulder. I cast him a scolding stare, then replied to my friends.

> Angelo says hi. We've had a big day. I'll text
> tomorrow if I have time, and let's catch up after
> I'm back from my HONEYMOON in Capri.

I tossed in a handful of celebratory emojis, followed by some beachy ones.

Angelo reached for my phone again, and I braced myself for whatever nonsense he was about to text my friends. Instead, he scrolled to my contacts, typed in his name, wrote "Amante" in the blank for a company name, then filled in his phone, address, and email. When he was done, Angelo selected himself as my emergency contact.

I started to protest, then decided it would be easier to just change it back to my father later. "Amante?" I asked, not recognizing the word.

He quirked a brow, so I went to my translator. The word meant "lover."

I blew out a sigh and Angelo smirked.

"Do you want mine?" I asked.

"I already have your phone and email, and now we have the same address, so—"

"Right," I said, a whole new world of panic hitting me at that realization. I chewed the inside of my lip and turned to the widow, focusing on the idyllic scenery blurring past the car.

CHAPTER 6

Angelo

*O*nce we arrived at the reception, I helped Catalina out of the car. To my surprise, she wrapped her arm around my hip as we headed into the lobby. I did the same to her, happy to not appear to be dragging her along. Cocktails and appetizers were already circulating by the time my bride and I arrived. The din of small talk filled the intimate, dimly lit space.

We were separated the moment we entered, which was fine by me. Catalina's sister scurried her off to the restroom, presumably for a hair or makeup touchup, and Eddie greeted me.

"Congratulazioni!" he exclaimed, handing me an amber-colored drink then slapping my back jovially. "Negroni," he added, identifying the beverage as my cocktail of choice.

"Grazie," I said, taking a healthy swig. We were joined by a few of my family's associates and some distant relatives, and I managed to swipe some of the appetizers as they circulated the room.

Just as I realized that a half hour had passed without me so much as glancing at my new bride, I felt a soft tap on my arm. I turned, wrapping an arm around Catalina and pulling me to my side before introducing her to the men I'd been talking with. I started the introductions in Italian, then translated for Catalina.

"These are some business associates," I explained before pressing a soft kiss to the top of her head. The way she'd been gazing up at me, her emerald eyes sparkling, the gesture felt alarmingly natural. "Did you sample the appetizers?"

"I'm fine," she replied.

I interpreted that as a no, so I grabbed a passing waiter, and asked him to bring a plate with one of each delicacy. Her father was paying, so she might as well at least taste the food. Besides, she was already too thin to be skipping meals while drinking alcohol. I leaned closer to Catalina, letting my lips brush her ear as I whispered, "What is your favorite cocktail?"

I figured to onlookers, the gesture would appear intimate, but in reality, I just didn't need people hearing me admit that I knew so little about my wife.

Confusion spread over her face as she turned to me. "Sex on the beach?"

My cock twitched at the innocence in her voice. "Let's save that for the honeymoon, kitten." I waited until her face flushed at the dual meaning of my words before tilting my second negroni in her direction. "Try this."

She sipped, then smiled. "Not bad." She started to hand it back.

"Keep it," I said.

The waiter returned with the plate of appetizers, so I held the plate in one hand, and used my free hand to feed her a bite of the bruschetta. Catalina accepted the offering, closing her perfect lips around the bread and biting off half. A soft moan escaped her mouth as she chewed. I bit back a smile.

"I love bruschetta," she said apologetically, butchering the pronunciation of the word.

I cringed. "Broo-skeh-tuh," I said, emphasizing the hard consonant of the C.

She repeated the word, then grabbed the remaining half of the tiny toast from the plate and ate it. Our guests had left us alone for the moment, so next, I offered her the skewer of fresh mozzarella, tomato, and basil.

"I could feed myself," Catalina said.

"The optics are better if I do it," I replied.

She opened her mouth and slid a bite off the skewer while I held it. I couldn't help but gawk as her lips closed around the food, especially as her tongue darted just past her lips. Catalina looked like a fucking porn star and she wasn't even trying to be seductive.

My mouth ran dry and I regretted giving her my drink. I tried to focus on anything but the thought of those gorgeous full lips wrapped around my cock, but the first thing that came to mind was Julia, my ex. She hated when I fed her bites of food. I never understood why, but I quickly learned that offering her a bite off my fork was likely to result in me being stabbed by said fork.

Thinking of Julia cooled my arousal faster than anything else could have.

The remaining appetizer was a meatball, but thankfully my mother appeared by my side right as I fed that to Catalina.

"Catalina, darling, you are the most gorgeous bride. I'm so happy this all worked out and so glad you're a part of our family." She gestured around the room. "And this is all amazing. Please tell your parents again how grateful we are for their contributions to all of this."

"Thank you, Mrs. Conti. And it was so nice of you to help with all of the arrangements. My family isn't really familiar with the area, so—"

"It's nothing," my mom said, squeezing Catalina's arm. "Now, I think the toasts are about to begin, so you two should grab some champagne and then head to your table."

I nodded in response, but my mom leaned closer. An odd expression crossed her face, and then she snatched the paper napkin from my hand and dabbed at my cheek. The remnants of Catalina's lipstick came off on the napkin. She flashed me her best "I told you so" look, then turned to take her spot at the table.

Well, at least we'd convinced someone that we were hitting it off.

Catalina's father gave the first toast, followed by my own father. My dad began in Italian, thanking everyone for coming, thanking Catalina's family for the wonderful day and for raising such a wonderful daughter. Then he translated to English. He turned to Mr. Alvarado as he continued in English.

"And as we thank you for letting your beautiful daughter join our family, we promise to treat her as one of our own. I speak for the entire Conti family, when I pledge to cherish and protect Catalina Alvarado Conti as if she were my own wife, sister, or daughter."

My father turned back to me as he translated the words into Italian. All of the men in the family—whether by blood or oath—stood, turned to Catalina, then bowed their heads. My father ended his speech with a toast to Catalina and the future of the Conti family, to which everyone toasted and cheered.

I turned to Catalina, who looked confused and embarrassed by the attention. "Welcome to the family," I said, hoping she understood the seriousness of what had just transpired. The arrangement was official. Catalina now had the protection of the entire Conti family at her disposal, and that was no small thing.

Catalina

I floated through the wedding reception as if watching someone else go through the motions. I didn't think this was what someone meant when they spoke of an out-of-body experience, but that's how I'd describe it. I wasn't participating, so much as watching a dream-like version of myself attend the event.

Despite the last-minute nature of the event, the finished product was remarkable. The Conti family had rented out a cozy meeting room of a local hotel for the reception. Thanks to the exquisite Roman architecture of the space, little décor was needed to make the room feel special. One wall overlooked a courtyard filled with colorful flowers, and vases of similar flowers filled the center of each table. A friend of the Conti family had provided all of the catering for the event, and the members of the band also appeared to be acquaintances of the family.

I'd never been one of those girls to dwell on fantasies about my wedding day, but when I had briefly considered the day, this was not what I'd envisioned. I would've jumped at the chance for a destination wedding, but a tropical locale would've topped my list. I supposed the fake story about me wanting to elope wasn't even far from the truth. The notion was so romantic to me, feeling such a pressing urgency to marry the one I loved that I forsook any traditional wedding preparations.

If I had planned a traditional wedding and reception, I would've orchestrated a much bigger event. I would've invited everyone I knew, and insisted the celebration be the most extravagant, outlandish event of the season. I would've demanded the type of party that snobbish socialites enjoyed for their quinceañeras. Not that my own quinceañera left anything to be desired, but I just figured a wedding should upstage that day, at least a little.

To an outsider, the event probably looked authentic. As far as

I could tell, the Contis had adhered to the Italian wedding tradi-tions, but there were also many American traditions mixed in. I didn't mind the absence of Puerto Rican traditions, if only because this wasn't real.

"Their family sure knows a lot of people," I commented to my dad as I watched Angelo greet one of the waiters as if they were long-lost friends.

"That's the whole point. They're well connected. Now you, too, are well connected."

I sighed and sipped my prosecco.

"I'd like a dance with my daughter," my dad continued.

"Why? This isn't real. We should save the father-daughter dance for my real wedding."

"The way you make life choices, this may be as close to a real wedding as you get, mija."

"Papi," I groaned and rolled my eyes, but followed him onto the dance floor.

After a dance with my father, Angelo stepped in. I hadn't seen him approaching, so I hadn't had time to panic about the forced proximity. But the second his hand clutched my hip, I shivered, already acutely aware of the heat radiating off him in waves. We danced like two teens in cotillion, our moves more formal than intimate, but I supposed it wasn't altogether inappropriate given the audience.

"Did you understand what was said during the toasts?" Angelo asked.

I frowned, already have forgotten the earlier parts of the evening. "I don't speak Italian," I finally stammered.

"My family officially welcomed you to the family. They've pledged to protect you. All of those men who stood up during the toast have promised to protect you."

"Those...I mean, every one of them is related to you?"

Angelo didn't answer right away. "Family means different

things in my world," he finally said. "All you need to know is that my part of the bargain is done. We will keep you safe."

The song ended just then. Angelo smiled widely, pressed his lips to the top of my hand as if we were courtiers from the Renaissance, then stepped back.

"Thank you?" I mumbled, still confused.

CHAPTER 7

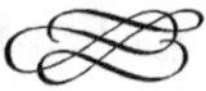

Catalina

*A*ngelo's driver friend dropped us off at the hotel where we'd be spending the night. Our luggage had been delivered earlier, which meant someone else had already been in the room. I only hoped they hadn't decorated the room with rose petals or something equally embarrassing.

Angelo hadn't spoken to me the entire drive to the hotel. He'd made a quick phone call—in Italian—then had stared out the window the remainder of the drive.

That was fine with me. I was exhausted, and somehow my buzz had already begun to fizzle into the foggy heaviness that always followed a boozy evening. I supposed it made sense that I was tired, though. I hadn't slept well since my dad had told me about the wedding, and I'd hardly slept at all the previous night.

I pulled out my phone, cleared my inbox, then read all the messages from Madison and Kristi. I ached to reply, but forced myself to wait. I wouldn't text my best friends on my wedding night if the relationship were real.

Instead, I focused on keeping my breathing level, and tried to tell myself I had nothing to be afraid of. It wasn't like I was a virgin. I'd been with four other guys. Each of them had different styles of love-making and very different skills in the bedroom. Each time, I'd adjusted. Just like I would this time.

Everything would be fine. Sex with Angelo would be no big deal. Maybe over time, I'd even grow to enjoy it. The guy was hot, after all. Well, at least he was when I didn't focus on the scary, serious exterior.

Besides, I knew how to pretend, even if I wasn't enjoying it. I'd done that plenty with Carlos.

I shuddered at a memory of my last few weeks with Carlos. He had become paranoid that I was cheating and interpreted every hesitation on my part as further proof of my guilt. In truth, I hadn't cheated, but the more Carlos screamed and accused me, the harder it was to fake my arousal and make myself be intimate with him.

Even in the end, I'd never truly believed Carlos would hurt me. Stupidly, I thought his delusional obsession was romantic, that he just loved me so much that it made him crazy. When he was too rough with me, he convinced me it wasn't his fault—it was mine. I was too beautiful, too sexy for him to control himself.

In retrospect, maybe I was a bit of a narcissist too, since I fell for all that crap.

But the difference with Carlos was that there had been a time when he was sweet and gentle. We dated, he bought me flowers, we made out countless times, and we gradually worked up to the actual sex. That relationship was nothing like my current predicament, stuck in a car with a man whose only condition of the fake marriage was that I service him on a regular basis.

I snuck a glance at Angelo, who was still staring out the window into the pitch black night. His head leaned against the seat back and one hand rested on his lap. His other hand was raised to his chin, as if he were deep in thought. Maybe he was.

For all I knew, he could be plotting his next murder or contemplating which demeaning sexual act he'd force me to perform first. His posture was casual, though. His knees were wide, in the typical man-spread pose, but no part of his body touched me.

Before I could contemplate what that might signify, the car jolted to a stop. Stefano said something and Angelo chuckled. The driver opened my door, offering me a hand to help me out. Angelo waited on the other side of the car, then started up the pathway towards the hotel lobby once I caught up. He clasped my hand, but in a way that seemed more to prevent me from falling than to show affection.

I could've sworn the doorman greeted him by name, but we walked straight through the ornately decorated lobby and into a mirrored elevator. Angelo dropped my hand the moment we were inside. A moment later, the doors slid open and another couple stepped into the small space with us. The woman smiled gleefully as she took in my dress, then gushed something which I assumed was congratulations.

I offered a smile, and Angelo thanked the lady, placing a hand on my back as he spoke. The couple exited the elevator a few floors later, but Angelo didn't drop his hand.

The elevator dinged as it slowed to a stop, and Angelo's hand pressed into the small of my back, nudging me into the hallway. He gestured towards the right, then used his phone to unlock the door.

I squeezed my eyes shut for a brief moment before entering. Angelo shut the door behind us, securing it with the chain. A lump rose in the back of my throat and I had the uncanny sensation that I was walking to my execution. I tried to focus on the tangible, like how pretty the room was. It wasn't massive, but the furnishings looked high-end and the décor was sophisticated.

A balcony sat across from the entrance to the room, and another door, presumably leading to a bathroom, was to the left. There was a small bar adjacent to the balcony, and a solitary bed occupied the center of the room. Knots of dread formed deep in my stomach at the realization that I would be sharing that plush bed with Angelo—after doing whatever debasing sexual acts he demanded.

"Your bags should all be here," he said, brushing past me and heading towards the bar. "I asked them not to unpack since we'll only be here for a night." He lifted the lid from the ice bucket, nodding approvingly when he saw it had been freshly filled. I wondered if he'd requested that, as well, and then I wondered if people always did the things he asked.

Angelo shrugged out of his suit jacket, and as he walked to the closet to hang the garment, I noticed a black holster strapped over his satin vest. Tucked neatly inside the holster was a big silver handgun.

I gasped, stiffening even more. Angelo slid the gun out of the holster, placed it on its side on the dresser, then set the holster beside it. As he began unbuttoning his vest, I couldn't help but wonder how I hadn't noticed the gun on his side earlier. Granted, we hadn't touched a ton, but we had danced to two separate songs. My arms had been at his waist and on his biceps, but I still would've expected to notice that.

I realized Angelo had turned to face me. He'd removed the vest altogether and his bowtie was loose around his neck. He looked like some movie star playing a spy. My breath caught in my throat as I tried to dismiss the weird mixture of fear and attraction.

"Do you need help with the dress?" he asked, his tone suggesting he had either already asked me something else or was just wondering why I was standing in the center of the room like a moron.

I shook my head. He turned back to the dresser, reaching under the hem of his pants leg and retrieving yet another gun. This one was black. He set it on the dresser next to the first one. A tiny choked sound escaped my throat.

Angelo swiveled to face me, his brows raised in an unspoken question.

"That's a lot of guns," I finally said, my voice squeaky.

His eyes flitted to the weapons, then back to me. He sunk into a chair by the bar and began removing his shoes. He arranged them neatly beside the dresser, then stretched his neck from side to side.

"It looks like there's a safe," I offered, pointing to the one I'd noticed when he'd hung up his jacket.

"I'm not planning on leaving the room tonight, so unless you're worried you'll shoot me, that seems unnecessary."

I opened my mouth to point out it wasn't *me* that I was worried about using the guns, but then closed it without saying a word.

Angelo began scooping ice into a glass, then inspected the selection of miniature liquor bottles. "Drink?" he offered without turning.

I considered the offer, certain I'd be less nervous if I had more alcohol. But I felt the start of a niggling headache from the drinks I'd already consumed. "Just some water would be nice."

I watched as he twisted open a bottle of water and poured it over the ice. He crossed the room in two long strides, handing me the glass before returning to the bar.

"Thanks," I mumbled, trying to focus on how well the suit fit him and not on the terror I felt about what my next hour may hold. "I'm going to take down my hair," I said after a moment of silence.

I took my water into the bathroom, sighing with relief once I was alone. Two small bags sat on the counter. The larger one I recognized as holding my own toiletries. The other presumably belonged to Angelo. I gazed at my reflection in the mirror, surprised to see my hair and makeup had held up relatively well. Before I could think better of it, I snapped a photo of myself and sent it to my friends with the message, "Just reached the honeymoon suite" along with a series of emojis.

I told myself I only wanted the brief connection with familiar people, but a larger part of me knew I also wanted some firm documentation of where I was and what I looked like, just in case no one ever saw me again.

I told myself to stop being stupid and began unpinning the tiara from my hair. My headache dissipated slightly by the time I'd removed every pin and elastic band from my hair, but I shook two ibuprofen tablets into my hand and swallowed them with a swig of water as an extra precaution. I wiped off my makeup, then twisted my hair into a loose bun on top of my head, securing it with a scrunchie. I rinsed a washcloth in cold water and held it against my face like a compress, inhaling the moist air.

I switched the faucet to hot, and then, feeling bold, I unzipped Angelo's bag. Peering inside I noticed all the usual suspects—deodorant, razor, cologne, after shave, toothbrush, and a few other small bottles. At the bottom of the bag, a hint of silver glinted and I reached for it. I pulled out the heavy, metallic object, quickly ascertained it was a switch blade knife, then dropped it back into the bag. I zipped up his bag, then washed my face with warm water before applying my eye cream and moisturizer. I brushed my teeth and longed to reapply deodorant, but such a task was impossible in the heavy dress.

I scolded myself for not having brought any clothes into the bathroom, then spotted two plush white robes hanging on the doorknob. Of course, if I came out of the bathroom wearing a robe, he'd assume I wanted to have sex. On the other hand, since that was clearly the plan anyway, it probably didn't matter.

I sucked in a breath and tried to reach the white buttons behind my back. I could touch them, but couldn't actually maneuver them through the tiny loops of thread securing them in place. I dropped my arms, stretched, then tried again, this time angling so I could see what I was doing in the mirror. I struggled a little longer, then gave up. There was zero chance of me getting out of this stupid dress without either a pair of scissors or another set of hands.

I gritted my teeth as I remembered Angelo's earlier offer of help, but I couldn't let my pride get in the way. The dress felt like a prison which was slowly crushing my soul. I needed out before I either lost my mind or the corset quite literally cut into my ribs.

I yanked out the scrunchie holding my hair, then steeled myself as I exited the bathroom. Angelo had turned off the overhead light, leaving only the dim glow of a lamp near the bar to illuminate the space. He sat in the corner of the room, a glass of amber liquid in his hand. He looked dark, dangerous, and undeniably sexy. If this were a movie, I'd saunter across the room, drop to my knees before him, unzip his suit pants, and suck his cock until he yanked me to my feet by my hair, tossed me onto the bed, and fucked me till I couldn't see straight.

Luckily, this was not in fact a movie.

And clearly, I could benefit from less TV in my real life, or at least fewer romance novels. Also, in a movie, I probably would've managed to strip down to my lingerie.

Angelo gazed up, his face void of any expression.

"So, it turns out I actually do need some help getting out of the dress," I said.

I wasn't sure he heard me until he crooked a finger, motioning for me to come closer. He stood as I did, and I turned my back to him.

"There's all these little buttons," I said, even though I already felt his fingers tugging at the material. It took him several minutes to undo the buttons, but as he finished that, I realized I still couldn't inhale deeply. "There might be some ties too," I said, remembering the damn strings holding the corset in place.

A moment later, the dress slipped down my chest. I relished the exquisite sensation of freedom, then tugged it back up over my breasts. I wore nothing but a white satin thong under the dress and didn't need Angelo seeing all that until he insisted.

"Thank you," I mumbled, turning back to face him.

Angelo's expression seemed darker, his breath heavier, but he licked his lips, then sunk back into his chair.

"I'm, um, really tired, it seems. Long day, right?" I babbled.

Angelo said nothing.

"I might just change into my pajamas now and…" my voice trailed off as I had nothing else to say aloud.

Angelo dropped his gaze to his phone in lieu of answering. I slowly backed away, grateful he wasn't watching as I rifled through my suitcase. I'd packed cute white lingerie, a sexy white nightgown, and a matching satin pajama set. I opted for the later. It wasn't remotely appropriate for a wedding night, but maybe it would be so un-sexy that Angelo would forget any thoughts of seducing me at all.

I locked myself into the bathroom to change, then used the toilet and washed my hands before emerging. I poked my head out first, then opened the door fully when I saw Angelo hadn't moved from the chair. I padded quickly across the room and climbed into bed, painfully aware he was watching my every move.

As I tugged the covers all the way to my chin, Angelo stood. I held my breath as he walked towards me, no, past me. He shut the bathroom door and a moment later, I heard water running. I debated pretending to be asleep when he came out, but I couldn't stomach the thought of keeping my eyes shut as he approached. I hated surprises.

When he emerged, he had stripped down to a sleeveless, ribbed T-shirt and his suit pants. The belt was gone, as were his socks. Angelo walked past me to the bar, refilled his glass, then checked his phone.

"I'm going to sit on the balcony for a bit. Do you want me to turn off the lamp?"

I tried to decipher possible meanings of his words, then heard myself say "okay." It seemed like the best response, since I had told him I was going to bed. But as darkness filled the room, I realized my mistake.

I watched through the sliver of moonlight as Angelo took his drink onto the balcony. He left the door open a crack, and sat on one of the chairs facing the darkness below. A moment later, the light of his cell phone illuminated his face.

I stared at Angelo for what felt like an eternity, my body growing more and more fatigued with each passing moment. I knew I'd never fall asleep, not with the uncertainty of when he'd return to the room and join me in bed, and especially not while wondering what he'd expect when he did.

But apparently, my exhaustion was stronger than my determination to stay awake.

Angelo

I gripped my drink so hard I feared I'd shatter the glass. A wiser man would stop drinking and go to sleep. Or at least switch to water. But I was not a wise man. Nope. Far from one.

I was the biggest fucking moron alive.

How had I gone from pledging to never date or pursue a serious relationship to marrying a stranger? I remembered the reasons my mom and Matteo had sworn it was a good idea, but none of them seemed to persuasive at present. So why had I fallen for them? Had I just forgotten the reasons I'd vowed to remain single?

I tipped the rest of the drink into my mouth, cringing as the ice clanked against the side of the glass. I prayed the noise hadn't woken Catalina, but I didn't dare look.

Even staring at the darkness beyond the balcony window, focusing on the quiet street and distant glimmer of boats on the Tiber River, I still couldn't shake the image of Catalina. Specifically, Catalina's back, as I unfastened the dress. The image haunted me...the way her creamy, bronze skin contrasted with the whiteness of the dress, the way the curve of her shoulders gave way to a tapered waist and the delectable hint of what lay just beyond. The vision of her thong peeking out when I untied the ribbons had instantly transformed my dick into a painfully hard rod.

Now, ten minutes later, after trying my damnedest to focus on all the unsexy topics I could muster, I still sported the erection. I'd take care of it before bed, if only to ensure it didn't pop back up overnight, but I didn't dare do anything until I knew Catalina was asleep.

I shuddered at the thought of her curled up in that bed, peacefully dreaming. She seemed so sweet and innocent that it almost felt wrong to slide under the covers beside her, but I wasn't about to try to sleep sitting up, either.

It wasn't just the sight of her that kept running through my mind, either. Her skin felt so soft, so warm. The mere act of touching her bare skin while unbuttoning her dress somehow comforted me more than anything else I'd encountered the past year. God, and then there was her scent. Catalina smelled like a bakery from heaven. I wasn't sure if she wore perfume or lotion or just had a naturally magical fucking aroma, but the woman smelled incredible, like flowers and freshly frosted cupcakes mixed with a hint of something wild.

The urge to lick her had been overwhelming. Maybe I should have.

I snorted at the image, picturing the confused, indignant reaction she'd surely have.

Technically, I supposed I could have touched her more,

indulged in my fantasies. Then I wouldn't be out here nursing a drink while my cock felt like it was trapped in a vise.

When she'd told me I couldn't sleep with other women during our "marriage," I'd had no intention of complying with her request, but my counter-demand seemed reasonable nonetheless. Catalina was my wife. I was absolutely entitled to sex with her now. Sure, she liked to argue about everything, but at the end of the day, I didn't think she'd protest. She might even enjoy it.

And if I hadn't been so fucking attracted to her, I might have tried something. But as it was, I could never. The only way sex with Catalina could help anything would be if the sex were terrible. Otherwise, the act would just further fuel my unhealthy obsession. The last thing I needed was to add dozens more visions, smells, sounds, and oh God, tastes, to my spank bank.

Besides, I wasn't oblivious to the way her hands trembled when she touched me. I saw the fear in her eyes when I neared her. I heard the terror in her voice when she asked about the guns. The last thing I wanted to do was hurt another woman.

I stood, gazing into the room. My eyes struggled to adjust after sitting under the moonlight for so long, but I eventually deciphered the shape of my new wife, huddled under the covers. She'd pulled the blankets all the way up to her chin, presumably out of modesty, and she was sure to overheat if she stayed that way. She wasn't moving, so I assumed she'd fallen asleep, but I didn't want to risk waking her.

I crept into the room, leaving the balcony door ajar. I went straight to the bathroom, indulging in a long, productive shower. The moment I dried off, I wondered if the noise from the shower had disturbed Catalina's sleep and, just like that, my dick was hard again.

I blew out a sigh and brushed my teeth. I was not about to jerk off a second time. My body could just take the hint. I changed into a thin pair of boxers, my usual summer sleepwear, then tiptoed back into the bedroom. I shut and locked the balcony, noting zero movement from Catalina. I set my phone and one of my guns on my nightstand, then carefully crawled under the covers.

I waited a minute, but the slow, steady rise and fall of Catalina's chest continued undisturbed. So I folded the covers down lower, made myself comfortable, and tried to think about anything at all other than the gorgeous angel asleep beside me.

CHAPTER 8

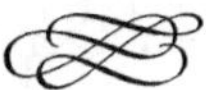

Catalina

I roused slowly in the morning, feeling the sunlight on my face before opening my eyes. I was groggy, and an icky taste filled my mouth, telling me I'd drank too much the night before. The rest of the details didn't hit me until I opened my eyes.

Sprawled out beside me lay Angelo Conti. He was shirtless, and his tan body contrasted sharply with the stark white bedding. He lay on his back, with one arm tucked behind his head, and the covers hit right at his belly button, leaving me unable to determine if he was wearing any clothes at all. His eyes were closed, and based on the steady rise and fall of his muscled chest, I assumed he was asleep. His face still bore the same serious expression he had throughout the day, though.

I tried to remember what time he had joined me in bed, but I didn't think I'd even woken. A flitter of panic washed over me as I considered that maybe I'd slept through it because he'd roofied me, but if that were the case, he probably wouldn't have re-dressed me after. As it was, my matching silk pajama shorts and button-down collared shirt were still securely in place. The comfy, white pajama set wasn't the sexiest I owned, but it was, at least, sophisticated. I had packed two different options that were more honeymoon-appropriate, but I had no intention of wearing those around Angelo unless he forced me to as a part of our stipulated conditions.

I watched him sleep for another minute, then rolled to the edge of the bed. According to the clock, it was nearly nine am. I wasn't sure when we needed to check out, but I was grateful for the chance to shower and dress before Angelo woke. I slid onto the floor then tiptoed across the room to the bathroom.

I grimaced when I saw my own reflection in the mirror. Black smudges beneath my eyes told me either I hadn't slept enough or hadn't adequately removed my wedding makeup. And my hair felt gunky and weird from all the products used to secure my up-do. I took off my top, then brushed my teeth while heading to the shower to see if I could figure out the fancy Italian faucet.

When I turned back to the mirror, I shrieked.

A bright red stain bloomed across the inside of the left thigh of my shorts. I swore under my breath and turned, confirming that the stain was also on the back.

Just fucking great.

I tugged off my shorts, and gritted my teeth at my blood-soaked panties. I yanked a robe around myself then held the stained garments in my hand while I switched on the shower faucet. I had expected the hot water to spray down, cleaning the blood from my clothes with the force of the water pressure, but that's not exactly how it worked.

The water that sprayed out was ice cold. And it didn't spray directly down. It hit my arm and the clothes, but also shot icy water into my eye. I shrieked again, jerking my body to the side to protect myself from the frigid spray.

The bathroom door flew open and Angelo rushed in. My eyes dropped from his panicked face to his very shirtless body.

"Jesus, are you okay?"

I looked back to his face and realized Angelo looked truly concerned. "Yeah, I'm fine. I just—"

"What the hell happened? I woke up and heard you scream and the bed was covered in blood and now…" his voice trailed off as his eyes wandered the room.

I followed his horrified gaze and realized that thanks to the freezing cold blast of water, or maybe thanks to my jerking away, blood had splattered on the shower walls, on my robe, and even on one of the towels hanging outside the shower. And now, since I was standing there like a moron, clutching my icy cold, sopping wet, bloody clothes in my hand, blood dripped onto the rug.

Just kill me now, I prayed.

"Sorry for waking you. I've got everything under control," I lied, shooing him to the door.

Unfortunately, he didn't budge. And nothing I did was going to force that man anywhere.

"What happened? How did you get hurt?"

"I'm not hurt," I insisted. I let my eyes wander around the room again. "God, this looks like a fucking crime scene."

"This looks nothing like a crime scene," Angelo said in a voice that was entirely too serious.

I was starting to question exactly how many crime scenes he'd seen when he added, "Unless the killer is a complete moron."

I gritted my teeth. "Okay, well, I can get it. You didn't need to see any of this." I motioned again for him to leave, but instead, he leaned past me, shutting off the shower. Then he grabbed my dirty clothes and tossed them into the sink.

I could've died seeing his hand now covered in my blood.

"Omigod, I'm so sorry," I gushed, turning on the sink to wash off his hand.

"It's not a big deal. I don't mind blood."

"Yeah, um, only surgeons and serial killers can say that with a straight face, so…" I stopped talking when I realized he might, in fact, have been telling the truth. Based on what I'd found online, Angelo was no stranger to shootings and death.

"I only meant I'm not squeamish. Where did all this come from anyway?" Angelo focused on me with a serious precision, causing me to tug the bathrobe tighter around my nude body. "If you're not hurt, then… oh." His expression changed the moment he figured it out.

"Yeah, well, I obviously didn't plan on my period starting up again last night, especially not quite so…dramatically. I mean, it's usually four days and it started like a week ago but was only two and I figured my body was just being weird about the stress over marrying a stranger, and…" I snapped my lips together, realizing I'd just given said stranger waaaaaay more info about my menstrual cycle than he needed.

I half expected him to gag and walk out, but instead, Angelo just stood there calmly as if waiting for me to finish my rant. When it was clear I had no intention of blabbering more, he spoke.

"Right. So, do you need to go by the pharmacy to pick up any…supplies?"

I relaxed a smidge. That was actually an incredibly thoughtful, and entirely unexpected, thing for him to say. "No, I packed stuff, and it'll probably be over by tomorrow anyway. But, um, I do need to get this stain out. I didn't pack enough clothes to ruin them, especially now that we're going to be gone so long."

"Okay." Angelo sucked in a breath, then turned towards the sink. "Well, first of all, that's not the best way to get fresh blood stains out. Just use hot water and a bar of soap." He waited till the water was hot, then scrubbed my soiled clothes with the bar of hand soap.

His pecs bulged as he scrubbed, and I bit my lip. The man was literally cleaning my dirty underwear, and here I was getting aroused by his stupid muscles. Clearly, I had issues. I walked past him, leaving the bathroom so I could see how bad the damage on the bed was.

Truthfully, it wasn't terrible. Just a few spots. But since the sheets were the whitest white I'd ever seen, the bright red flecks of blood were impossible to miss.

"What should I do about the bed?" I asked.

"Don't worry about the bedding. It's the honeymoon suite. Housekeeping will just think we had a much more entertaining night than we did," he paused while I scowled. "And I'll leave a good tip. It's fine."

He held up my shorts, which were now stain-free, then draped them over a towel rod beside my panties. "When we check in to the villa, we can send our clothes out to be laundered. And we've got a couple hours before the ferry leaves, so we could hit up a shop or two to buy more clothes."

I started to protest, but he'd already wandered back towards the bed. He sat on his side of the bed, reaching for the phone. "Take your shower. I'll order breakfast and then we can check out after we eat."

Angelo

I told Stefano that Catalina needed more clothes for the honeymoon, and he drove us to a section of town with several shops in a row. The first one appeared to carry lingerie and sleepwear, so I figured Catalina could tackle that alone. I helped her out of the car, then opened my wallet.

"I need to make some quick calls, but I'd be shocked if they don't have at least one salesperson who speaks English. Just start in that store and work your way down the row. I'll join you in a few," I said, gesturing to the closest shop. I pulled a stack of euros from my wallet, folded them in half, and handed her the bundle.

She made no move to take the money.

"This should be more than enough, but if you need more—" I began.

"I'm not taking your money," she said.

"Pretty sure you're not supposed to keep using Daddy's charge card once you're married."

A twitch of her eye told me she had not thought of that.

"I have my own credit cards."

I didn't know what kind of money librarians made, but I suspected it wasn't enough to cover high-end Italian boutiques. Still, I wasn't about to broach that topic on a busy street when we had limited time. "The exchange rate is brutal when you pay with cards. Just take the cash, and we'll sort it out later."

She hesitated, then agreed.

I watched her head into the store, then turned back to Stefano.

He bit back a smile. "Fun wedding night?" he teased.

I rolled my eyes and paced along the sidewalk. I didn't actually have calls to make, or anything else to do, to be honest. I just needed space from Catalina. Something about that tiny, quiet woman was so overwhelming. I couldn't breathe near her.

"She's gotten under your skin," Stefano said.

I shot him a look that was supposed to shut him up, but he remained undeterred.

"I mean, if you're taking her lingerie shopping already, I assume things went well."

"She got..." I began, then stopped. My driver did not need to know the inner details about my new wife's menstrual cycle. Although, for that matter, I wasn't sure *I* needed to know either. The entire time I'd been with Julia—over a year—I'd never once had a single conversation with her about what went on with her body or when. I wasn't even sure if she actually got a period. I thought maybe she took medicine or something to stop it, but I'd never thought to ask.

"I'm not taking her shopping. She's on her own. We are just driving her," I finally said to Stefano. I checked my phone, but for once, I had no unread texts or emails. I blew out a sigh, then gazed up. "Are you coming to Capri?"

He shook his head.

"Do you know who is driving us there?"

Stefano grinned. "Your parents thought you'd like to be alone with your new bride. The villa should be well stocked before you arrive and then you can just hibernate in your little love nest until it's time to fly back to the U.S."

I scowled and paced further down the sidewalk. I needed a distraction so my mind wouldn't keep flitting to images of Catalina sampling various new undergarments.

Catalina

A feeling of unease washed over me as the ferry pulled away from the dock in Naples. Everywhere I looked, the scenery was gorgeous. But as the waves lapped at the edges of the boat, I couldn't shake the dread. What sane person willingly travelled to an island with a criminal she just met?

Angelo passed the first few minutes of the boat ride on his phone. By the time he gazed up at me, I'd begun busying myself taking photos. I tried to focus on how gorgeous the pictures would look on my Instagram feed, even without filters, but in the back of my mind, I also noted the value of having some documentation of where I was. For all I knew, these picturesque moments would be my last.

"We should take a photo for your friends," Angelo said, frowning. "Or for your stalker."

I swallowed in response, then moved to step closer. The boat lurched over a rogue wave and I stumbled, slamming into Angelo's side. He was built like a brick wall, but his arm roped around me with an instinctual chivalry that kept me upright.

"You okay?" he asked.

I nodded. "Yeah. Sorry."

Angelo took my phone and angled it towards us, framing the perfect selfie. My hair was blowing in the breeze, and my dark sunglasses obscured the worry in my eyes. Behind us, craggy rocks of the island dotted the background.

"You'll need to stop with the social media," Angelo said as he returned my phone. "Once the world realizes we're married and that you're no longer fair game for toying with, there's no point of keeping it up."

"I like the pictures," I said, grimacing at the childish tone in my voice. "I like taking them, editing them, and I really like seeing my story unfold over time. Haven't you ever heard of photo-journalism?"

"Documenting your every move isn't really conducive to the lifestyle you'll have as Mrs. Conti," he replied, dismissing all of my protests with a single wave of his hand.

I opened my mouth to reply, but let it go. I focused my attention on the fast-approaching land. I'd seen pictures of Capri before, but I'd never really felt drawn to it, at least not any more than any other Mediterranean site. Honestly, Santorini had been pretty high on my list. I supposed there was a chance I would've chosen it as a honeymoon destination if I'd had any actual say in the matter.

But as we drew closer to Capri, I couldn't recall why I'd never added it to my travel bucket list. I'd never seen a more striking cerulean sea, and the massive rocks jutting out from the water only emphasized the beauty of the island. A spattering of colorful buildings dotted the coastline and instantly warmed me to the island more than the stark white structures I'd always seen in pictures of the Greek Mediterranean. The picturesque beauty facing me was, quite literally, breathtaking.

I was nearly dizzy with anticipation by the time the ferry docked, and I gripped the railing to avoid stumbling as we lurched to a stop. I gazed to the side and realized Angelo was watching me. He didn't look away when I caught him staring, but I also wasn't sure how long he'd been focused on me. I felt heat rush to my cheeks.

"It's, um, quite pretty," I said, embarrassed for my obvious awe at the sight. "You've probably been here so much that you don't even notice anymore, but—"

"You never get used to this type of beauty," he interrupted, still staring at me.

He offered a hand to help me off the ferry. The process of gathering our items and traveling from the port at Marina Grande to our actual villa took nearly two hours. I was exhausted and parched by the time Angelo unlocked the door to our villa. A concierge walked ahead with our luggage, and Angelo motioned for me to enter next.

I took two steps into the room, then stopped abruptly. Directly ahead, gauzy white curtains danced in the breeze as the sliding door to the balcony had been left open. Just outside, a narrow paver patio led to a small infinity pool. The edge of the pool dropped like a waterfall, lending the illusion that it poured directly into the Mediterranean. We were up high in the hills, but our villa seemed to jut out directly over the water.

I made my way outside, not even noticing the interior of the villa. I paused on the balcony, inhaling the salty sea air, then traipsed down the two steps onto the patio. From this view, I could also see a small dining table, two lounge chairs, and a hot tub off to the side of the pool. The space appeared to have been carved into the side of the rocks, leaving complete privacy on both sides. This outdoor space could only be seen by someone looking down from a plane or gazing up from a boat.

Back here, we would be completely alone.

I startled, suddenly aware that I was not the only one by the pool. I turned to see Angelo standing beside me, his hands thrust into his pockets and his dark glasses still covering his face.

"I hope this is alright. A friend recommended this place and I figured we would at least have some privacy if nothing else," he said.

"Yes, it's gorgeous," I said.

"If you'd like to change, we can go out for dinner, or we could order in," he said, pointing back to the unit.

I snapped out of my trance and nodded. As exhausted as I was, going out seemed like the safer option. "I'll get changed," I said. I started back inside, pausing to note that the interior of the villa was nearly as idyllic as the outside. A small seating area, with a plush white sofa and matching chaise occupied the center of the room. Sapphire blue throw pillows and artwork accented the space and mirrored the outdoors. To the right, just past a half wall, there was a large bed in similar white and blue tones.

A single mahogany door offered privacy from the rest of the space. I assumed that was the bathroom, and where I'd apparently be headed to change. I didn't love that I had so few options for true privacy for the next two weeks, but I had to acknowledge that this would be the perfect location for a honeymoon if it were the real thing.

I changed into a turquoise sundress, then a car came to take us to dinner. Angelo gazed at me as I climbed into the car, and I half expected him to say something, but instead he just cleared his throat then looked away.

At the restaurant, he ordered an Aperol spritz for each of us, then offered to translate the menu. "Or I could just order for you," he said. "Do you have any allergies?"

I laughed so hard I nearly spit out my drink. This muscular, intense looking mobster did not seem like the type to inquire about food allergies. And yet, here we were.

I wasn't sure what sounded good at the moment, so I just told him to order. I hadn't eaten much the past few days, what with the stress of the wedding, so I was famished. Anything would probably taste amazing. The Aperol spritz was by far the best I'd ever tasted. It was fizzy and sweet, and just strong enough.

The waitress had brought a small bowl of olives with our drinks. I asked Angelo if that was an appetizer.

His lip twitched as if that was an odd question. "That's the aperitivo. The antipasti is next."

I nodded, as if that meant anything, but a few minutes later, the waitress set a charcuterie platter on the table between us.

"In Italy, we have a saying that eating brings on the appetite. So you begin a traditional meal with lighter items to help spur your appetite," Angelo said, sampling a thin slice of meat and a cracker.

I nibbled on some of the meats, crackers, and cheeses, but hoped some real food would come soon. Angelo ordered wine for himself and water for me. I figured I should avoid more alcohol until I had something in my stomach to soak it up.

For the primi, which Angelo explained was more like a side dish in America, we had ravioli Caprese. Apparently, that was one of the foods for which Capri was famous. The pasta was lighter than I'd have expected, and the fresh tomato and basil sauce topping the cheese-filled dough was so exquisite that I couldn't help but moan with delight. Angelo said nothing, but appeared uncomfortable with my enjoyment of the meal. I groaned inwardly, wondering if he was one of those men that thought women should live off of salad and yogurt or something.

"The secondi is basically the main course," he said. "This is pezzogna all'acqua pazza."

I nodded, but had no idea what any of that meant. Luckily, he went on to explain.

"It's a locally-caught fish in some sort of tomato sauce. I also ordered some calamari for you to try."

"I've had calamari before," I said, but once I bit into the dish, I realized how wrong I was. The calamari I'd had before tasted more like onion rings made from rubber bands. This calamari practically melted into my mouth.

"Mmm," I groaned.

Angelo sipped his wine, his expression a mixture of bemusement and stress. I decided not to pay any attention to him and just focus on my delicious food. We were splitting everything, including the roasted mushrooms and a side of pan-fried asparagus. I was starting to fill up, when the waitress delivered another platter.

"Insalata course," Angelo said.

"Salad after the meal?" I confirmed.

He nodded, then dipped a portion of the salad onto each of our plates. The base of the salad was arugula, and it was topped with cherry tomatoes, cannellini beans, olives, cucumber and red pepper. The dressing was a simple vinaigrette, but like everything else we'd tasted, it was exquisite. I was still eating the salad when a plate of fresh fruits and cheeses arrived.

"Formaggi e frutta," Angelo said. "Hope you're not full."

I chuckled, but managed to sample a bite of each item on the plate. Somehow, we'd managed to go an entire hour without discussing anything of substance. We'd talked about our favorite foods, and what we ate back home, but we hadn't really touched on anything serious. Now that I'd been fortified with a billion calories, I decided to broach more personal topics.

"So, what exactly do you do for work?" I asked.

Angelo swallowed the last sip of his wine, as if needing a moment to think. "Depends on the day," he finally said. "My family owns a large shipyard in Bridgeport, so I do a lot of work with imports and exports. I also run a construction company though."

"You work construction?"

A frown flitted across his face. "Uhh, well, I run the company. I don't actually do any of the heavy lifting, if that's what you mean. My background is in business, so…"

His voice trailed off as the waitress brought two steaming mugs of the darkest espresso I'd ever seen, plus a plate of cannelloni. I rubbed my stomach, already envisioning how nauseous I'd be after eating the rich dessert.

"Is black coffee at bedtime a tradition here too?" I asked.

Angelo shrugged. "It'll help you digest the dessert. Caffe is usually served with the dolce course. After this, we'll have a digestivo. Capri has the best limoncello you'll ever taste," he promised.

I sighed, then downed the rest of my food.

We were both quiet on the way back to the villa, then Angelo announced that he was going for a swim. For a moment, I thought he meant in the ocean, which made no sense since the beach was much further than it appeared, and surely wouldn't be safe in the dark night. But then, Angelo emerged from the bathroom in a pair of fitted swim trunks.

He dove into the pool, his body making nary a splash or a sound as he broke through the surface of the water. I lingered at the edge of the balcony, watching as he began to swim laps. Angelo's technique was flawless, as far as I could discern, and I couldn't help but wonder if he'd been a competitive swimmer in his younger days. I didn't dare break the spell by asking though. Instead, I simply watched, mesmerized.

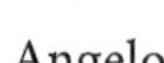

Angelo

*B*eing alone with Catalina in the most romantic villa in all of the Mediterranean was pure torture. On our first night, I'd been relieved when she chose to go out to eat at a restaurant over ordering in. But then, all throughout the meal, I had to listen to her moan with pleasure at every bite.

She hadn't eaten much since the wedding, so I'd expected her to be hungry. But since I wasn't sure what type of food she enjoyed, I'd merely guessed at what she might want to eat. I hadn't anticipated her making so many sounds as she chewed. I could only assume that any girl who was that vocal with her enjoyment of food would be really loud in the bedroom. It didn't help matters that she'd worn this ridiculously sexy sundress that revealed her cleavage, hugged the curve of her hips, and displayed her delicate shoulders.

I'd gone for a swim after dinner, certain I'd need to fully exhaust myself before sleeping next to her. I still had to jerk off in the shower, but thankfully she was sound asleep by the time I joined her in bed.

The next morning, I woke before Catalina. I'd planned two days' worth of stereotypical tourist activities for us, hoping that would be adequate to fill her Instagram feed and convince people our relationship was legit.

We started with breakfast in Piazza Vittoria in Anacapri. Catalina didn't disappoint, groaning her delight at the croissants, fresh fruit, and even the cappuccino. We wandered around the town while our food digested, then rode the chairlift up to the peak of Mount Solaro. Despite my many trips to Capri, I'd never actually ridden on the chairlift. The views were breathtaking, but I preferred watching Catalina gasp with awe as she took in the gorgeous vista.

We downed another coffee at the café at the top of the peak, then walked back down the mountain slope, pausing for pictures in front of a small chapel perched on the mountainside. We strolled through the center of Anacapri, then took a car to visit the Sphinx of Villa San Michele. After a light lunch, we returned to the villa to rest. Catalina lounged by the pool for a bit, then we went to the Piazzetta for cocktails. We brought dinner back to the villa.

We'd kept busy enough during the day that I hadn't felt any pressure to actually talk with my new wife, aside from translating for her where necessary. We'd made polite conversation about the various tourist attractions, but that was the extent of it. I didn't mind the silence. I'd never been one to succumb to pressure to fill a void in conversation, but I got the impression Catalina was accustomed to nonstop chatter.

While we ate dinner, I asked her about her family. That seemed like a safe topic, and it kept her chatting the entire time we ate. She'd enjoyed the limoncello the day before, so I'd ensured we had more in our villa fridge. I poured a drink for each of us, then Catalina gasped.

"I just realized I've been rambling for like an hour straight," she said, cringing.

I offered a polite smile, trying to convey that I didn't mind, but she still looked flustered.

"Tell me about your family. You're the oldest too, right?" she asked.

I nodded.

"Did you get along with your siblings growing up?"

I opened my mouth, then closed it. My relationship with my siblings had been strained over the years, for sure. I supposed I'd always been friendly with my brother Matteo, who was closest in age to me, but I also suspected he'd always preferred our sister to me.

Being the oldest in the family, I was expected to take over the family business. Surprisingly, that didn't seem to be the root of my problems with my siblings, as neither of them wanted any part in the family business. Matteo reluctantly joined when forced, but he neither had the desire or stomach for the type of work we needed to do to succeed in our world.

"We all get along now. I wasn't my sister's favorite when we were children," I finally said, hoping she didn't ask what changed our relationship. I wasn't about to tell her that my sister now worshiped the ground I walked on since I shot someone to save her life.

"Why not?" Catalina asked. "Did you deserve it?"

"Deserve what?"

"To not be her favorite. I mean, were you nice to her?"

I considered the question, then answered honestly. "Sometimes. My sister lived a very different childhood than I did. I always had so much responsibility, and she just flitted through life partying and thinking only of herself."

"That wasn't exactly her fault though. And wasn't she younger?"

I shrugged. "She married a man who spent years of his life trying to undermine my relationship with my dad and stealing parts of my business."

"Luca Marina?"

"Marino," I corrected.

"Do you think she married him to make you mad?"

"No," I laughed.

"Why is that funny?"

"Did you not see them at the wedding?"

"I was a little distracted," she explained.

"Well, you'd know what I mean if you saw them together. I've never seen a couple more obsessed with each other."

"Obsessed? Or in love?"

"Both."

"So do you get along with them now?"

"I do," I said. Then I quickly rose to my feet and began cleaning up dinner to avoid further discussion.

We went to sleep early that night, then spent the next day lounging at the beach. When we'd left the villa, Catalina had been wearing a bright magenta sarong and a wide-rimmed black straw hat. She looked pretty, and a bit cosmopolitan, but nothing about her appearance was particularly unnerving. When we'd settled into our chairs at the beach though, Catalina lifted her sarong over her head, revealing a skimpy magenta bikini covering her tanned body.

I turned away, swearing under my breath. My own trunks were not nearly thick enough to hide my response to her nearly-nude body, so I didn't turn back until I'd successfully occupied my mind with stressful, work-related thoughts. Catalina read a book—literally starting and finishing the novel before sunset, and I made a few phone calls.

As evening neared, she put on her sarong and I threw a button-down over my shorts. We strolled along the beach, then went to the Punta Carena lighthouse for drinks and dinner at sunset. Had I been on a real honeymoon, I had no doubt that this precise outing would precede a night of unbelievable lovemaking. As it was, we had a nice meal then headed back to the villa in silence, both of us keeping our hands to ourselves.

Catalina showered and then emerged in her pajamas. Instead of the dorky shorts and tee shirt combo she'd worn the last two nights, a flimsy white gown was all that covered her. I sucked in a ragged breath, my dick turning to stone. I was about to say goodnight and move away when she turned to me, a quizzical expression on her face.

"My friends and family call me Lina," she finally said.

She lingered, gazing at me until I realized her words were a clear invitation. Then I nodded, and she made her way to bed.

I wasn't sure I'd ever fall asleep.

CHAPTER 10

Catalina

I'd fallen asleep before Angelo, again, but I awoke to a pitch black room a short while after. I knew I hadn't slept for long, but when I saw Angelo still wasn't in bed beside me, I checked the clock. It was after two am. I rubbed my eyes, then rose from bed. Since the villa wasn't large, it didn't take long for me to spot him by the pool.

Maybe it was my exhaustion, or maybe I was just fed up with the pained awkwardness between the two of us. We'd spent days together, and getting Angelo to talk with me was like pulling teeth. And now he was hiding from me? It was ridiculous. Even a fake marriage couldn't survive if he was never going to be honest with me.

The screen door made the slightest squeak as I scooted it open. Angelo swiveled as if expecting an assassin, then calmly turned back to face the pool. "I have to go," he said into his phone, his voice louder now. "Yeah, me too," he added to the caller.

He set the phone beside him, not acknowledging me in the

slightest. It didn't matter, since his words confirmed my suspicions.

I gazed at the pool shimmering by his feet. Thanks to the lights, the water glowed a serene shade of turquoise. Beyond the pool, I could see only blackness, accented with a spattering of tiny lights in the distance.

"That's your idea of discretion?" I finally asked, sick of waiting for him to offer excuses. "Hushed calls to your girlfriend? This is supposed to be a honeymoon."

Wordlessly, Angelo picked up his phone. He toggled to the recent calls, raising the device for me to see.

I stepped closer, confirming that the latest entry purported to be a call to "Eddie." But that meant nothing. Angelo could've easily changed the contact name for precisely such an occasion.

Feeling bold, I leaned forward and tapped on the contact, then pressed the button to air the call on speaker. Shock registered on Angelo's face, but he didn't have time to say anything before "Eddie" answered.

"Jesus, I'm up, okay man?" said a gruff, distinctly male voice.

I cringed apologetically. I didn't know Angelo well enough to gauge how angry he'd be over this, but in my defense, the hushed middle of the night call was suspicious.

"Alright, just checking," Angelo said without missing a beat, clicking to end the call.

I waited in case he was going to say something else to me, or maybe yell, but instead Angelo was silent. I decided to be mature.

"I'm sorry," I said, my voice quiet now. "It's the middle of the night, and you snuck out to make hushed calls by the pool. I just assumed…"

Angelo gazed up at me, his expression unreadable. He stood slowly, and my heart thudded as he reached his full height, towering above me. I stiffened, anticipating a lecture, or possibly worse.

But what he did was shove me.

Shrieking, I toppled sideways into the pool, the terry cloth bathrobe pooling around me like a parachute. My head didn't go under the water, but the shock of it all stunned me enough that I floundered for a moment before planting my feet on the bottom of the pool. I untangled myself from the robe before it managed to drown me. I flung the now-heavy garment onto the dry concrete.

Sopping wet, I peered up at Angelo. I wanted to scream at him. I felt the anger boiling just below the surface. But I said nothing. The look on his face was one I didn't recognize. He bit back a smile and his eyes almost seemed to twinkle.

Was I seeing a playful version of Angelo?

"I can't believe you did that," I said, and I meant it. Pushing me into the pool was the last thing I expected him to do.

"Sorry," he said, sounding anything but apologetic. "Let me help you."

I accepted his outstretched hand and he started to hoist me out of the pool. A moment later, he pulled back his hand, causing me to flail backwards into the water. This time, the splash soaked my hair.

"Oh my God! I really cannot believe you just did that!" I shrieked. I slapped the water, hoping to spray him, but only a few droplets reached his legs.

"Oh come on, it's refreshing."

"Refreshing? Why don't you get in if it's so refreshing?"

Angelo crouched on the edge of the pool. "I was in it."

"Just your feet," I pointed out.

I reached for his hand again as if seeking help out, and this time, maybe he would've actually hoisted me out of the pool. But I didn't give him a chance. Instead, I tugged as hard as I could. Angelo teetered off balance, but instead of flopping into the pool as I had, he maneuvered into a half dive once it became clear he couldn't avoid the water.

After his playful reaction a few minutes before, I wasn't

expecting anger when he emerged to the surface. But his outright laughter still surprised me.

"I did not see that coming," he admitted, shaking the water off his head like a dog.

"Yeah well, it's not fun. Is it?"

He cocked his head to the side then splashed me. Now that I was already drenched, the shock of the cool water didn't jolt me. I flung water up in his face, then dove under the surface to make a quick escape. Angelo followed me to the shallow end, pinning me against the wall by placing one hand on either side of me.

"Let's get one thing straight," he began. "Eddie is many things to me, but a lover is not one of them."

I stilled, acutely aware that only a matter of inches separated our faces. The last time we'd been this close was probably our wedding, but I hadn't been able to concentrate on anything then. Now, I noticed the droplets of water coating his thick, black lashes. He had a small, almost whitish scar beneath his left eye, and a day's worth of stubble surrounded his full lips.

Angelo Conti was definitely an attractive man.

And on paper, he was mine.

In reality, though, probably not.

"Do you understand?" he asked.

I opened my lips to speak, but didn't remember hearing the question.

"Eddie, not my girlfriend," Angelo repeated.

"Right," I said, my voice rushing out like an exhale.

Angelo waited a minute, then dropped his arms, opening up escape routes on either side of me. But for some reason, I didn't move. We both stood there, staring at each other as if under some wacky spell.

Angelo was the one to break the silence. "Your lips are turning purple. Why don't we move to the jacuzzi?"

Instead of waiting for my answer, he turned, tugging my hand so I followed him towards the concrete steps leading out of the pool. He released my hand once we reached dry land, making his way over to the dials for the hot tub. A low rumble emitted from the motor, then bubbles began to fill the small pool.

I glanced down, suddenly aware that the gauzy white nightgown clinging to my flesh was completely see-through. It was the perfect attire for a real honeymoon, but made for terrible swimwear. I tried in vain to cover myself, crossing my arms over my chest, but that only caused my breasts to jut up higher.

Angelo stood on the edge of the hot tub, making no attempts at subtlety as his eyes slowly roamed up my body as though inspecting every damp inch.

His attire—a simple pair of black boxer briefs, was much better suited for the pool. Even though the shorts clung to him, the darker fabric concealed what it needed to, and I couldn't imagine he'd want to hide the rest. Angelo's torso looked like it was carved from stone. If the whole life of crime didn't work out for him, he could probably make a decent living as a swimsuit model.

"You're freezing," Angelo said, his eyes seemingly locked on my nipples, which had hardened to points. "Get in."

"Bossy," I mumbled. But the steam misting out of the jacuzzi beckoned to me, so I stepped in, gasping as the heat permeated the numbness of my toes. I lowered myself to one of the benches, instantly relaxed. My eyes drifted shut as I settled back. The combination of the jets massaging my sore muscles, the soothing heat, and the rhythmic sound of the motor worked together to erase any stress of the last few days.

The water sloshed higher as Angelo climbed in, but I didn't open my eyes. He sat beside me, groaning like he'd just tasted the most delicious dish of his life.

"I can't believe you pushed me into the pool," I said.

His chuckle was barely audible over the rumble of the jets. "I can't believe you called Eddie."

I opened my eyes, gazing at him. "For all I knew, it was Susie or Stella or Sarah."

"What's with the S names?"

I splashed my hand into the water. "I don't know. Not the point."

"Why is it so important to you anyway, that whole monogamy thing?"

"I think you'll find most people value monogamy in a marriage."

Angelo scowled. "Maybe, but we don't have the most traditional arrangement. And the last I checked, there was a difference between monogamy and celibacy."

My stomach clenched. He was right, but that didn't change my feelings. Angelo gazed at me expectantly, clearly wanting more of an explanation.

"I hate hypocrisy," I finally said. "Like, why make a big show out of all these promises if you can't keep them? Don't tell the world you're going to love and cherish someone, if you're going to turn around and disrespect them by sleeping with half the city. It's not that hard to be faithful."

Angelo's expression suggested he disagreed, but he kept that to himself. "So, I'm guessing Carlos cheated on you?"

I shook my head. "No." Then, I actually thought about it. "Well, maybe. I don't know. That's not why it bothers me so much."

"Why then?"

I took my time answering, unsure how much I wanted to divulge. "My dad is…" I paused, searching for the right words. "He treats my mom like a prized possession. And at home and in his work, he goes on and on about respect, how it's the most important thing in the world. But everyone knows he's cheated on my mom, like multiple times. It's mortifying. She knows it, I know it, the entire world knows he's had these affairs, and it's painful watching her try to pretend she doesn't see the way people look at her, the pity in their eyes when they look at this pathetic woman and wonder why she isn't enough for him or how she's too stupid to see what he's doing."

I paused, feeling my anger rise up. "I just want to strangle him sometimes. Or at least shake him until he realizes what a hypocritical ass he is," I said through clenched teeth.

Angelo quirked a brow. "Wow. Tell me how you *really* feel."

I turned away, embarrassed by my outburst. I didn't want to say any more, didn't want to risk telling Angelo how much he reminded me of my dad, how I could easily see him telling the world he was mine only to humiliate me by dating half the women in Manhattan.

The rumble of the jets and gentle bubbling of the water was the only sound for a long time. I glanced at Angelo, noted his eyes were shut, and wondered if he'd fallen asleep. But then he moved, his hand reaching out through the water, settling on top of mine.

◈

Angelo

I could've fallen asleep in the jacuzzi. Everything about it was soothing, and I knew the second I left its warmth, I'd be wide awake again.

Fucking time change.

I couldn't get out of the tub yet anyway. I hadn't brought a towel outside when I called Eddie, not intending to swim, and I couldn't think of any other way to hide my massive erection from Lina.

God, she was like a literal wet dream, standing there all sweet and innocent in that see-through negligee. What was she doing with a gown like that anyway? That was the sort of lingerie I'd expect to see on a real honeymoon, not on whatever fucked-up trip we were on.

She was supposed to be ugly. Or at least annoying. I didn't know how to fake a relationship with the freaking goddess sitting next to me, especially when she was pouring out her heart in some doe-eyed tale that just begged for someone to swoop in and rescue her.

I tried to think about work, tried to concentrate on her story about her dad, but I absolutely could not get the image of her perfect fucking nipples out of my mind. I'd already known she had killer tits. Round, perky, and just enough to fill my hands without overwhelming her petite frame. But seeing those nipples poking through the stupid nightgown? Holy fuck. I about came on the spot.

It was ridiculous. I'd seen nipples before. Tons of nipples. I'd always assumed nipples were nipples, right? Not much variation. But nope. I'd been dead wrong. These nipples were different.

This girl was different.

And with her? Somehow I was different, too. She poured her heart out to me, practically begged for comfort. The normal Angelo would've taken that as an invitation to fuck her brains out. Normal me would've kept her coming until she didn't have a care in the world. But this new, weird version of Angelo just held her fucking hand.

"Will you tell me the truth about something?" Lina asked suddenly, jolting me from my incoherent thoughts.

I nodded, pulling my hand back to my thigh.

"Is there someone else now?" she asked, her bold blue eyes pleading with me.

"Someone…" I repeated, trying to understand the question.

"Do you have a girlfriend? Or I mean, someone on the side, or whatever?"

"Oh." I shifted more upright. "Um, no?"

"Is that a question? You don't seem certain."

I laughed at her tone. "No, it's not a question. I just didn't expect my wife to be asking about my girlfriend on our honeymoon."

She sighed. "I guess you don't have to tell me."

I flung my hands in the air, inadvertently spraying us both with water. "I am telling you. You want honesty? I haven't dated anyone since my last girlfriend. A couple one night stands, yeah, but.." I stopped talking before I humiliated myself further.

"You really loved her?"

"No," I confessed. "At first I thought I maybe did, but the more time passed, the more I wondered if I was only with her because she seemed like the type of person I should be with." I didn't say aloud the rest, how she was actually the worst possible person for me to be with, but that I hadn't realized that fact until it was far too late.

I could tell Catalina wanted to ask me more, but I wasn't about to let her push further into my history with Julia.

"How did a nice girl like you end up with a guy like Carlos?" I asked, turning the tables on her.

Lina laughed, and it was the sweetest sound imaginable.

"Why is that funny?"

She turned to me. "Have you never seen him? The guy is hot." She drew out the single syllable of the last word for emphasis.

I rolled my eyes. I had seen Carlos before, and I really didn't see the appeal. "He's short," I finally said.

"Well, so am I, so it was kind of perfect."

"I suppose he had some monster cock too," I teased.

"Ahh, more like magical," she said, her dimples popping.

"If you're into assholes with big dicks, I guess we'll make the perfect couple then."

Lina raised an eyebrow, cast a glance down to my shorts, which were thankfully concealed by the bubbling water. Then, she giggled maniacally.

I waited a moment before pressing further. "Seriously though, you had to have realized what he was like before things got so—"

"Intense?" she supplied before pausing for a minute. "Yeah, I mean, there were red flags from the start. I don't think I ever actually considered what we had to be serious. But I was fresh out of a totally different kind of relationship and I needed that confidence boost Carlos gave me. He was so proud of me, he wanted the world to know I was his. He needed to know where I was, what I was doing, every second of every day."

"He was controlling and possessive," I summarized.

"Yeah, a little. But it was flattering. And that feeling of being wanted so much was flattering."

I cringed, wondering how such a seemingly normal, mentally-stable woman could describe a sociopathic stalker so lightly.

"You think I'm unhinged now, don't you?" Lina asked.

I nodded.

"Well, I blame Harry. He ruined me."

"Harry," I repeated, confused.

"He's British," she said, as if that answered any questions. "He was my boyfriend before Carlos."

"Okay."

"He was a professor at my university and I could've sworn he was the love of my life," she continued.

"He was older?" I guessed.

Lina nodded. "Not a ton though. He was thirty one."

My age, I thought. "And at the time, you were..."

"I was twenty-two, but super mature for my age."

I laughed at the notion than *anyone* could be mature at twenty-two.

"I'd never had a serious boyfriend, and whenever I went on dates with guys my age, it felt almost like I was babysitting. They just wanted to get drunk, fool around, and play video games. I just needed someone I could talk to, you know?" She paused, but not long enough for me to answer.

"Harry taught my nineteenth century English lit class, so we read all the gothic novels and moody romances. I'd never read Wuthering Heights in high school and it's just so captivating, right?"

I nodded as if I had any idea what she was talking about.

"I fell in love with all of the books. I just devoured them, really, and so I kept going to Harry for more recommendations. And then after I read each one, of course we had to meet up to discuss."

"Of course."

"Harry could talk for hours about a book, but he always wanted to hear what I thought about it, too. Maybe it was the professor thing. When I was with Harry, I felt like the most fascinating person alive. He valued my brain, unlike all the dumb frat guys that just wanted to get in my pants."

"So the love of your life was completely platonic?"

"No. the third time I went to his office to discuss a book, he kissed me. And then he apologized because, well, he was my professor and that sort of thing was frowned upon. But we both felt the connection, so the next time we wanted to talk about a book, I met him at his apartment. We'd barely covered the basics of Frankenstein before we made love."

"Sounds idyllic," I said, my voice dripping with sarcasm.

"It was," she agreed, missing my sarcasm. "The whole secret component was hot, for sure. But after the semester ended and he wasn't my professor anymore, I asked him why we were still hiding. And he made the point that it would look suspicious if we came out as a couple right after the class ended. So we waited another semester."

"Wait, and this entire time, you're not dating anyone else?"

"Of course not."

"But you were in college."

She shrugged. "Yeah, that part sucked. I was dying to introduce him to my friends. Or even go out to dinner with him or dancing or a bar. All we ever did was meet up at his place, sip wine, talk about a book and then have sex. I couldn't even sleep over because then people would be suspicious."

"What happened at the end of that semester?"

"Harry still didn't want anyone to know about us. I confronted him and basically he admitted he was embarrassed to be with me. He played it off as the age difference, but the message I got was that I was such a loser that he couldn't handle people associating him with me. Then Carlos came along and wanted nothing more than to show me off to the world."

"And the rest is history," I supplied.

She shrugged, then settled back against the headrest, letting her eyes drift shut.

"You should get inside, get some sleep."

Catalina wrinkled her nose. "I'd love to see the sunrise, but I am sleepy. What's on the itinerary for tomorrow?"

"You can sleep in then relax out here by the pool or something. I need to handle some work in the morning, but I made dinner reservations."

Lina appeared to consider that, then yawned. I stepped out of the jacuzzi, wrapped a towel around my waist, and then held her hand as she climbed out. Wordlessly, I offered a towel to her.

"Why were you making secret calls out here anyway?" she asked, accepting the towel.

I stared unabashedly at her perfect figure until she covered it with the towel, then tried to recall how to speak. "There's no secret. I just didn't want to wake you so I went outside and kept my voice down."

"Why were you awake in the middle of the night?"

"It was morning in Connecticut. I don't do well with the time change so I figured I'd make sure Eddie was up since he has to tackle all the work I'd be doing if I were home."

"And what work is that exactly?" Catalina tilted her head to the side in a way that told me she wasn't expecting a truthful answer. "Construction, or…illegal gambling?"

"Nice try," I commended. "I think I already told you everything you needed to know about my work."

"I thought criminals could tell their wives everything. Spousal privilege and all."

"I could. I choose not to. My last relationship didn't exactly instill trust and I just met you."

She frowned, but shuffled inside the room.

We both changed into fresh pajamas then lay down in bed. I didn't expect to fall asleep, but just after I saw the first rays of the sun peeking through the blinds, I drifted off.

CHAPTER 11

Catalina

By some miracle, Angelo was still asleep when I woke around ten. I lay in bed for several minutes, debating my next step. His back was to me, so I supposed there was a chance he was awake and just not moving, but based on the steady rise and fall of his ribcage with his breaths, I was willing to bet he was unconscious. I tried to recall if he'd gone to bed without a shirt. Surely he had, but wouldn't I have remembered that? It wasn't every night that I slept next to a twin of Adonis.

Well, I guess as long as this marriage lasted, I would be.

I rolled out of bed, then made my way to the bathroom. Angelo had said we didn't have any real plans, so I figured it would be a good day for me to explore the town. When we'd strolled around the island on our first day, I'd noticed several shops I'd wanted to visit. I could grab a souvenir for my friends, and maybe some cutesy trinket for Valeria, too.

My hair had dried funky after the late-night dip in the pool, so I combed some conditioner through it and then twisted it into an off-center knot above my head. I clipped a yellow flower barrette onto the side, then dressed in a matching pale yellow tank top with only one shoulder strap and a pair of white capris. I giggled at the irony of my pants choice—capris in Capri, then moved on to my makeup. Once I was ready to go, I stepped out of the bathroom.

I fully expected to find Angelo awake, but he hadn't moved from the bed. I grabbed a pair of strappy sandals and my purse, then crept out the door. I hesitated after I shut the door, wondering if I should've left him a note, then dismissed the idea. He could just call when he awoke.

I strolled down the side streets towards the main piazza, snapping photos of charming windowsills and balcony railings dotted with flowers, then focusing my camera on views of the sea peaking between the colorful old buildings. I bought a coffee and a croissant with a sliver of dark chocolate baked right in the middle of the buttery goodness, then devoured the flaky treat as I walked.

I ducked into two separate shops just to browse, but ended up buying random trinkets at each. The shopkeepers were so friendly, and so far, they all spoke English. After the second shop, I planned to stop for another coffee and maybe text Angelo to see if he was up. I didn't peg him for a big fan of shopping, but I thought he might enjoy browsing through the gallery in town, or maybe checking out the bookshop I'd spotted.

But the second I left the store, before I could call him, a hand reached out and yanked me by the bicep.

"Ouch!" I yelped.

The hand released me right as I turned to see Angelo. His jaw was set in a firm line and fury filled his eyes. I rubbed at my arm, trying to decide what to say, when he flung his hands in the air and began muttering some rant in Italian. I was about to walk on to the next shop and let him throw his tantrum in peace, but he switched to English.

"Jesus Christ, Lina. I woke up and you were gone. You just fucking left, no note, no way for me to find you, nothing."

I considered what he was saying. "Wait, how did you find me?"

He scowled. "I tracked your phone, obviously. But that's not relevant. You can't just disappear."

I opened my mouth to explain, but he kept lecturing me.

"The whole point of this fucking ridiculous arrangement is for me to watch you. The entire reason you and I are stuck together is so that I can keep you safe. I can't keep you safe if you wander off alone. Do you understand that at all, or are you really that stupid?"

I bit back tears and started towards the villa. "I guess I'm just that stupid, because I thought we were actually connecting last night. I guess I was wrong. Sorry you're stuck with me." I finally said.

"Lina!" he barked, sounding like a parent scolding a child.

I didn't slow down. I kept going as fast as my stupid sandals would carry me, all the way back to the villa. And then, I ignored Angelo the entire afternoon, securing my earbuds and blasting my favorite Latino tunes while tanning by the pool.

If Angelo wanted to see how bad it could be to be stuck with me, that was fine by me. I didn't need to be friends with my stupid fake husband.

⁂

Angelo

After starting my day with a near heart-attack upon waking and realizing that not only had I slept through my first call, but that also, my wife had disappeared without a trace, the day had somehow still gone downhill. Lina had apparently decided to wander into town—alone—to go shopping. Thank God I had already set up GPS tracking on her phone, since she hadn't left a note or bothered to answer my calls.

I'd found her relatively quickly and even though my first reaction at the time had been relief, somehow that had come out as anger. Honestly, I was still pissed. Lina knew she was in danger. She knew I was in charge of keeping her safe.

I would never survive if I failed her like I had Julia. I was determined to protect Lina if it was the last thing she did. But how could I do that if she snuck away every time I fell asleep?

Lina had resolved to ignore me the rest of the day, which was fine by me. I had a lot of work to catch up on, and since I'd planned for us to take a private boat tour of the area the next day, this was really my only chance to tackle all of my pending projects. Given the lack of advance notice of my wedding, I hadn't been able to clear my schedule for the entire honeymoon.

I didn't want Lina to stay mad at me though, so I resolved to ensure both of us made it to the restaurant for our dinner reservation. Around five thirty, I marched out to the pool deck, where Lina was roasting herself like a marshmallow, rotating to a different side every half hour or so. I stepped in front of her until her eyes popped open, then I gestured for her to remove her earbuds.

Surprisingly, she did.

"We're leaving for dinner at seven, so you should start getting ready. Reservations are for seven thirty."

"I'm not hungry," she said, moving to resume her music.

"I don't care," I replied. "You're going whether you want to or not. You can choose if you're wearing a sweaty bikini or a nice dress."

Lina blew out a sigh, then gazed at her phone.

"Look, I didn't mean to hurt your feelings earlier. I was worried when I realized you'd left alone."

She said nothing, but she slowly rose from her chair,

stretched, then headed inside to shower. I supposed that was a small victory.

The restaurant I'd chosen was near the water, and right in the center of the Piazza. It was a gorgeous night, so we were dining alfresco. Lina had been quiet on the way to the restaurant, and said nothing as we sat at the table. I recognized the look in her eyes by this point though. She appreciated the ambiance. This place was quintessential Italian, and if the food was as good as I remembered, she'd love that, too.

The waiter brought us both waters with our menus. Lina immediately reached for her glass, chugging like she'd just been rescued from a deserted island. I ordered some bruschetta while we browsed the menu, and Lina tackled it with a similar hunger. Unfortunately, as she tipped the bread to rip off a bite, a glob of tomato coated in olive oil and balsamic glaze slid off the toast and down the front of her dress.

Instantly, her cheeks flushed bright red. The reaction was so marked that I laughed out loud.

"Oh that's funny to you? Me ruining my dress? Learning the person you're stuck with is clumsy?"

My smile faded as quickly as it had appeared. "It's not ruined. I have a solution back in the room that'll make it good as new."

Lina's expression was dubious. "You're a laundry expert?"

"No, but I have more experience getting stains out of clothing than you'd expect," I said, not realizing until I shut up how that sounded. "I mean, with work, I..." I stopped again, certain that was no better.

She cleared her throat and dropped her eyes to her menu. Since everything was in Italian, it was clear that she was just avoiding stare.

"I wasn't laughing because of the stain. I just had this vision of you telling me you thought a man named Harry was the love of your life," I said. "Harry," I repeated, grimacing.

Lina gazed up, her expression softening.

"And I didn't mean what I said earlier. I was…" I paused as the waiter approached. I asked him, in Italian, to give us a few more minutes to look over the menus. Then, as he started to turn, I told him we'd like a bottle of prosecco to start.

He nodded politely and left us.

I sipped my water, trying to regain my train of thought. "I thought we connected last night," I began again. "And then when I woke up and you were gone, I panicked. I worried something had happened to you and that it would be all my fault." I swallowed hard to stop myself from telling her the rest, that I had a sordid history of letting bad things happen to the women who got close to me.

"Well, I'm fine," she said.

"I'm glad. And that's what I should have said when you came back," I admitted. "But I was stressed out and worrying makes me cranky, so I lashed out. The point is I didn't mean it."

She gazed around us uncomfortably. "No, you were right. It was the truth, anyway."

I nodded, accepting that I should just let it go and move on to a less awkward topic. But I still didn't feel right, with her not knowing everything.

"It's not though. You might be stuck, but I'm not. I didn't have to agree to this. And if I don't like it, I don't have to stick it out. I can leave at any point," I said. "I don't have a crazy ex gunning for me. And I don't have a sick father."

"Then why did you agree to it?" she interrupted.

I shrugged. "I don't want my dad to write me off as unstable just because I'm single, but other than that, I said yes because I had no real reason not to."

She seemed to accept that. The waiter returned with the wine, showing me the label and waiting for my nod of approval before popping the cork. I asked him to take our photo once he finished pouring, and I handed him Catalina's phone. He lifted the phone, then I motioned for him to wait.

"Dobbiamo brindare," I said to the waiter. *We should toast.* I lifted my drink and Lina did the same.

"To my wife," I began. "There's truly no one I'd rather be stuck with in this life."

The waiter smiled and snapped our picture, likely having no clue what I'd said.

Lina burst out laughing before even sipping her wine. "Too soon," she said. "Too soon."

I pressed my lips against the champagne flute to keep from smiling too widely. If I'd any doubt my words were true, hearing her melodic laughter would've cleared it up. I had the feeling I'd do anything to make this woman laugh.

She seemed relaxed and I wondered if maybe, she'd already forgiven me. Rather than push my luck, I asked what made her decide to become a librarian.

Lina smiled. "I love reading. Books make me happy, so I knew I'd be happy at work surrounded by books. But I also get to bring other people happiness by helping them find books they love too."

"What would you say if someone doesn't like reading?" I asked, certain she'd read between the lines and realize I wasn't a fan of books.

"I'd say they just haven't found the right book yet."

I liked that answer, but before I could press her further, the waiter came to take our order. When he left, Lina was eying me.

"What?" I asked, unable to tell what she was thinking.

"Before the wedding, remember when you asked me about my expectations?"

I nodded, although it was a bit fuzzy.

"When I said you had to be faithful, you said you expected me to perform all traditional wifely duties or something like that. Did you just mean cooking and cleaning?"

I quirked a brow, unsure of what she was getting at.

She sipped her prosecco, still eying me. "I guess at the time, I sort of thought you meant that you expected sexual favors from me."

I reached for my wine to avoid laughing at how uncomfortable she appeared even asking about it. My own past crassness did make me cringe though. In my defense, that had been a hard day for me, and I was in an uncharacteristically bad mood. "Well, you did forbid me from fooling around with anyone else, so it seems like a reasonable request."

Her lips parted as a barely audible gasp slipped through her lips.

I debated saying something else, but kept quiet in hopes of watching her squirm a little longer. She was adorable when she was trying not to say the first thing that came to mind.

"So..." Lina began after a delightfully long pause. "Did you change your mind?"

"About?" I pressed, although I knew exactly what she meant.

Her cheeks flushed. "Well, we've been married nearly a week, and you've received zero payment on your terms, so I guess I'm just wondering if you no longer expect...that...while we're married, or..." her words trailed off.

She bit her lip, drawing my eyes to her mouth. I watched the way her teeth dragged across the rosy flesh and I wondered if she'd bite her lip that way if I made her come. No, *when* I made her come.

Her eyes focused on my own as she waited for me to respond, but I simply added that into my fantasy too, telling myself she wouldn't be one of those women that closed their eyes during sex. No, Lina would gaze right back at me with those piercing emerald eyes as I shattered her with orgasm after...

"Angelo?"

Her soft voice penetrated the daydream, snapping me back to the infinitely less pleasurable reality. I dropped a hand to my lap, casually rearranging my now bulging erection as I crossed my legs. I gazed around us, wondering how none of the many passersby seemed as distracted by Lina's presence as I was.

"Why are we having this discussion here, in the middle of the piazza?" I asked her, genuinely curious.

Lina shifted in her seat, taking in our surroundings before focusing back on me. "Because I want to know now. And it's not like anyone is listening anyway. They all speak Italian."

I declined to point out that the vast majority of Italians possessed at least a working familiarity with English. "So you want to know why I didn't demand sexual favors the second we left that church?"

She squirmed at my directness. "Well, yes."

I cocked my head to the side, trying to ascertain how offended I should be by her question. "It's a very different thing to say something like that than to actually do it. I was just having a bad day. I never intended to touch you."

Lina seemed relieved by my answer. "So it's not me," she finally said, her voice so soft I almost missed her words. "I mean, you were looking right at me when you said it, so I figured I didn't completely repulse you, but then—"

"You were worried you repulsed me?" The idea was so ridiculous that I couldn't help but laugh.

She shrugged.

"Do you turn off a lot of guys? Like, they just aren't into that pretty, damsel-in-distress look you've got going on?" I teased.

"You think I'm pretty?" she asked, already beaming with pride.

I rolled my eyes. "You know you're a knockout. You can't go anywhere without men falling over trying to stare at you. Don't think I haven't noticed." I gazed pointedly to the table beside us, where two men in their late forties were openly gawking at Catalina.

"That might be the nicest thing you've ever said to me," she replied, tugging her sundress further down her thighs.

"Well, I'm a nice guy," I lied. Then, I turned back to the other table and glared. "Posso aiutare?" I snapped, asking the men if I could help them, in the least helpful tone ever. I waited until they turned back to their own food before meeting Lina's gaze again.

"I'm not really in the habit of forcing women to sleep with me. I prefer my partners willing. And this might come as a surprise to you, but I've never really had trouble finding a willing partner," I said.

"That doesn't surprise me at all. You're a handsome guy. You wouldn't have to force me."

I bit back a laugh right as Lina's face turned even redder, revealing she probably hadn't meant to share that sentiment out loud. She squeezed her eyes shut, then averted her gaze once she opened her eyes again.

"Good to know," I said, before motioning to the waiter to refill her water.

CHAPTER 12

Catalina

We returned to town in the morning, grabbing a light breakfast before boarding a private boat at the port. Angelo chatted amicably with the guide while I settled into a seat on the boat. After a few minutes, Angelo joined me at the front of the boat. Side-by-side loungers were perched on the bow of the boat, so we could relax together, without actually touching.

Not that I would've minded the touching. Somehow, I'd completely forgiven Angelo for his angry outburst the day before. I was no stranger to men hurting me or my feelings and then trying to win me back with over-the-top apologies, but Angelo seemed different. His apology felt sincere. Also, it was a challenge to stay mad at a man who looked as good as Angelo did that morning.

Angelo wore a white linen button-down with his khaki shorts, but he'd left the top several buttons unfastened, showing off his tan, muscular chest. He reminded me of a movie star, some hunky, dark-haired guy pretending to be a rich mob boss, not an actual criminal. I'd gone with my skimpy white bikini with gold fasteners, so I went ahead and lifted my cover-up over my head.

I smirked when Angelo's eyes widened as I revealed the swimsuit. It wasn't completely indecent, but it definitely wasn't one I'd wear around my grandma, for instance. Angelo cast a glance at the skipper, as though worried he'd be ogling me and might crash the boat. Luckily, the man seemed focused on the water.

We toured around a few different tourist sites, then joined a line of boats waiting to enter the famed blue grotto. I diligently photographed each stop, in part to keep up the ruse of the real honeymoon, but also because I really did want to document these gorgeous sites. Even if the honeymoon wasn't real in the traditional sense, I was really here—exploring this watery haven.

When we finished our tour of the blue grotto, we returned to the open seas. We drank limoncello and devoured fresh fruits, cheeses, crackers and meats. I told Angelo about some of my favorite trips to the Caribbean and Mexico, and he shared a couple stories about his childhood vacations to Palermo and Capri.

"Do you do a lot of business in Italy?" I asked, switching subjects.

Angelo shook his head, then refilled my glass.

"So why do you go to Italy so often?"

"We have family here. When I was a child, my grandparents lived in Rome and had a vacation home in Capri. We haven't been to Capri as a family since my grandfather passed, over a decade ago. But a few of our business associates live in Palermo, so we visit them sometimes too."

I was about to ask a follow up question when the skipper said something. Angelo nodded, then stood upright, bracing himself on one of the metal poles.

"This is a good spot for snorkeling, if you're interested," he said.

I hesitated. We appeared to be in open water, with nothing of particular interest nearby. Did Angelo really expect me to just jump off a boat and trust him and some stranger to get me back on board?

Angelo shucked his shorts and began unbuttoning his shirt the rest of the way. He glanced at me, then dove off the boat. I gasped, not daring another breath until a full minute later, when Angelo broke through the surface, grinning widely.

"Come on. It's gorgeous down there!" he said.

I gazed at the skipper, who offered a pair of flippers and snorkel to me. Reluctantly, I accepted both. The skipper tossed Angelo's into the water beside him, and Angelo treaded water while adorning his feet and securing his mask. A moment later, I was bracing myself for icy cold water as I leapt off the boat.

Surprisingly, the water was refreshing. Cool, but not frigid. Thanks to the crystal clear water, we could see hundreds of feet in any direction. I didn't notice a ton of marine life initially, but as we progressed, we did see a variety of fish and some cool rock formations underwater.

I lost track of time as we snorkeled, but by the time we climbed back on board, we were ready to head back towards the port. I stretched out on a lounger, drying my suit as we made our way back.

When we returned to the villa, I showered while Angelo returned some business phone call. As I twisted my wedding ring to rinse sand out from under it, I made an intriguing discovery. I already had a tan line from my wedding ring.

Angelo

*S*pending the day on a boat with Lina had tried my self-restraint. Her non-existent bikini combined with the memory of her saying I wouldn't have to force her was nearly enough to make me ravish her on board. I'd kept my sunglasses on so she couldn't see me leering at her, but I wondered if she could still sense my incessant staring. Luckily, the skipper had been there. I maybe couldn't have controlled myself, if we hadn't had an audience.

After we both showered, we ordered dinner to eat at the villa.

I watched Catalina lick her fingers after she chewed the last bite of mussels. Her eyes drifted shut and she groaned.

"Why is the seafood so much better here? Seriously. I don't get it. We live on the coast, too."

"Different coast?" I suggested. "Or better olive oil." To be honest, I wasn't sure why, but Italian food definitely tasted better. Although, watching Lina eat did rouse my appetite, just not for food. At least when we were in restaurants, I could keep my body in line by the sheer fact that we were in public and nothing untoward could happen.

Here, we were alone. Technically anything could happen.

And after her comment the day before, I didn't think she'd stop me if I tried something.

I pushed those thoughts away and reached for my wine glass, taking a small swig before scooting my plate to the side.

"I wanted to talk to you about a few things before we left our little paradise," I said, dropping my tone to signify the seriousness of the topic.

"Uh oh. The last time someone used that tone with me, it was my dad telling me I'd have to marry some stranger."

"Right. Well, nothing I have to say is quite that terrible. I just thought we should go over some logistics." I paused and she forked another bite into her mouth before gazing up expectantly.

"Obviously we'll live together, so I've arranged for Eddie to oversee the process of moving all of your things in by the time we return. Your dad mentioned—"

"What's your policy on pets?" she interrupted.

I clenched my jaw together. "No pets."

Catalina flashed me puppy dog eyes.

"Non-negotiable. You are the only kitten welcome in that house."

"How about a puppy?"

I shook my head. It was one thing to take on a woman, another altogether to bring a damn dog into my life.

Catalina sipped her wine, then giggled. "Okay, it's possible I was only messing with you. I don't have time for a pet right now anyway, what with my schedule at the library."

I suppressed an eye roll. Of course she was just teasing. But at least that brought me to my second point. "So you plan to keep working?"

"Umm yeah. That's how I make money."

I frowned. "As long as your work doesn't pose any security risks, I'm fine with you continuing." I paused long enough to ignore her eye roll. "But you do understand that, on paper, we're married now, right? You don't need to make money."

She seemed surprised by this. "Oh? You're gonna be my sugar daddy now?"

I refilled my wine glass, certain I'd need all the alcohol in the world for this discussion. "That's literally our arrangement."

"No, our arrangement was for protection."

Touché. "True, but the way I'm protecting you is by marrying you. And being married, what's mine is yours, right?"

"Oh? So one of those guns is mine?"

I felt my eyes widen.

"Okay, bad joke. I won't touch those. But seriously, I don't need you to support me. I can buy my own stuff and pay you rent or whatever."

"I've seen your paycheck. You cannot afford to pay me for half of my house, or anything else. And that's fine. No one would expect my wife to have any financial responsibility. That's not how we handle things in our family."

"How have you seen my paycheck?"

Shit. I hadn't meant to disclose that. "My associates did some digging into you. I need to know everything about you in order to keep you safe."

I expected some sassy question, but she said nothing.

"I'll give you a credit card, but I'd prefer you use cash as much as possible. I'd also appreciate if you don't ask too many questions about my finances. Just know that we have plenty."

"I never thought you were broke, but how rich are we talking?"

I sighed, then opted for a vague version of the truth. "Depends on the day. But you won't need to worry about money. Okay? Can we move on to the second topic?"

"Ooh, what's the second topic?"

I cringed, hating that she seemed excited. "Carlos."

"Oh."

I showed her the pictures I had of Carlos and his various associates. She supplied the names of a couple guys, but she knew surprisingly little about his actual work. I didn't want to scare her, but I figured she could better keep herself safe if she knew what she was up against. Lina knew he was "up to no good," as she put it, but she was clueless about the extent. When I called him a gang leader, she rolled her eyes dramatically.

"What, is he like your competition?"

I clenched my jaw. "No. I don't do shit like that. My family runs a legitimate business. I'm not a drug dealer. Carlos is."

"I would've known if he were dealing drugs."

"I would've thought that as well, but apparently not. He's been in the marijuana business for ages, but now he's got a broad turf for heroine, too."

"Heroine?" her eyes widened.

"He's also been linked with stolen guns and stolen cars." I paused and turned to her. "The point is, he's dangerous. And he has a wide network of equally dangerous morons ready to do his bidding."

"Okay," she mumbled.

"This guy has an ego the size of Texas. He's not used to people telling him no. You did just that, and you tripped his ego. He's not going to let that go."

"Well, then I guess it's good I married you."

"Yes, but that's not enough. You still have to take precautions. I can protect you better if you stop working, at least until—"

"No," she interrupted. "My dad said the whole benefit of marrying you was that I could keep my same job and same friends. If I have to live in some stupid tower like a captive princess, then what's the point? We might as well let Carlos kill me."

I rolled my eyes at her excessive dramatization. "My house is nice. It's hardly a prison."

"Don't you mean our house?" she corrected.

I chuckled. If nothing else, this woman was going to keep me on my toes.

CHAPTER 13

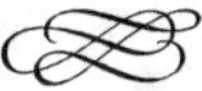

Angelo

The next day, we lounged around the villa then ventured to town to look at a few shops. Apparently, Lina had spotted a bookstore and some art studios the other day on her solo adventure. She finally seemed more comfortable with me, which I appreciated, although maybe it was just that I'd let her choose what we do for the day. I did notice she started snapping photos of the two of us without me prompting, and at one point, she even reached for my hand.

I stiffened at the realization that she wanted to hold my hand, but then she swung our hands up and took a photo, releasing my hand a moment later. I shook my head, trying to think reasonably. Of course she wasn't just randomly holding my hand. We weren't a real couple.

Except, parts of it were starting to feel real. And at least to the outside world, we were actual newlyweds. I was fed up with the incessant leering from all of the local men. As far as they knew, we were enjoying our real honeymoon. Catalina was my wife, and yet they gawked at her as if I weren't right beside her, as if my ring wasn't on her finger.

Catalina chose the restaurant for dinner, and though the place was rowdier than I would've preferred, the change of pace was nice. A live band began playing right after we ordered our entrees, and Lina gazed wistfully at the dancefloor.

"I don't suppose you dance," she said, quirking a brow.

I did not dance. I knew how to dance, of course, but I absolutely never would choose to do so in public. Or, honestly, in private. But somehow, I couldn't say no to Lina. I motioned to the waiter to save our table, then reached for her hand. She squealed like a school girl, then practically dragged me to the dance floor. To my relief, the music changed almost as soon as we reached the center of the floor. The fast paced dance beat transformed to a romantic slow song. I made a mental note to tip the band greatly for that small mercy.

A flash of disappointment crossed Lina's face, but as I placed a hand on the small of her back and guided her to me, she didn't pull away. We weren't as close as I'd prefer to be, but I also couldn't drag her into me the way I'd like without her feeling how much I wanted her for real. Still, being this near to her at all, especially while she was actually awake for a change, was a treat.

Our food arrived on our table right as we finished our second dance together, saving me from having to maneuver a fast song with her.

Lina spread her napkin over her lap, then dug into her food, appearing thoughtful as she chewed. "How did you envision your wedding?" she asked right as I forked a bite into my mouth. "I mean, like if it was the real thing?"

"I never really spent a lot of time thinking about my wedding," I answered honestly.

"Weren't you with your last girlfriend for over a year? You must have at least talked about it."

I tensed, instantly annoyed at the mention of Julia. "She might have thought about it, but I really didn't. I'm not sure I would've had a lot of say in the planning anyway. I assume my mother and bride would perhaps split the tasks."

"Hmm," she said, chewing another bite before continuing. "I always thought I'd enjoy a destination wedding, so I guess in a way, that's what we did. Did you ever daydream about your honeymoon?"

I nearly made a crude comment about how I'd fantasized about the nonstop sex, but then I stopped myself. I could answer this question completely honestly. "Actually, I always planned to honeymoon in Capri."

"Really?"

I nodded.

"I can see why. It's gorgeous, romantic, and there's tons to do. And don't get me started on the food," she said, right as the waiter returned.

He frowned, probably picking up on her reference to "food" in his broken English. I ordered after-dinner drinks and gelato for us, then told the waiter everything was good so far.

"Should I try to learn Italian when we get back?" Lina asked. "I mean, that's something your real wife would do, right? Oh, and you could learn Spanish!"

Her enthusiasm was adorable, but no good could come from any wife of mine understanding everything I said in Italian. Technically, I was fluent, but the only time I spoke Italian outside of Italy was when I needed my conversation not to be understood by others in the area.

"I think there are a lot of similarities between the languages," I said. "But maybe we don't need to rush into anything just yet."

"Yeah, it would be crazy to rush into something," she agreed, fidgeting with her wedding ring. After a moment, she gazed up, and we both laughed.

I was about to reply, but caught a man from a nearby table staring at Lina again. I shot him my scariest glare and he shifted his chair away, but he'd probably turn back as soon as I stopped watching him. The same guy had ogled her when we were dancing, and another one had been checking her out earlier when she went to the restroom after we ordered our appetizer.

As Lina sampled the gelato, her soft moan reminiscent of a kitten purring, two more men gazed at her.

I paid the bill the second she finished eating, then rushed her out of the restaurant. Even as we walked through the busy piazza, it seemed like every man was leering her.

"Do men stare at you like this in America?" I asked. Italian men in general could be less subtle in their appreciation of a beautiful woman, but this seemed extreme.

Lina gazed around her, as if oblivious that anyone had been looking. After a moment, she shrugged. "Sometimes guys ask me out, sometimes they flirt, and sometimes they just check me out and then go about their day. As long as they're not creepy about it or refuse to back off when I say no, I don't let it bother me. It's sort of flattering."

"Flattering? No."

"Well, it doesn't hurt anything," she said.

I couldn't believe she'd just put up with that sort of attention for so long. "How can you say that? It's disrespectful for them to gawk you like you're some piece of meat. And it's disrespectful to me because…" I paused, realizing I sounded like a petulant child.

"Why?" she asked, further fueling my frustration.

I stopped walking and dragged a hand through my hair. I felt the last iota of my self-control slip away as Lina gazed up at me, her bold, pouty lips just begging to be kissed.

"Because," I said, gripping her hand and tugging her to the side of the street. "You. Are. Mine."

I paused only long enough for her to comprehend the seriousness of my punctuated words. "I don't like when other men look at my toys, especially when I'm not even allowed to touch them."

"That's what I am to you, a toy?" her incredulous tone stoked a fire in my belly.

I took another step closer, forcing her back to the wall. Busy street be damned, Lina's eyes were on me now.

I shook my head in disbelief. Did she really not see it? Did she really not know?

I drew in a ragged breath before answering. "No. You are everything to me, Lina."

Her expression didn't falter as she replied. "Good. But either way, I never said you couldn't touch me."

The moment I processed what she'd just said, my lips crashed into hers. The feel of her soft, warm lips willingly opening for me made my heart race. Lina tasted like fresh strawberries and all I could think about was getting more. God, I wanted to devour her right there and then.

The sweet scent of her vanilla lotion, the steady thrum of her heartbeat, and the heat of her breath on my cheeks created a dizzyingly potent cocktail, rendering me completely helpless. I couldn't think straight, let alone control myself, not while my every sense was monopolized by Lina.

I wanted more. No, I *needed* more.

I didn't kiss Lina like a newlywed, poised to enjoy a lifetime of kisses with my bride, but rather like a man heading off to war, uncertain of what the future held or if I'd ever get the chance to touch her again. I kissed her like this was my last day on earth and she was all of my final requests wrapped up on one beautiful package. I kissed her in a way that would leave me without any regrets, even if this was the last time she let me taste her.

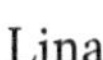

Lina

*H*oly fucking fireballs.

Angelo could kiss.

Sure, we'd been flirting, exchanging witty banter and such for a couple of days now, but I still hadn't been sure if the attraction was all in my head. Had we gone another day without him touching me, I probably would've combusted. Or molested him in his sleep.

Again.

But the second his lips met mine, I was gone. Granted, I couldn't have escaped if I'd wanted to, with my back against a brick wall and Angelo's broad arm planted on one side of my head, pinning me in place. But obviously, I didn't want to. Kissing Angelo was the best kiss of my life.

God, it was like, the best sex of my life, and it wasn't even sex.

Where did he even learn to kiss like that?

His tongue clashed against mine and I moaned. Yep, like, actually moaned out loud. On a public street. And when he shifted, his body pressing against mine, I swear I almost came. I could feel every glorious inch of him…and that was saying a lot.

Angelo was the one to end the kiss, pulling back ages before I was ready. His face lingered less than an inch from mine for a full minute, and it took all of my self-control not to yank him back to me. Once he'd caught his breath, he pushed off the wall, dropping the arm from beside my head.

I shivered at the sudden loss of his warmth, but before I had time to process what had just happened—or remember how to walk—Angelo had clasped his hand around mine and began tugging me down the street.

I practically had to jog to keep up. I was already winded from the exquisite make-out session, and I was painfully aware that my skimpy panties were now soaked. Besides, my high-heeled wrap sandals were cute, but not exactly practical for speed-walking.

"Can we slow down?" I asked.

Angelo glanced at me and frowned, but switched to a slightly more reasonable pace.

"Where are we going in such a hurry?"

"The villa," he said.

I stopped walking, pulling my hand free of his grip. "So, why do we have to run there?"

Angelo stepped closer, and my stomach fluttered excitedly just from his proximity.

"Because I don't want our first time to be in an alley, but if I'm not inside of you in the next five minutes, I might die," he said.

His deep voice sent shivers down my spine, and once I'd processed his words I was more than ready to speed up again.

"Yeah, okay," I said, reaching for his hand so I didn't stumble while scurrying along the cobblestone path.

After a minute, I recognized our location. We were only a few minutes from the villa, but I also knew I was just begging for a broken ankle if I kept running in those shoes any longer.

"Hang on," I panted, stopping abruptly. I braced myself on his forearm before bending down to untie my sandals.

"What are you doing?" he asked as I clutched the straps of both shoes in my hand.

"I can run better barefoot," I said. And without waiting for an answer, I took off.

An instant later, my feet left the ground.

"Not a chance," Angelo growled, sweeping me into his arms. "There could be glass or rocks."

I flung an arm around his neck to steady myself, but he'd already resumed a brisk walking pace.

"You can't possibly carry me the rest of the way."

"Can and will," he replied, not even breathing harder.

"I weigh more than you'd think."

"Your shoes weigh more than you," he replied, tossing me a little higher in his arms.

I settled against his chest, not feeling even close to as ridiculous as I should, being carried down the street like a child. In Angelo's arms, I was safe.

"Key," he mumbled, freeing his wallet from his pocket without somehow dropping me.

I retrieved the keycard, then laughed out loud.

Angelo gazed down at me, a hint of a smile breaking up his always serious expression. "What's so funny?"

"You're a week late, but isn't this how you're supposed to carry your new bride?"

Angelo grinned, then jiggled the handle while I waved the key in front of the lock. He kicked the door open wider with his foot, using the same foot to slam it shut behind us.

He slid his shoes off, then carried me straight to the bed. He tossed me down caveman style, and I half expected him to jump on top of me, but he didn't. Instead, he stared at me, the look in his eyes almost predatory.

I held his gaze for a minute, then pushed up to my elbows, suddenly shy. My movement seemed to snap Angelo out of a trance.

"Sorry," he mumbled. "Just looking at you."

He gripped the hem of my dress and tugged it upwards. I opened my mouth to tell him the zipper was in the back, but he hoisted it over my head before the words came out. Angelo lifted my arms above my head, causing me to settle back against the fluffy white blanket covering the bed. He paused again once the dress reached my arms, leaving them pinned in place above my head by my own attire.

Angelo sucked in a harsh breath and I watched as his eyes roamed down my body. He'd seen me in a swimsuit before, but I supposed this was very different, even if the coverage was the same.

"You are gorgeous," he said, almost as if the observation surprised him. He finished removing my dress and dropped it onto the floor beside the bed before straddling me, still fully clothed.

"I was promised something that requires your clothes to come off," I reminded him.

He lifted my hand to his shirt, so I began unfastening the buttons, working my way down from the top. With each button, my hands drew closer to his groin, and my pulse increased exponentially.

Angelo shucked the shirt once I'd unbuttoned it, and I splayed my hand out across his abdomen, feeling the taut muscles beneath the sleeveless undershirt. My fingers looked comically small on his large frame and a hint of panic washed over me as I started to think about what else might be bigger on his body.

He gripped my hand and placed it on his belt, so I obediently unfastened the buckle. Feeling playful, I tugged the entire belt through the loops, slapping it dramatically against the covers beside me like a whip.

"Kitten, we can have lots of fun with that later, but this time I think we should try it without the toys," he said.

I would've asked what fun he envisioned with a belt, but he placed my fingers on the fly of his pants and my breath caught in my throat. The pants hadn't appeared tight when he'd worn them to dinner, but now the fly strained in a way that made me certain the zipper was moments away from popping open.

I forced myself to unfasten the button, then just let my hand linger there, barely stroking the massive bulge beneath the thin fabric. As eager as I was to see it, touch it, even taste it…, I was even more terrified.

I fumbled with the zipper, inching it down slowly so as not to hurt him. I couldn't lower his pants very far with him still on his knees, straddling me at the rib cage, but I decided that didn't matter.

My mouth watered at the sight of Angelo's package so close. I'd never really thought anything about the male genitalia was particularly tantalizing, but Angelo looked good. He wore bright white briefs with blue trim and it occurred to me that he could have a profitable career as an underwear model if this whole life of crime didn't pan out for him.

I traced his full length with my fingers, giggling as Angelo responded with a sharp hiss. Unable to wait any longer, I gripped the waistband of his briefs, lowering them just enough to free the first few inches of him. I smiled at the sight of the swollen purple tip, craning my neck to reach it with my tongue.

Angelo flew backwards and onto his feet, nearly falling over thanks to his pants still stuck at his knees.

I pouted dramatically. "You're kind of a tease, flaunting it in my face and not letting me touch it."

Angelo snorted a laugh. "If that perfect fucking mouth of yours touches me now, I won't last a minute."

I was tempted to take his words as a challenge, but then he lowered his briefs to the ground, showing me his full length.

"Oh fuck," I breathed, feeling my eyes widen at the sight. Angelo's cock was beautiful to be sure, but it was also, well, proportional to the rest of him, both in girth and length. There was no chance that beast of a cock would fit inside me.

"I'll go slow," he promised, clearly sensing my apprehension.

"I.." I started to protest, but all coherent thoughts left my brain as Angelo stepped closer and slipped his fingers into my panties.

He stroked right along my core, eliciting shivers, then he pinched my clit and pulled back his hand. But before I could protest, he began sliding my thong down my thighs.

"Your panties weren't this wet after I pushed you in the pool," he said, his voice soft, as if he were offering me praise. From the way he stared at me, I thought he was.

I didn't have time to formulate a response. He'd already gripped my thighs and tugged me down to the end of the bed, planting his face between my legs. Angelo lapped at my pussy as if trying to soak up every last drop of my juices, but of course it didn't have that effect. The tip of his tongue prodded just inside my entrance, then he flattened the base of his tongue for a series of long, hard strokes.

"Oh God," I panted, already dangerously close to climax before he even touched my clit. How that man could take me from zero to sixty in a matter of seconds was a total mystery, but one I very much looked forward to investigating further.

Angelo's hands reached up by body, pinching my nipples through my silky bra. Then, his lips closed tightly around my clit. He sucked it before hammering it with short direct strokes from the tip of his tongue.

My body exploded into wave after wave of pleasure so intense that I could've sworn I levitated off the bed.

By the time I came down from my high, Angelo had already removed my bra. He stretched out on top of me, shifting slightly to the side so he kept me warm without squishing me. Then, he kissed me. And just like before, it was exquisite.

His tongue exerted just the right amount of pressure and moved exactly the right way. Maybe it was because I was still all tingly from the best orgasm of my life, but I truly thought I could kiss this man for hours. His hand found my breast, and as soon as he rolled my nipple between his thumb and forefinger, my post-orgasmic bliss was instantly replaced with a tightness deep in my core.

Angelo broke off the kiss, dropping his head to my breast instead. The second his tongue swiped my sensitive skin, the tension in my body ratcheted up. I moaned, the expert strokes of his tongue on my breast reminiscent of his mouth's amazing work on other parts of my body, moments before. I bent my knee, angling closer to Angelo's torso as he returned his mouth to mine. His touch was everywhere, yet somehow I desperately needed more of him.

Angelo must have felt the same, as he suddenly shifted, positioning himself directly above me. I roped my legs around his waist, pulling him closer, but he pulled back.

"I don't want to hurt you," he growled through gritted teeth. "Let me go slow." He rose to his knees and positioned himself at my entrance.

I bit my lip in anticipation, then sucked in a breath as he pushed in the first inch, then another. We moaned in unison as he glided in a little further. He felt incredible, but I knew I'd taken maybe half of his full length so far.

"See? You fit perfectly," I teased, already feeling a little dizzy with pleasure.

Angelo sunk half an inch further as he laughed.

"Just do it," I urged, eager for him to start moving freely. Sure, it might sting for a second, but at the moment, I didn't care. I wanted to feel all of him inside me.

Angelo dipped his head, nipping my breast again, then started to shift his hips.

And then it hit me.

"Wait!" I cried, my voice already breathy.

Angelo froze, a panicked look on his face. "Are you okay? Was that too much?"

"No, I," I cringed, hating that I was ruining the moment. "I'm fine. But, um, shouldn't we get a condom?"

He blew out a sigh. "You're not on the pill?"

The accusation in his voice was a tad much, given the circumstances. "No. Why would I be? Until two weeks ago I was single. I didn't know I was going to marry some strange sex god. Don't you have condoms?"

Angelo lifted off of me. "Sex god, huh?"

I watched as he crossed the room, rummaged around in his toiletry bag, then pulled out a strip of condoms. He ripped one apart from the rest while walking back towards me. He looked dangerously good walking around naked, his cock at full attention. I licked my lips right as Angelo dropped the foil packet on my bare stomach.

I tore open the package, resisting the urge to taste him before rolling the latex down his length.

⁂

Angelo

I shuddered as her fingers rolled the condom onto me. I was so tightly wound that I wouldn't last for long, especially if I let her keep touching me.

I gripped her wrist and held it to her side as I hovered over her. I'd been trying to go slow, to gently stretch her body to accommodate me, but my willpower was waning. And from the way she writhed against me, Lina wasn't a fan of the slow-but-steady route, either.

I kissed her, relishing her sweet taste, then thrust into her.

This time, I moved inside her, pushing a little further on each thrust.

"Yes," she panted. "God, yes. Angelo!"

The sound of her voice, all breathy and unguarded, was nearly enough to send me over the edge. I was determined to give her more, to bring her to climax again before letting myself give in, but my body wasn't cooperating. Lina felt too good. Her warm, wet pussy hugged me tighter with each move. I picked up the pace of my thrusts, focused only on restraining myself so as not to hurt her.

I reached between us, groping at her beautiful breast, rolling the hardened tip between my fingers. Lina moaned again, her eyes fluttering shut, and her breaths came faster. She was close.

My vision blurred as the pressure building deep inside me threatened to take over. Right when I realized I couldn't hold off any longer, Lina's nails pierced into my hips.

"Fuck, Angelo. Yes, yes, yes!" she screamed. Her hips bucked wildly and her pussy squeezed me like a vise.

My orgasm hit me like a freight train, intense almost to the point of pain. The jolts of pleasure vibrated through me over and over until I was completely spent. I waited a minute, then pulled out of her warm sheath, collapsing face down on the bed beside her.

I tried to collect my thoughts, or at least form one rational sentence to speak aloud, but I was speechless. I'd been with a lot of women and sex had never felt like that. I'd never come so hard, either.

"Well that was unexpected," Lina said, interrupting the silence of the room.

I lifted my head and quirked a brow at her.

"No offense, but you come off like a total narcissistic asshole and you're actually quite the generous lover."

I bit back a laugh and pushed off the bed. "Offense taken," I said, making my way to the bathroom to ditch the condom. "And first thing tomorrow, you're going on the pill."

Lina was smiling when I returned to the bed. "I have nothing against the pill, but I think it'll have to wait another week until we're back in the States," she said.

I shook my head. "No. There's doctors here. We take care of it tomorrow."

She shrugged, noncommittal.

I gazed at her, lounging on the bed completely naked. She was gorgeous from head to toe, for sure. My eyes stilled on her breasts. They were without a doubt the best breasts I'd ever seen —perky and full, with creamy smooth skin and pert nipples.

"Your tits are real," I said aloud, clearly still in a post-coital stupor.

Lina clutched one breast in each of her hands, still smiling. "Is that a question?"

"No. I'm certain. In your swimsuit, I wasn't sure. They looked too perfect to be natural."

"And now they're not perfect?"

I laughed at the ridiculousness of the notion. "Still perfect. But now that I've touched and tasted them…" my voice trailed off as she moved her hands again.

"I feel all sticky," Lina said, rolling off the bed onto her feet.

"You gonna shower?"

She shook her head. "I think I'll take a swim. I wouldn't mind some company. Or at least a lifeguard."

She walked straight out of the room onto the veranda, diving into the pool without pause.

CHAPTER 14

Catalina

J felt like I was on fire before I dove into the pool. I'd already come twice and still I was burning with desire so strong that I had to literally submerge myself completely in cool water to simmer down.

God. Where had that come from? Like, how had we not noticed we had that intense of chemistry before? Even as I kicked back and forth in the water, I couldn't help but feel a slight pang of regret that we'd squandered a full week in this romantic villa without having sex. All those times I'd been lounging by the pool, we could've been making love. Instead of leisurely strolls along the beach or through the town, we could've been fucking like animals.

What a waste of time!

I'd had good sex before. Well, I'd had what I thought was good sex. Compared to what I'd just shared with Angelo, everything I'd done before wasn't even in the same league. And that just didn't make sense because it wasn't like I was a virgin. I thought I knew what I liked. I hadn't climaxed every single time I'd made love to Harry or Carlos, but I had sometimes.

Except, sex had never before been like that for me. These orgasms with Angelo put every other orgasm to shame.

Even just thinking about it now made my innermost muscles throb.

I heard a splash, but didn't dare turn. If I saw Angelo before I'd fully cooled off, I'd probably jump him all over again. And we couldn't have sex in a pool. Not without birth control, anyway. Although, there was the morning-after pill…

My lungs burned with the need for fresh air, so I breached the surface, inhaling deeply. I smoothed my hair back out of my face, then turned to where Angelo stood, watching me from the shallow end. His beautiful, massive cock dangled between his legs, tempting me like a lollipop in a candy shop. Clearly, Angelo didn't find the water too cold.

"Do you always swim laps in the nude?" he asked.

"I needed a moment," I admitted.

He didn't acknowledge my words, but rather just watched me. I tried to remember how to swim, but I could barely recall how to breathe with Angelo's intense gaze on me. After a minute, I kicked to the side of the pool, supporting my arms on the edge.

"I'm not much of a swimmer," I confessed.

"You seem to be doing okay," he replied. "Did you grow up with a pool?"

"Yeah. You?"

"Uh huh. But I was the only one in my family who ever used it for laps."

"Does your current house have a pool?"

"No," he said, a hint of sadness in his voice.

"Is there room to add one?"

There was a brief silence as he appeared to consider the question. "Yes." He paused again. "Can I ask you a personal question?"

The man had literally sucked my clit until I came less than an hour before, so it seemed odd that now he was hesitant to get too intimate, but I just nodded.

"Do you always come like that?"

I felt my cheeks flush with shame. I tried to remember how I'd acted when I came, or at least what I'd said or done. But I had no idea. It was all a blur. "Was I loud?"

Angelo parted his lips as if trying to formulate an answer. "You were perfect. I didn't mean your volume."

"You didn't?"

He swam closer, wrapping his arms around me and pulling me to him. "No. I, uh, I guess I meant more the fact that you came. Twice, if I'm not mistaken?"

I blushed, but nodded.

"Don't be embarrassed. I liked that. A lot. I was just curious if it's always that way for you."

He must have sensed that I still didn't understand the question, because he kept elaborating.

"Some women take forever to orgasm. Some don't come at all during sex. I want to know if you always climax twice with a guy or maybe if this was perhaps, good for you too?"

Relief washed over me at the last word of his question. Good for me *too*, he'd said. I thought he'd enjoyed it, but now I knew for sure.

"It was good for me too," I confirmed. "And no, I don't think I've ever come twice in one…um…round."

A grin spread across Angelo's face. "Seems like we will have to try to recreate that then. Or maybe even beat the record."

"I'm always up for a challenge," I agreed, letting him carry me out of the water to a nearby lounger.

Angelo

he last few days of the honeymoon were vastly more exciting than the first several. As promised, I found an Italian doctor willing to prescribe Lina birth control pills. Unfortunately, due to the irregularity of Lina's cycle and the timing of her starting the pills, the doctor recommended a backup form of birth control for the next two weeks.

Still, instead of spending the next several days sampling the local cuisine and exploring the island, I spent my time sampling Lina and exploring her body. We made love on every surface of the room, as well as a few choice spots in the privacy of the back patio.

The time together felt exactly like I'd imagine a real honeymoon would feel. Well, except for the fact that we still really didn't know anything about each other.

Lina was opening up to me more each day, but I learned nearly as much from the things she didn't tell me. She was feisty, for sure, but she had little sense of self-preservation. Once aroused, she'd try to rush through the foreplay even though she was the one who would be sore after, and when I put the brakes on things, she'd actually pout.

Lina also made no effort to keep herself hydrated, fed, or rested. I wondered how much of my protection duties would actually entail the more basic tasks of ensuring my wife remembered to eat in between our marathon lovemaking sessions.

I couldn't believe how responsive she was, though. I'd never before been with a woman who orgasmed so often or easily, and I loved that. The more she came, the more I wanted to make her come again. It was a glorious cycle.

On our last night in Italy, Lina's best friends called. Her face lit up when she saw the video chat light up her phone screen, then she quickly frowned and glanced at me, as if having forgotten my existence.

"It's fine. I'll call them when we're back in town," she said, her voice betraying her words.

'Just answer," I suggested. "I need to check in with Eddie and Rico anyway."

She hesitated, then clicked to answer. A beat paused, then her friends shrieked.

"Is that really you?" one of them asked.

"Are you back home?" said the other.

Lina's smile widened. "I'm still in Italy. We leave tomorrow though."

"Where's this mystery man of yours?"

Lina turned and gazed at me. I shrugged, so she angled the phone towards me. I waved and forced a smile onto my face, then made my way out to the balcony, sliding the door shut behind me. I wasn't sure how exactly she was going to explain everything to her friends, but she didn't need me eavesdropping. Besides, I needed to have a similar heart-to-heart with my friends.

As far as Eddie and Rico knew, I'd agreed to marry Lina as a friend. I trusted them to protect her regardless of the nature of my intimate relationship with her, simply by virtue of the oath they'd taken. But I also suspected they'd take it a step further if they knew my happiness was actually tied to her safety now.

I called Rico first, not wanting him to feel left out since he hadn't been able to attend the wedding. It was early afternoon back home, so he answered quickly. I heard construction sounds and loud music in the background, but he told me to hang on, and then a moment later, the sounds were muffled.

"In my truck now," Rico explained. "How's it going? You home yet?"

"No. We leave tomorrow."

"Right. How's the honeymoon?" he snorted as if that were a ridiculous question.

I appreciated the easy opening. "Well, that's actually why I was calling. I know I was vague about my history with Lina and just told you the gist about this arrangement, but…" I paused. What exactly did I say? I couldn't exactly tell him I'd started banging my wife and now everything was different, but technically that was really all that had changed.

I sucked in a breath, then started over. "Being alone for the last couple of weeks, Lina and I realized we actually have more in common than we thought. We've gotten closer, and—"

"No way!" he interrupted. "Are you telling me you're hitting that? Oh my God. I fucking called it."

"I'm not hitting anything," I snapped. "I mean, we're not fifteen. Have a little respect. She's my wife."

"Yeah she is," he said, as if that were the punchline of some dirty joke.

I rolled my eyes. "And what do you mean, you called it? You've never even met her."

"I've seen pictures. She's fucking hot. And those ti—"

"I swear to God, Rico, if you finish that sentence," I cut him off.

He chuckled.

"Look, you guys don't need to make a big deal out of it. I just figured you should know that this is real for me. I'm not just in it as a favor for my dad."

Rico started to say something, but Lina stepped outside and I stopped listening to my friend. She hesitated by the door until I patted the lounger beside me. She padded over to me and curled up in the tiny crevice beside me.

"Listen, Rico, I've got to go, but I'll check in tomorrow sometime," I said, hanging up without waiting for a response. I set my phone on the concrete beneath the chair, then wrapped my arm around Lina.

"How are your friends?" I asked. "And what are their names again?"

"Madison and Kristi. They're good. They seemed surprised that you were real."

"Oh? They thought you made me up?"

"That's unclear. They definitely both think you're hot though."

"Hmm. Good to know, but I'm taken."

She gazed up and blushed shyly.

We were both quiet for a moment.

"So how does this work when we go home? I mean, I just move into your house but then go about my life like before?"

"Not exactly. If you want to keep working—"

"I do," she interrupted.

"Then we'll need to figure out a way that I can get you there and back every day, or hire someone to drive you."

"I can take a bus."

"No, you can't. My job here is to protect you, and that means figuring out a way to keep you safe on your way to and from work or wherever else you go."

She didn't protest, so I assumed she accepted this.

"What's my job then?" she asked. "If your job is to protect me."

I grinned. "I mean, you're doing a pretty good job of fulfilling the wifely duties I was envisioning, so I can't really think of anything else."

Lina frowned. "So you're going to work full time, pay for everything, keep me safe, and I just have to be available for sex on occasion? That doesn't exactly seem fair."

I shrugged. "That seems like how a marriage should be."

"Maybe in nineteen-fifty."

"I don't understand why this bothers you. I said you could work if you want. Or you can just have more time for your friends or hobbies. Seems like a good deal to me."

"Because I want to contribute," she said.

I considered that. "Do you clean?"

She tensed.

"What?"

"Well, don't you have a cleaning lady or something?"

"No. I don't trust strangers in my house," I replied.

"Then how do you keep your house clean now?"

"I clean it." I didn't love cleaning, but I was meticulous about it.

"Hmm."

"What does that mean?" I asked.

"Umm, just that I'm not great at cleaning. I mean, I could probably learn, but it doesn't come naturally to me. I'm sort of a messy person by nature."

'Oh, God." I couldn't help but cringe.

"Ooh!" Lina sat up and turned to face me, an excited grin on her face. "I'm a great cook. I can cook for you."

I traced my finger along her smooth skin, nudging the strap of her dress off her shoulder and then letting my finger roam along the swell of her breast. I decided not to tell Lina that I too, was an excellent cook. We could surely take turns in the kitchen. For now, I wanted to enjoy my wife one last time poolside in Capri.

I shifted Lina so that she was on top of me, swirling my tongue around her pink nipple, groaning with delight as it swelled and hardened in response to my touch. I moved to the other breast, nipping her skin before licking the pebbled bud until a soft moan escaped Lina's lips. She pushed herself upright, straddling me. I helped her maneuver my shirt up over my head before pulling her down to kiss her.

Before Lina, I'd never enjoyed kissing a woman. Kissing had always been a seemingly unnecessary precursor to the main course. I did it willingly, but only to get my partner ready for what I really wanted. With Lina though, I wanted to kiss her. I relished the feel of her lips against mine, the taste of her tongue, and the warmth of her breath.

I longed to kiss her for hours—except I doubted I'd ever achieve that goal, because every time I kissed Lina, I grew so aroused that I felt like I'd combust if we didn't do more. Luckily, Lina seemed to feel the same way. She broke our kiss, leaving my lips grasping for more like I was a fish abruptly yanked from the water. But then she inched her way down my body, shucked my shorts to the ground, and swirled her perfect pink tongue around the swollen tip of my cock.

"Oh fuck, kitten," I hissed right as she wrapped her lips around me, sucking the first inch or so into her warm mouth. "You feel amazing."

Her responding "hmm," came out like a purr, vibrating through my groin. I thrust my hand into her hair, letting the silky strands cascade over my fingers as her head bobbed up and down. She peered up at me and those beautiful emerald eyes nearly made me come in her mouth. I grinned, then squeezed my eyes shut, determined to last a minute or two longer.

When I was sure I couldn't handle any more, I gripped her shoulders, forcing her off of me. She pouted, and I briefly considered the possibility that she wanted me to finish that way. Maybe Lina was too sore for another round with me inside her anywhere else.

But then she flicked a condom onto my chest.

"Where did that come from?" I asked.

She smiled sweetly and held out her hand. Then she rose to her feet, and let her dress fall to the ground. I slid the condom over my erection and positioned myself for her to climb back onto my lap, but then I had a better idea. I climbed off the chair and made my way around to the steps leading into the pool.

Lina watched me quizzically, not moving until I had submerged myself just past my knees and gestured for her to come to me. She quirked an eyebrow but approached obediently. I patted the edge of the pool right in front of me. She slowly lowered herself to the concrete, still eying me warily. I pressed a hand into her belly, nudging her backwards enough for my tongue to access her pussy. I lingered just long enough to ensure she was wet enough for what I had planned, then I slid my hands under her butt.

Lina braced herself on her palms as I brought the rest of her body towards me. Once she trusted I wouldn't drop her, she roped her legs around my back and draped her arms over my neck. I kissed her again, then shifted her weight so I had one hand free. Lina was a lightweight to begin with, but with the added buoyancy from the water, I had no trouble supporting her with one hand while using my other hand to guide my cock to her entrance.

"Tell me if it's too much," I said, already worried I'd somehow hurt her. It took all my self-restraint to ease into her, rather than just impaling her on my throbbing cock.

"You could never be too much, Angelo," she whispered as we came together. "I think I was made for you."

I bit back a groan, the mixture of her words and the intensely exquisite feeling hitting me like a freight train. Every part of Lina wrapped around me and squeezed, from her pussy to her thighs to her arms. I probably could've just stood there, fully surrounded by her, and still reached climax within a matter of minutes, but I didn't dare try.

Instead, I slowly raised and lowered her, letting my arms work instead of my hips. Lina moaned into my ear and I loved that already, I knew her body so well. I could gauge how close she was by the way her pussy tightened around me. I was tempted to hold back, to make it last longer, but I didn't want to risk making her sore. And besides, the rhythmic sloshing of the water as I moved further in and out of her body was too erotic for me to restrain myself any longer.

My hips joined in with my arms, and I fucked her like our lives depended on it for a full twenty seconds. Lina's cries were so loud when she came that I couldn't help but wonder if she'd woken the neighbors. I didn't bother to quiet my own moans either, focusing instead on the intense onslaught of sensory delights hitting my body both from the inside and outside.

I didn't pull out of her right away, either, instead carrying her across the pool where we'd left a towel earlier in the day. Carefully, I lifted her onto the side of the pool, gazing admiringly at the swollen pink lips of the pussy now at eye level. I pressed one chaste kiss onto her there, then hoisted myself out of the water, collapsing onto my back beside her.

"So…if it's in the budget, I think we should get a pool," Lina said after several minutes of silence.

"I couldn't agree more," I said with a grin.

Catalina

The trip home from Italy was exhausting. We began with a ferry from Capri to Naples, then a high speed train ride to Rome, followed by a flight back to New York. Angelo's friend Rico picked us up at the airport and drove us to the house, and I was so exhausted by the time we finally arrived that I barely noticed any of the details of my new home.

The next day, I'd slept so long that Angelo was already breaking for lunch by the time I woke up. He called to check in and to reiterate his request that I stay home until he got back. Normally, I'd resent the patronizing tone, but I was still so sleepy that I didn't care. Besides, I hadn't yet fully explored my new house.

Angelo had given me the basic tour the night before, but everything looked different in the light of day. I'd expect a man like Angelo to live in a poorly lit, ultra-modern house filled with dark wood and stark open spaces, but this place was homey. I supposed that was thanks to his sister, who had designed it all.

There was a wide backyard, contained with a tall privacy fence and a solid line of trees. In the front, stood a charming porch with two upholstered rocking chairs and a wicker table in between them. I envisioned drinking my morning coffee on the porch, or splitting a bottle of wine with Angelo there after a long day's work. Inside, the house had a traditional layout. The first floor housed the laundry, kitchen, dining room, bathroom, office, and living room. Upstairs there were three bedrooms and two more bathrooms.

Angelo's friends had moved my stuff into the house, but had simply left the boxes either in the living room or the guest room, depending on the label. I appreciated that they hadn't unpacked anything, since I couldn't stomach the invasion of privacy that their combing through my belongings would've entailed. But I also didn't exactly have the energy to unpack everything. So instead, I opened all the boxes. For the upstairs ones, I dumped everything onto the guest bed, figuring that way, I could slowly tackle the pile over the next few weeks.

Unfortunately, I'd told the library I'd return to work the next day, so I really didn't have a lot of time to unpack. When Angelo came home from work, I didn't miss the terrified look in his eyes when he spotted the piles of stuff, but he at least pretended to be okay with me taking my time organizing it all.

"You could take a few more days off work," he suggested as I set my alarm that night before bed. "Give yourself more time to recover from jet lag and settle in."

"Oh? This coming from the guy who left for work at the crack of dawn this morning?"

He snorted, then turned off the light.

The next morning, Angelo dropped me off at the coffee shop next to the library before heading to work. I tried to convince him to come inside, to at least meet my best friends, but he insisted he had some meeting he couldn't miss that morning.

Still, I enjoyed pastries and coffee with Madison and Kristi while catching them up on all my gossip before starting my shift at the library. We only had a half hour, so I couldn't get into all of the details about Angelo, but I promised they'd meet him soon. They'd already seen the photos I'd shared on social media, which included some gorgeous Italian vistas—and even more breathtaking sights of my new, handsome husband.

Thanks to the events of the last week, I didn't really have to lie to my friends. I could honestly tell my friends that yes, I'd rushed into the marriage and no, I still didn't know everything about my new husband. Most importantly, I didn't even have to pretend I'd spent the last week enjoying phenomenal newlywed sex. They could read it all over my face the moment they brought it up.

"So, we're talking best sex of your life?" Madison asked.

"Obviously, or she wouldn't have married him for it," Kristi replied for me.

"I'm sure she didn't marry him just for the sex," Madison retorted, continuing the conversation as if I weren't right there.

Kristi shrugged. "There's worse reasons to get married."

Yes, like because your father forces you to, I thought.

I pushed to my feet before they could press me for any further details. "So good to see you both, and I can't wait for you guys to meet Angelo. He can be a little quiet with new people, but you are going to love him and obviously he'll adore both of you." I leaned down to hug each of them, desperately hoping the latter part of my sentence proved true. Then, I scurried next door to the library.

My first few hours of work flew by, and I nearly forgot to take my lunch break. I had forgotten how much I enjoyed the simple rhythm of the library. The low din of voices, the familiar scent of the books, and the crisp organization of everything within sight somehow managed to both soothe and energize me. I also loved catching up with my coworkers and seeing all of my regular patrons.

After lunch, I was shelving books in the adult nonfiction section when Dave, another one of the regulars, came to say hi.

Dave was a professor at a nearby college campus. For as long as I'd been employed by the library, Dave had preferred to work in the library study carrels rather than his tiny office on campus. In a typical week, I saw him at least two or three times, so we'd become friends over the past year.

"Lina, how are you?"

"Hi! I'm great. How are you?"

"Doing well. I was starting to worry about you. You've been gone for what now, six weeks?"

"Eh, just a month," I began. I was about to tell him why I'd been out, but he started talking again.

"I thought about you last week when I saw that news article about South Carolina. The book banning stuff?" he said.

I cringed. We'd bonded over our mutual hatred of any sort of restrictions on books. "Ugh, yes. I saw that. It's ridiculous."

Right as I said that, my boss walked by. Faye was exactly what you'd picture when you thought of a librarian. She was older, and her gray hair was perpetually pinned above her head in a tight bun. She wore long floral skirts with crisp button down blouses, and her glasses always dipped low on her nose.

She glared at me as she passed, but I wasn't sure if it was because I was talking with someone, or because we were being loud.

"Sorry," Dave said once Faye turned onto another aisle. "Didn't mean to get you in trouble."

"No, it's fine." I wasn't worried about Faye, and she certainly couldn't penalize me for speaking with a patron.

"Well, I'd love to catch up with you more, but I guess we need to find a new place to meet up and chat," Dave said. "Honestly, I'd been meaning to work up the courage to talk to you about it lately anyway. Maybe we could meet up for a drink when you get off work sometime."

I hesitated. I enjoyed talking with Dave, but in the same way I appreciated my chats with all the regulars. I'd never considered spending time with him outside of the library.

Dave continued, unfazed. "Or would you want to grab lunch with me sometime?"

I felt my eyes widen, and he quickly amended his invitation.

"Or we could just do coffee."

"Oh," I said. I quickly replayed all of our past interactions in my mind. How had I never before realized Dave was flirting with me?

Dave grinned up at me expectantly, but his face morphed when he saw my expression. "Sorry, don't worry about it. I must've misread the…"

"No, I'm sorry for any mixed signals," I interrupted. "I would love a coffee but um, actually, I'm married. So I don't know that—"

"Married?"

I held up my hand, showing the ring.

"Uh okay. Wow. That's huge. I…can't believe I didn't notice that before."

"It's new," I explained. Then, I recalled that actually the ring was some sort of family heirloom, so I continued. "New to me, I mean. The ring."

He quirked a brow, and I realized that sounded weird.

"Not that someone else had it before. I'm the first wife." I cringed, then pressed my palm to my forehead. "I am so sorry for making this so awkward. All I meant to say was that I am flattered by the invitation and don't want to give you the wrong idea when I'm already taken."

Dave cleared his throat and turned to his shoes. "Understood."

I should've just shut up then, but I didn't. "This reminds me that I need to get a new name tag now that I'm officially Catalina Conti."

I also still had a stack of paperwork awaiting in the library office that I needed to complete once the legal name-change went through. Initially, the process of formally changing my name seemed an unnecessary hassle, particularly if the arrangement was only for a year, but Angelo had insisted that the Conti name itself would help secure my safety. So I'd agreed, and he assured me he had a guy who could fast-track the forms.

Dave smiled politely. "I didn't think many women changed their names for marriage anymore. What did you say yours is now?"

"Conti. It's Italian."

He nodded. "Is that a common surname?"

I shrugged. "Maybe in Italy. I don't think it's super common here. My husband does have a big family though."

"What's his first name?"

"Angelo. Angelo Conti." I couldn't help but smile just speaking my husband's name aloud.

Dave's expression changed. He abruptly broke eye contact and gazed to the side. He didn't speak for a moment, and then another patron approached and asked me for help finding a book.

I offered a polite nod and smile to Dave, then led the patron to the young adult fiction section. I figured Dave would head out before I returned to my desk, but instead, I found him pacing in front of it.

"How long did you and Angelo date before the wedding?" he asked abruptly.

I tightened my stomach, suddenly uncomfortable with the line of questioning. "Oh, gosh, I don't know the exact amount of time. Not long, I guess. When you know, you know, right?" I said, an awkward laugh punctuating my words.

"Have you spent a lot of time with his family?"

"Um, no, not really. I've met them all, of course, but—"

"Do you know much about the family business?" Dave had dropped the casual conversational tone. Now his voice reminded me of what he'd use for an interview, or perhaps an interrogation.

"Yes, they own a shipping company and some ports. Do you know them?"

"I know *of* them," he replied.

The way he said it made my skin crawl. "What do you mean?"

Dave looked around as if checking for witnesses. Instinctively, I took a large step backwards.

"You know I teach criminal justice, right?" he asked.

I hadn't known that, or at least I'd forgotten if he'd told me. I knew Dave was a teacher at the university and I thought he was in the social studies department, but for some reason I'd assumed he was more of a history expert.

"I stay on top of the local news about crime. The real world makes for some interesting examples in class. Angelo's father, Marco Conti, is a suspected boss in the organized crime world."

I dropped my head, trying to hide my lack of surprise. "I appreciate your concern Dave, but Angelo has nothing to do with his father. And even if he did, well, suspicions don't mean anything. If Marco was involved with organized crime, he'd be in jail."

Dave's frown tightened.

"I need to go to the back to work on some new orders, but, um—"

Dave reached for my wrist. "Angelo does not have a good reputation, Catalina. I don't know what you've gotten yourself mixed up in, but you should get help. I have some friends on the force that could talk to you about your options."

I stared at Dave's fingers on my arm until he took the hint and released me. "I don't know what you think you've heard about my husband, but he's a good man."

I strode into the back room before Dave could say anything else. I helped Faye with the remaining orders, and couldn't tell if Dave ended up leaving or was still working. So, when Faye told me I could head out early, I made a beeline for the bus stop. Angelo had been planning to pick me up after work, but I didn't want to wait around at the library and risk another run-in with Dave.

Nope. What I needed was to get home, and fast.

Angelo

I was about to leave for the day when Lina texted to say she'd finished early and was taking the bus home. My nostrils flared as I read the message a second time, trying to decide if this was her idea of a joke. Then, I clicked on my wife's location and confirmed that she was, in fact, moving along the least-direct route possible towards the house. Thanks to the inefficiency of the public transit system, we made it home around the same time.

Lina greeted me with an uneasy smile, then asked about my day.

I shook my head, trying to tamp down my annoyance. "I told you I'd pick you up. You don't just text me a change in plans. Did you already forget why we're married?"

"Because I'm irresistible?" she replied, her joke failing to lighten the mood.

"Catalina, I'm serious. I can't keep you safe if you don't follow the rules."

"There's rules now?"

I clenched my jaw. She knew the danger she faced. I'd explained it all, along with the importance of her not wandering around the places Carlos knew she'd be without someone who could keep her safe by her side. I didn't have time to act like a husband, fulfill all of my regular work duties, and babysit a woman who was going to fight my efforts at every turn. But I also couldn't stand the thought of letting something happen to her.

"Do I get a punishment for breaking these rules?" she taunted, still clearly misjudging my level of annoyance.

I considered her words, then nodded. "Yes, actually. That might help you remember next time. Get undressed and wait for me in the bedroom."

Lina didn't move. I could practically see the thoughts turning over in her mind, but I didn't have the patience to wait to see if she decided to obey. I lifted her off the ground at the waist, tossed her over my shoulder, and marched her into our bedroom. She squealed as I plopped her onto the bed, but quickly scrambled to try to sit up. I swung a leg over her waist, pinning her in place. I yanked her top over her head, then unfastened her bra.

The sight of this beautiful woman, now topless, squirming beneath me momentarily distracted me from my plan. I'd intended to be decisive and efficient in my punishment, not playful, but it took all of my self-control not to fill my palms with those perfect breasts.

I unfastened my belt, and as I tugged it free of the loops in my pants, I saw Lina's eyes flare with a hint of fear. "I'm not going to hit you," I snapped.

"Oh, because punishing me in bed is so much healthier?" she taunted back.

"No one would ever accuse of me of having healthy relationship habits," I said, roughly grabbing her arms and lifting them over her head. I twisted the belt around each wrist, then secured it along the bedpost, tightening the knot securely.

When I dropped my hands to my side, Lina immediately began to shimmy around, as if trying to free her arms.

"The more you move, the more it'll tighten and chafe. If you hold still, it might not even leave a mark," I said. I held high confidence in my knot-tying abilities, and I trusted the restraint would hold regardless of what she tried. But the leather really could hurt her if she fought. Besides, I preferred she not stretch my favorite belt.

I pinched each of her nipples, enjoying the surprised gasp I got in return, then climbed off of her. "I'll be back in a few," I said. "Don't move."

I chuckled to myself as I returned to the kitchen. I'd bought steak to grill that night, so I marinated the meat and stuck it back in the fridge. Then, I poured myself a drink. I sipped it slowly, trying not to think about the half-naked woman in my bed. When that challenge proved too hard, I returned to the bedroom.

Even though I knew she couldn't have moved, I was surprised to see Lina still positioned on the bed, her arms trussed up above her head. She stared at me, an indignant look in her eyes, and I regretted having left her pants on this long. I approached wordlessly, reaching for the waistband of her leggings. She tried to kick at me, so I yanked her pants down halfway, restricting her movements. She winced as the leather of the belt dug into her wrists.

"You should hold still," I warned. "I don't want you to be sore."

"Isn't that the whole point of a punishment, to hurt me?"

I frowned. "No, I just want to make sure you remember today."

My answer seemed to confuse her, but she held still long enough for me to remove the rest of her clothes. I began undressing, then paused when I felt my phone in my pocket. I snapped a photo of her naked body, grinning as I pictured all the fun I could have with that image any time we were apart.

Lina scowled. "What was that for?"

"Memories," I teased, moving on to my pants. I still hadn't decided what exactly I wanted to do to her. Seeing Lina like this made me desperate to make love to her, but for that, I didn't just want to be inside her, I also wanted to feel her arms and legs wrapped around me. She'd need to be a fully willing participant and so far, she probably wasn't.

Instead, I straddled her, letting the weight of my thick cock rest against her bare breasts. Her breathing increased and her nipples had hardened, so I at least knew I wasn't the only one feeling aroused. I stroked myself a few times, then swiped her lips with my thumb.

"Open your mouth, kitten."

Lina snapped her lips shut, gazing up at me with a proud defiance in her eyes. I pinched her nipples and she gasped again.

"Not to sound cliché, but we could do this the easy way or the hard way, kitten." I rolled her nipples between my thumbs and forefingers as I spoke, but kept my eyes on hers. After a moment, her lips parted the slightest bit.

"Good girl," I praised, noting the way her mouth opened a little further at the compliment.

I shifted my hips and placed the tip of my cock inside just inside her mouth. She didn't lick it or take it further, but she also didn't try to bite it off, so I considered that a win.

"There are all sorts of unsavory people on the bus," I said. "And I can't keep you safe when you're on a public bus with god-knows who else. So from now on, when I tell you I'll pick you up from work, the only way you're getting home is with me. Do you understand?"

She mumbled an incoherent response around my dick.

"I'm sorry. I couldn't understand that. Can you say it again?" I asked, grinning mischievously.

She glared in response, and I pulled back, freeing her mouth for words.

"I'm an adult capable of making my own decisions, and..." she began.

I cut her off, shoving my cock back between her lips. "No. You are my wife. Mine. So you can make your own decisions about what you do in your job, when you take your lunch break, even what shoes you wear. But I make the decisions about your safety. Because it's my job to protect you."

She didn't have a response to that. I moved my hands back to her breasts, silently rewarding her for taking me deeper. I wasn't sure if she realized she was doing it or not, but her tongue now swirled around the head as I gently thrust in and out. I couldn't imagine a sexier sight than the world's most beautiful woman, with the most magnificent lips wrapped tightly around my cock.

I reached for my phone again, snapping another picture before she even fully realized what I was doing. When she did, her eyes flared. She widened her mouth to protest, but I thrust in further, so all that came out was a muffled gag. I pulled back quickly, then dropped my phone on the bed beside us.

"Don't worry, kitten. That photo is for my eyes only. I don't share."

She didn't look convinced, but I kept moving further into her mouth with each thrust. She'd adjusted quickly to my size, but I could tell from her sensitive gag reflex that she wasn't accustomed to letting a man have the control during fellatio. I tried to hold back, especially when I noticed her eyes starting to water.

Everything about the experience was too erotic for me. Her mouth was too warm, the dampness just right. If I closed my eyes I might've been able to last another minute, but I couldn't stand the thought of not staring at her while my body rushed to the finish line.

I fought the primal urge to let my seed shoot straight down the back of her throat. Instead, when I knew I was on the brink, I pulled back abruptly, finishing all over her perfect breasts.

Her cheeks flushed red, and from the way she was panting almost as hard as I was, I could tell for certain that she was aroused. Lina enjoyed being bossed around. She got off on not being in control almost as much as I needed control to get off.

I went to the bathroom for a washcloth, pausing before cleaning her up to take one last picture. Then, before she could say anything, I buried my head between her legs. I debated untying her first, but decided I liked the power too much. I enjoyed the way she writhed against me, first chasing more pressure, then yearning for a break, I brought her to the brink of orgasm, then pulled back, smirking as her eyes flitted open, filled with frustration.

She opened her mouth to protest, but before she could, I reached for her wrists. I released the knot securing them to the bed, but didn't bother untying them from each other. Her arms fell limply around my neck and we kissed, long and hard. Then I sunk my cock deep into her wet pussy. She cried out at the suddenness of it, then found my lips again, kissing me through her next moan.

Lina came fast, and I quickly followed suit. After I caught my breath, I untied her wrists. The leather had left red imprints on her bronzed skin, and I kissed each mark, rubbing my thumbs over the skin to help bring back the feeling.

"You have a weird way of teaching lessons," she said. "I'm not sure if you were trying to convince me not to take the bus, or…"

"Lina," I said, hoping my eyes conveyed the seriousness of the situation. "Do not test me on this. I am not playing games with your safety."

She gazed back at me as if having completely forgotten the entire reason we'd married in the first place. My chest constricted with regret. I'd promised to keep her safe and I wasn't even sure how to do that. Not now, anyway. Not after falling for her.

"I should go grill the steak," I said, rolling off her and stepping into the first pair of shorts I found.

CHAPTER 16

Catalina

I awoke the morning after my first day back at work with a familiar twinge of soreness between my legs. Since my first time being intimate with Angelo, I hadn't exactly given my body a break, nor did I plan to. Surely, I'd eventually adjust to him. If not, well, *whatever*. Sex with Angelo was worth any potential consequences I had to face. He was that good. And the worst part was that I never had enough. The more orgasms he delivered, the more I craved.

None of it made sense.

The shower was running by the time I dragged myself out of bed. Apparently, Angelo had already completed a full workout in the home gym in our basement before I even peeled my eyes open. I yawned and thought about coffee. I craved that familiar warmth, sure to soothe and wake me.

But there was something else I craved more.

So, I made my way to the bathroom, stripping off my nightgown as I reached the door. Angelo's back was to the door, and steam filled the room. My breath caught in my throat as I drank in the sight of him. Soap suds trickled down his back, over the swell of his muscular buttocks.

Holy fucking shit.

I was still frozen in place, admiring the view, when Angelo turned and caught me staring. His chuckle came out as a low rumble in his throat, then he motioned for me to come closer. I didn't hesitate to join him under the hot spray of the shower.

"Morning," he said. "Did you sleep okay?"

"I…think so?" I said, still distracted by him and his proximity.

"I was about to get out, but I can help clean you up first," Angelo said with a wink. He reached for a loofah, sudsed it up, and began washing my back. When he reached my neck, he started on my front, moving from my stomach upwards. My nipples hardened the second he made contact, but he didn't linger. Instead, he just eyed me viciously and moved on to my arms.

I jerked back as the soap hit my wrist, the stinging sensation catching me off guard. Angelo froze, and we both gazed at my wrist. Faint red marks circled my wrists like bracelets, and the left arm had a small cut on the side of my wrist.

"I warned you not to pull to hard," he said.

He had, and yet… I sucked in a breath, feeling like I should be mad or ashamed or something. But instead, all I felt when I stared at my wrist and thought back to the night before was…arousal.

Before I could speak, Angelo's lips wrapped around my nipple. I pressed my palm against the cool tile wall, bracing myself.

"Didn't mean to hurt you," he said between delicate nips and languid strokes of his tongue. "Guess I'll have to make it up to you."

I would've replied, but he'd moved on to my other breast. A moment later, Angelo dropped to his knees and hoisted my left leg onto his shoulder.

I shrieked, gripping his hair with one hand and pressing harder into the wall with the other as his tongue delved deep into me, soothing any soreness I'd felt minutes before. Angelo clenched my hips with both hands, both steadying me and holding me squarely above his face. He licked, sucked, and teased my clit until I was panting and dizzy.

"I need to make a phone call in one minute, so you're going to come for me right now," he said, pulling back only briefly before resuming his delicious torture.

A burst of annoyance rushed through me. I was about to explain he couldn't order me to orgasm on command, except... apparently he could.

Everything about Angelo's bossiness turned me on, whether I wanted it to or not. My body began tightening, and each stroke of his tongue felt more powerful, and more targeted. I felt myself climb higher and higher and then, pleasure detonated in my core, scattering throughout my body.

Angelo held me tightly to his mouth until my orgasm subsided. Then, he delicately lowered my leg to the ground and rose to his feet. He leaned in, and I thought he was going to kiss me, but instead, he just paused by my ear.

"Good girl," he whispered, before stepping out of the shower and wrapping a towel around his waist. "I'll make breakfast," he called, leaving the bathroom.

I nearly collapsed onto the bench at the far end of the shower. *How was I so captive to this man?*

I finished my shower, put on makeup, and dressed before heading to the kitchen for breakfast. Angelo had already finished his phone call, and a plate of scrambled eggs and fruit sat on the table next to him.

"Is that for me?" I asked.

He nodded. "Sorry if it's cold. I didn't realize—"

"It's fine," I said, sitting down and starting to eat. I couldn't recall a time that a man had ever made breakfast for me aside from that first morning after, when they're all desperate to impress. I chewed in silence for a few minutes, since Angelo seemed to be working on something, but I was never very good at silence.

"So, you actually cook," I finally said.

Angelo gazed up from his phone, a wry grin on his face. "I'd starve if I didn't."

"Right." I supposed that made sense. "I'm not a bad cook either though, and I feel like you work more than me, so I'd love to handle dinners if…"

Angelo stared at me, awaiting the rest of the sentence that would never come. I had no idea what I was trying to say, except that I felt like I needed to contribute something to this whole arrangement. Finally, he nodded.

"Sure. Just order whatever groceries you need and have them delivered," he said. He glanced at his watch, then stood. "Will you be ready in a half hour?"

I shoved the last bite of fruit into my mouth and carried my plate to the dishwasher. "Yep. Just need to do my hair."

When I finished drying my hair, I heard voices in the living room. I emerged to find two men standing with Angelo. Their backs were to me, but he seemed relaxed with them in a way that made me assume they were close friends or family. They all turned as they heard me approach.

"Lina, you remember Eddie and Rico, right?"

I didn't really, having met each of them briefly and only once, but I nodded and smiled regardless.

Angelo pointed to the taller of the two men. "This is Edoardo Conti. He's a cousin. His dad Vincenzo was at the wedding.

"My dad's a couple years younger than Marco," Eddie offered.

Angelo moved on to the other man, patting him on the shoulder blade. "This is Federico Regio. He picked us up from the airport," he reminded me.

I nodded, vaguely recalling that fact.

"We met in elementary school and have been friends ever since. He joined the family about…" Angelo paused and glanced at Rico. "Maybe ten years ago?"

Rico nodded, then extended his hand to me.

I shook his hand, but noticed the absence of any wedding ring. "So who are you married to?"

Rico grimaced and shook his head.

"Uh, these guys are both single. You'll see why once you get to know them better," Angelo teased.

"But if he joined the family…"

Recognition washed over Angelo's face. "Not that kind of family, kitten."

"We work together," Rico offered. "All of us."

"Right. Eddie and Rico both work with the family," Angelo said. "You can trust them with anything, okay?"

I nodded again, knowing full well I wouldn't trust them until they'd earned it. I understood in Angelo's world that trust was some sort of business arrangement, but for me, it was personal. I needed to really know someone to trust them.

"They'll both drive you sometimes when I can't," Angelo continued. "So I figured we could all take you to work today. You ready to go?"

"Uh, yeah." I grabbed my purse, then Angelo gripped my hand and practically dragged me to an SUV waiting in the driveway. He rode in the backseat with me, holding my hand the entire time, but largely ignoring me for his friends. As we neared the library, they finally asked some questions about what I did at work. Based on the nature of their inquiries, I suspected they'd never before set foot inside a library.

"I could help you guys get library cards," I offered. "They're free, and then you can check out whatever books you want."

Angelo grinned at me, then pressed his fingertips on my cheek, angling my face to his. He kissed my lips, then climbed out of the car, walked around, and opened my door. He escorted me through the first set of double doors marking the entrance to the library, then stopped.

"Are you okay? You seemed quiet."

"I'm fine. I just didn't realize your friends were driving us. Or are they coworkers? Or relatives?"

He sighed. "They're all three."

I shrugged.

"I grew up with them. They're good guys, and I'd trust them with my life." He paused. "More importantly, I'd trust them with yours. They know about Carlos, and they know what he looks like. They'll keep you safe when I'm not around, okay?"

Everything Angelo said filled me with unease, but I simply nodded.

Angelo squeezed my shoulders and pressed a kiss to my forehead. "Rico will pick you up after work today. He'll be in the same car as now, right out front. If you need to leave earlier or later, just text. I programmed his number into your phone. If you need anything else and you can't reach me, call either of them. No taking the bus. Understood?"

I smiled at the memory of the consequences of that decision, but promised to ride home with Rico. Then I headed off to an uneventful day at work.

Angelo

Rico, Eddie and I rolled through our errands in record time. I made it home by mid-afternoon, and immediately went to the guest room to tackle the mess. For some reason, rather than leaving her shit in boxes until she had time to unpack fully—or just taking a couple days off work to unpack like a normal person—Lina had decided to dump everything onto the bed in the guest room. She explained that she planned to put away a few items each day.

Unfortunately, Lina didn't appear to love organizing or cleaning tasks. And since a decent chunk of her work day involved arranging books in an orderly fashion, Lina typically already reached her fill of organizing long before she returned home to me.

I wanted to be patient, but the sight of all the clutter was enough to drive me insane. So, I spent the next hour repackaging all of her nonessentials into boxes. I moved her clothes into our closet, and set a framed photo of Lina's family and one of her with her two best friends on the nightstand in our bedroom. Then, I stacked the remainder of the boxes into the closet in the guest room. The next time Lina had a day off work, she could unpack the rest. I was not about to stare at piles of stuff until then.

Giada and Luca stopped by that afternoon. I'd only expected Giada, but since Luca was headed back to Italy for an extended trip, I supposed I shouldn't have been surprised that they didn't want to be apart. I greeted them both and offered them drinks, then sat down to look at the design options Giada had brought me.

While Giada and I talked shop, focusing on our newest flip, Luca made his way to my back yard. I wasn't comfortable with him freely roaming my house, and he clearly wasn't comfortable talking on his phone inside my house, so it was win-win. At one point, Giada scampered to the guest room to grab a pillow to show me what "damask" fabric was, and I found myself watching Luca. He'd recently taken over his family business, and he looked stressed all the time. Not that he'd ever been the picture of calm, but he seemed particularly miserable as of late.

I planned to ask Giada how he was doing once we finished our official business, but instead, she caught me off guard by asking how things were going with Lina.

"Fine," I said, caught off guard by her sudden curiosity.

She quirked a brow. "I happened to notice your guest room appears completely unused."

"We haven't had any guests for…well, ever."

Now my sister frowned. "I overheard Mom say something before the wedding about how you could give Lina the guest room if she'd be more comfortable. It seemed weird at the time that you were planning on having separate rooms from your wife."

"Maybe you heard wrong," I lied. "I don't remember that."

Giada cocked her head to the side. "I'm the youngest kid in a family built on secrets. I'm a master at eavesdropping. I don't mishear things." She then relaxed her expression and continued. "But I'm also kind of a snoop and I'm guessing from the state of your bedroom that married life is going well."

I grimaced, instantly thinking back to everything Lina and I had done in our bedroom the night before. I had no clue what we could've left out, but I also really didn't want to talk about anything even remotely pertaining to sex with my baby sister.

"I need alcohol," I said, making a beeline to the fridge. Luca came in right as I was offering Giada her choice of whiskey and vodka.

She shook her head quickly, casting an almost worried look to Luca. I paused, trying to remember if I'd actually seen my sister consume any alcohol at the wedding or since. I turned to her just as she rubbed a hand over her stomach. She didn't look any different, but the way Luca's expression changed right then sent off alarm bells in my head.

"You should get some rest," he said to his wife, rushing to her side.

"Are you pregnant?" I blurted out, my voice sounding a bit disgusted, but only because I knew the things they'd have to be doing to make a pregnancy happen.

Luca and Giada exchanged a glance, and then a wide smile spread over my sister's face.

"We're telling the family at the dinner tomorrow, so keep your mouth shut until then."

"Yeah. Of course," I promised. "Congratulations?" I heard the word come out like a question, but I hadn't meant it that way.

Giada smiled and tugged me close for a hug. Luca shook my hand, and then the two of them left, leaving me free to down another drink.

CHAPTER 17

Catalina

Angelo was three drinks deep by the time I got home from work that day. Apparently, he'd learned his sister was pregnant—but that he wasn't supposed to share that news with anyone before a family dinner the next day. He already knew his brother was expecting a baby, although I wasn't sure if his brother was even still dating the mother of his child.

I'd already been nervous about the prospect of a dinner with Angelo's entire extended family at his childhood home, so I joined him for the next drink, eager to relax my mind.

"I feel like we were all just kids, and now they're both having kids of their own," Angelo mused. "It's weird."

I tried to picture my sister Valeria as a parent someday, then wrinkled my nose. I understood exactly what he meant. "Do you want kids?" I asked him, acutely aware that this was a conversation we probably should have had before the wedding. Well, except that before the wedding, we hadn't intended to stay together any longer than necessary.

Angelo cringed at the question, then shrugged. I pretended his answer didn't sting, and I was a little surprised to see how much it did actually bother me.

"I honestly haven't thought much about it," he finally said. "Up until a couple years ago, I assumed I'd get married and have a couple of kids just because that was the expectation. But after Julia, I never planned to settle down, and…"

I stroked his arm, letting his words trail off. This was a conversation we needed to have eventually, but not now. Not after we'd both been drinking. And not when I was already nervous about meeting the whole extended family.

As it turned out, my worries were unfounded. The dinner went smoothly, and the entire Conti clan had welcomed me with wide smiles and warm hugs. I'd expected the night to be filled with awkward moments, but everything felt natural, almost as if Angelo and I were no longer faking the relationship.

Over the next week, I'd settled into a comfortable groove. I was back at my usual schedule at work, and at home, life was good. Angelo and I had established a delightful routine that I hoped would be sustainable. Angelo started each day in the gym, but finished his workout early enough to save time for a quick round in bed—or the shower—with me. Then, he cooked a delicious breakfast for both of us while I got ready.

Rico drove me to work most days now, but that was okay. I was slowly getting to know him, and he seemed like a decent guy. I knew Rico carried a gun, but other than that, he didn't strike me as some tough mobster. For that matter, neither did Angelo most of the time. Yeah, he was serious, but I couldn't really picture him breaking the law. As far as I could tell, all that mafia stuff was just rumors.

There weren't wads of cash under the bed, drug dealers wandering in and out of the house, or prostitutes delivering a share of their earnings like I'd expect if my husband were actually some mob boss.

Our life was a normal, newlywed life. I tended to get home before Angelo, so I had time to make dinner. Angelo usually ended up doing more work in the evenings, but we almost always made love again before bed.

I hadn't managed to pry any more details about work out of him, but Angelo was opening up to me about other areas of his life. He told me more about his childhood, and we went to lunch with his brother and sister on a Sunday when neither of us was working. Angelo joined Madison, Kristy and I for a boozy brunch on a Saturday, and he even drove us all to a few shops after we drank too many mimosas. Really, life was good.

In the back of my mind, I realized my relationship with Angelo wasn't technically real. As far as I knew, we still had an expiration date. Once enough time had lapsed and the threat with Carlos was gone, Angelo and I could divorce and move on our way.

Theoretically, we wouldn't have to if we didn't want to, but since we hadn't discussed it, I couldn't say with certainty where Angelo stood on that. If it were up to me alone, well, I would stay put. This fake marriage was by far the best relationship I'd ever been in. The only downside was my lack of certainty about whether my husband felt the same way.

I shimmied back and forth to music in my head as I shelved the last few books. I only had a half hour left of my shift at the library and then I was heading home to cook a romantic dinner for Angelo.

"Catalina."

I jumped several inches at the soft voice, dropping the book from my hand.

Dave bent to retrieve the book, an apologetic smile on his face as he handed it to me.

"Thanks," I mumbled, wheeling my cart towards the nearest aisle.

"Wait," he said.

Against my better judgment, I did.

Dave extended a manilla envelope to me. "One of my friends in the department showed me this. You should read it."

"What department?" I asked.

"Police."

Angelo's name was scribbled on the outside of the folder, so I didn't have to guess that part. "You were asking about my husband?"

"I'm worried about you. You're not safe."

I rolled my eyes and handed the folder back to him. "There's nothing you could show me that would change my opinion of Angelo."

"So he told you about his last girlfriend?"

"Yes," I said.

My answer seemed to surprise Dave. He took the folder back. "Okay then, I'm sorry for wasting your time. You're clearly not the person I thought you were."

I should've let it go, but his tone rubbed me the wrong way. And I was fed up with men treating me like shit just because I didn't share their romantic feelings.

"Seriously?" I snapped. "I thought we were friends. That's a crappy thing to say even if you are mad I won't go out with you."

"This has nothing to do with a bruised ego. I legitimately thought you must not know that Angelo murdered his last serious girlfriend."

His words didn't make sense. Angelo had been devastated about Julia. There was no way he was faking that emotion. Dave had to be confused. "What are you talking about?"

"You didn't know she was killed?"

"Of course I did," I said.

"But Angelo didn't tell you he was arrested? Initially they planned to charge him with her murder."

"Why would Angelo have been charged with murder?"

Dave frowned. "Because he was the one who killed her."

I opened my mouth to protest, but he continued.

"Angelo never denied that part. He admitted to the police that he pulled the trigger." Dave paused. "I thought you said he told you."

"He told me he loved her and that she died. He didn't say—"

"That he shot her point blank in the face, then once more in the shoulder for good measure?" Dave thrust the folder back at me. "Angelo's family has a lot of friends on the force, or they might have looked a little harder into his story that he was defending his sister."

My mind dwelled on the realization that Angelo must have been there, must have had to watch her die, if he was almost charged in the crime. For a moment, that image filled me with pity. Then, I snapped back to what Dave was saying.

"Did Angelo tell you she'd been meeting with an undercover cop in the months leading up to her death?" he asked.

I opened and shut my mouth, but no words came out.

"Think about it, Lina. He's in the mafia. She was working with an undercover agent. Then Angelo killed her. How does any of that make him a good man?"

I accepted the folder with a shaky hand, then stared at it like it was toxic.

"You shouldn't bring this home. Read it here and give it back to me," Dave suggested.

Wordlessly, I stumbled to the library's family bathroom, locked the door, then read the investigation notes about a horrifying murder of a young woman.

By the time I emerged from the bathroom ten minutes later, I'd vomited twice, but cried none. In the end, it was the photos that did me in. Even in black and white, the image of that poor girl's brains splattered on the patchy grass was gruesome. I couldn't imagine my Angelo playing any part in that, whether it was self-defense or not. But the police notes said Angelo admitted he held the gun that shot her. He admitted to pulling the trigger.

He admitted doing it twice.

Angelo

Rico texted that Lina wasn't feeling well, so I'd hurried home. She hadn't answered any of my texts, and Rico said she hadn't given him any details except to say she was sick, and that she hadn't spoken or looked at him the entire drive home.

But as I walked through the door, familiar cooking sounds greeted me. I sighed with relief, assuming that meant she was better. "Honey, I'm home," I called out, fully embracing the cliché of normalcy I'd become.

"In the kitchen," she replied unnecessarily.

I stepped out of my shoes, then hurried to the kitchen to see Catalina. Her back was to me, and she appeared to be tearing greens for a salad. I'd hoped she'd turn to greet me, but when she didn't, I roped my arms around her waist, kissing her on the side of the neck. She stiffened at the contact, but said nothing.

"You okay?" I asked, backing off.

"Yes. Great," she replied, her voice a bit too high pitched.

"Rico said you weren't feeling well."

"I guess lunch didn't agree with me. I'm good now."

"How was work?"

"Good. Nothing of note."

I frowned at her odd phrasing, but decided to let it go. No matter how comfortable I felt with Lina, we were still in that getting-to-know each other phase.

"Should I open some wine?" I offered.

"Sure. Thanks."

"Red or white?"

"Whichever."

I glanced over at the stove to see what she was cooking and then selected a bottle of red. I poured two glasses, setting Lina's beside her. "Can I help with something?"

"No, I'm just running behind. I'll have it all ready in five minutes. Sorry."

I sighed, nearly certain something was wrong. What I was less sure of was whether it was something I'd done or if she was just upset in general.

I sipped my wine, admiring the view of Lina from behind as she cooked, then topped off my glass. As she finished plating up everything, she finally turned to me.

"Hi," I said, happy to see her face.

Lina flashed me a fake smile and carried our plates to the table. I grabbed the wine and followed her, but stopped her before she sat down.

"Hey," I said. "I can tell something is wrong. Talk to me," I said, reaching for her hand. She tugged it away, wiping her palm on her jeans.

She glanced furtively around the room, then shook her head. "I'm fine, really. Too much caffeine is all."

Lina sunk into her chair, gulped her wine, then began stabbing at her food.

I leaned back in my chair and watched, no longer hungry.

When she finally looked up, she frowned. "You don't like it? I'm sorry. I can make you something else." Lina started to stand.

"No, sit. It's great," I said, shoveling bites into my mouth and moaning like it was the best thing I'd ever had. We went on like that for another five minutes, and then Lina stood to carry her plate to the kitchen.

I decided I was done guessing and followed her into the kitchen. The second she set down her plate, I grabbed her hips and hoisted her onto the counter. I stepped forward, planting a hand on each of her thighs and stepping between them.

"Let me go," she protested.

"Not until you tell me what's wrong," I said.

Her eyes bounced around the room in a panic.

"Are you afraid of something? Jesus, is someone here?" I asked, my hands starting towards my gun.

Lina snapped her eyes shut. "No one is here."

"Talk to me baby, please," I begged.

She didn't answer right away, but I sensed from her deep breaths that she was working up the courage to say whatever she had to say. After an eternity, her eyes opened and peered straight into mine.

"I planned for tonight to go very differently," she began. "I was so excited to see you and I spent half the day thinking about last night."

"Me too," I said, feeling my dick jerk to attention at the brief mention of the night before. We'd fucked on the kitchen counter and Lina had come three times—once around my fingers and then twice in a row squeezing my cock like a vise and soaking me. It was the kind of sex that was so good, we should both be floating on the clouds for days. I couldn't believe we were arguing about anything right now.

And yet, here we were.

"But then I saw something, and now I can't think about anything else," Lina continued. "I know you can't talk openly about all of your work stuff and whatever, but I need to ask you about something else. And I need you to be honest."

"I don't understand. What did you see?"

"That's not important now," she insisted.

I sighed, a mixture of annoyance and impatience clawing at me. "What's your question?"

Lina swallowed audibly. "Did you kill your last girlfriend?"

My throat ran dry and I stumbled one step backwards, then another. I peered around the room, then spotted the bottle of wine. I emptied the remainder into my glass, then began gulping. "I can't discuss this in here."

I walked out of the kitchen without another word.

CHAPTER 18

Catalina

I slid off the counter, steeled myself with a few deep breaths, then poked my head around the corner. Angelo sat on the couch, his head thrust between his hands. I made my way to the armchair across from him, sitting tentatively. He waited a moment, then gazed up at me. I held my breath, awaiting the lie.

Instead, all he said was one, breathy word.

"Yes."

Angelo stared back at me, as if expecting me to run or scream or do something else dramatic. But his honesty was so unexpected that I just sat there, like the idiot main characters in horror movies who run up the stairs instead of out the front door when the knife-wielding psychopath appears.

I waited for Angelo to elaborate, but when it became clear he wouldn't, I pressed onward.

"On purpose?"

His mouth twitched as if the question confused him, but then he responded. "Yes."

"How?"

His gaze dropped to his lap, where he wrung his hands together. "It was complicated. I thought it was the only option I had, and…"

"No, I mean, what was the cause of death?"

"Oh. Gunshot wound to the head. There was also one to the shoulder, but that was unnecessary, it turned out." He reached for his wine glass and drained the rest of it. "But you already knew all this, didn't you?"

It wasn't so much a question as an accusation.

"I saw the police notes," I admitted. "I want to hear your side."

"I have no side. Nothing more favorable than the police version of events, at least." Angelo stood and began pacing.

I tried to remain still, but every time he neared me, I flinched.

"I'm not going to hurt you," he snapped.

"I know," I lied. "But could you sit down at least? You're making me nervous."

"No, I can't sit down while I relive the worst day of my life," he said. "Because that's what it was, okay? It was an impossible situation and my choices were all shit, but I did what I did and now I have to live with the consequences."

He kept pacing. I kept flinching. Finally, he thrust a hand into the holster at his ankle, and tugged out a gun.

I shrieked, but he'd already set it on the coffee table. I stared at it, feeling my eyes go wide.

"Take it," he said.

I shook my head, terror now coursing through my veins.

"Do you know how to shoot it?" he asked.

I hesitated, then nodded.

"Okay, well, I can't tell you all of this if you're going to be afraid. So hold the gun if that makes you feel better."

"It won't."

"Then set it someplace else. I don't care."

I paused, then reached for the gun. Pointing it at the ground, I lifted it and placed it on the bookshelf behind me.

"Better?" he asked.

I shrugged. "I wasn't afraid of you." That was partly the truth.

"You should be. Julia never was, and look where that got her."

"Please sit," I begged. "Just tell me what happened."

His reluctance was palpable, but he sat. "You want to hear what you already read?"

"Is there more?"

Angelo shrugged. "My sister was spectacularly naïve growing up. And she had a reputation for being this good little catholic girl. So when she was engaged to Luca, an undercover cop approached her. He prayed on her Catholic notions of right and wrong to get her to talk about Luca."

"Did she?" I asked, already invested in the backstory.

"No. Giada worships the ground that man walks on. She'd never say anything bad about Luca," he said. "Me, on the other hand, she hated. So she told the agent to look into me. Then, the agent approached Julia. But he asked *her* for details about Luca."

I frowned. The police notes hadn't included any of this information. I wasn't quite sure why it was all relevant, but I didn't dare interrupt again.

"Julia didn't know much. Luca keeps his business private. But she shared what she could. And that was her first mistake." He gazed up and locked eyes with me. "You never talk to the cops, especially about someone else. If she'd blabbed about me, I maybe could've protected her, but the second she ratted out Luca..."

Angelo shook his head. "Her next mistake was in getting caught with the cop. My sister recognized the cop and so then she knew Julia was talking with him too. Julia tried to get to Giada, like she wanted the two of them to bond over it or something. Giada told Julia she was going to tell Luca, which I'm sure she would have since she tells him everything. And Julia figured Luca would kill her once he spoke to Giada."

"Would he have?"

Angelo shrugged. "Hard to say at that point, since Julia hadn't yet told the cops anything useful. But then Julia panicked and decided she had to kill Giada if she didn't want Luca to find out."

"No," I whispered.

"She hired some two-bit hitman, but he fucked up and shot Luca when he was driving Giada. Luca crashed the car, but instead of killing my sister, the accident just gave her a head injury and amnesia. Julia started acting strange, and I was about to break up with her, but then she started going over the top with her research on regaining memories. It was like an obsession. And that gave me pause."

Angelo paused right after saying the word.

"I started to look into her finances and I had her followed. I figured out pretty fast what she'd done. If I told Luca, he'd have killed her in a heartbeat. Well, except he probably would've taken his time."

I grimaced. "He's a monster."

Angelo offered yet another casual shrug. "If someone tried to kill my wife, I wouldn't respond well either."

I wondered if I was included in that sentiment, or if he was referring to some future, real wife. Angelo paused, and I wasn't sure if he was done, but I decided to ask my question. "None of this was in the police story. I don't understand how all of this relates to what I read."

Angelo swallowed. "This is the part I didn't tell the police." He rubbed his eyes, then gazed back at me. "This is what I've never told anyone."

My pulse drummed harder, in part because I needed to know the connection, how he went from having this knowledge to everything that happened that day in the field. But I also relished the awareness that he trusted me with some new information.

"So you didn't tell Luca when you found of what Julia had done?" I confirmed.

"No. He found out later, of course, but I wanted time to figure out what to do. I could've let him kill her, could've washed my hands of the whole debacle. But that didn't sit right with me. We were still technically together. She was sleeping in my bed every night, and as much as I knew she'd betrayed me and my entire family, I couldn't shake the feeling that I'd betrayed her too."

Angelo squeezed his eyes shut. His breathing became ragged, and when he opened his eyes again, they were damp and red. He wiped his eyes again and cleared his throat, but I could tell he was struggling. And something about the sight of this big, powerful man trying so hard not to cry was wrenching a hole in my chest.

I moved to the couch beside him, squeezing his hand in mine.

Angelo gazed at me, his expression an odd mixture of sorrow and gratitude. Then, he continued.

"I thought about sending her away, but it would never work. Giada would never be safe, and Luca would've killed me if he'd found out. Hell, my own father might have killed me. And I couldn't trust Julia. There just wasn't a single scenario where Julia didn't have to die."

My stomach fell as Angelo said the last word and my hand went limp around Angelo's. His back vibrated with tears he wasn't releasing, but I couldn't comfort him more. I needed to know for sure.

"Wait, are you saying you planned to kill her?"

He shut his eyes, not speaking for a full minute. When he finally stared back at me, he nodded.

"Would you feel better holding that gun now?" he asked, his voice even.

I licked my lips, but said nothing.

"I knew it had to be done, and I knew that it had to be me. That was the only way I could ensure it was quick and painless. I didn't want her to see it coming, didn't want her to be afraid." A tear slid down his cheek and in an instant, my empathy returned.

"Angelo, you were being compassionate. She tried to kill your sister. You kept her safe the only way you could." I meant that he'd prevented her from being tortured for her crimes, but he didn't interpret it that way.

"If I kept her safe, she wouldn't be dead!"

I squeezed his hand to calm him. "From what you're telling me, there's no scenario where she could've stayed alive. She made the choices that led to her own downfall, not you."

He frowned, but said nothing.

"So why did you decide to go to the park to do it?" I asked after a long silence.

"I didn't. I was trying to figure out a way to take care of her without getting caught."

"Take care of her...as in—"

"Kill," he said bluntly.

"Julia was going paranoid, asking me questions about Giada and her memory, telling us all that Giada might generate fake memories. I could tell she was getting desperate, so I played on that." He paused. "So I told Julia that Giada called me and said she got her memories back. I said that my sister wanted to talk to me about her."

"What did she do?" I asked, growing impatient.

"She told me not to go, said my sister was making things up. Julia asked to meet with Giada alone first. I acted casual and said fine."

Angelo stopped again and rubbed his forehead. "I set her up. I left one of my guns out on the dresser where she'd see it, under some of her clothes. I wanted her to take it, and she did. I picked the park. I chose it because of the cameras overlooking the parking lot and the bathrooms. I told Julia to invite my sister hiking or something. Then I told Luca that Julia was acting weird. I asked him to come keep an eye on Giada, just in case something went wrong."

"You wanted to protect your sister," I said.

He nodded and continued. "I got to the park early, had Eddie drop me off so no one would see my car. I waited until Giada and Luca arrived. For my plan to work, Julia had to try to shoot my sister somewhere that a camera could see, but I figured when she saw Luca there too, she'd panic and try to do it right away. I was right."

"I'm so sorry," I mumbled, and I meant it. The whole story was awful. I sometimes thought my family was a mess, but this was worse. Way worse.

"The only surprise is that Julia actually aimed for Luca. I guess that makes sense, since she was always convinced he was evil. For a brief second I thought about letting her try. Her aim was shit anyway, so she probably wouldn't hit him, and then Luca would've shot her and ended it all real fast."

"Why didn't you?"

"Because my sister jumped in front of Luca." He shook his head as if he still couldn't believe it. "So I took the shot. And even though I knew how to handle a gun, I freaked out and fired twice."

The pain in his voice was palpable, and I couldn't let him suffer any longer. I crawled onto his lap, wrapping my arms around his neck and pulling his face tight to my shoulder. My heart felt like it would burst for this poor, beautiful man, and I wasn't sure how to react. I hadn't expected honesty from him, and certainty hadn't expected all of that story. So maybe that was why I felt only love where an hour before it had been nothing but fear.

I held him for close to an hour, before he finally nudged me off his lap, insisting we should go to bed.

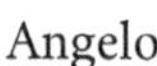

Angelo

*A*s I brushed my teeth, I couldn't remember ever before feeling this drained. I felt like I'd bared my soul, and had nothing left to give.

"Can I ask you a question?" Catalina said later that night, replacing the cap on her toothpaste.

I turned to her, not sure I could handle answering anything else. I'd never talked to another person as much as I had her.

"You could have just told me it was self-defense. Or, defense of your sister," she corrected. "You could have given me the exact story you gave the cops."

I nodded, then lifted my shirt over my head.

"So why didn't you?" she asked. "I would've never known that wasn't the whole story."

"But I would know."

She peered expectantly, those emerald eyes demanding more.

"You deserve to know the truth about the man you married. You need to understand what I'm capable of," I finally said.

Lina frowned as if my words made her sad. "I know what kind of man you are, Angelo. You may not see it, but I do."

"You're not safe with me."

"You're not going to hurt me," she countered.

I wasn't sure that was true, but I didn't have the energy to argue. "People in my life get hurt."

"I'm not her, Angelo. I'm not Julia. I'm not going to the cops. I know how this world works and I'm not going to put you in a position where the only way you can save me is by killing me."

"You don't know what the future holds," I said.

I waited for Lina to reply, but instead, she slipped the straps of her black negligee off her shoulders. All the breath whooshed out of me as I watched it tumble past her breasts, over the curve of her hips, then pool on the ground.

"Make love to me Angelo," she said, her voice barely above a whisper.

In my mind, I already was. I'd buried myself so deep inside that tight, pink pussy that I didn't remember my own name, let alone my past sins.

But in reality, I couldn't. After the night we'd had, the way I was feeling, no way. I needed to join a cage fight, drink till I passed out, or face-fuck a hooker until she gagged on my cum. I couldn't be loving. I couldn't be gentle.

I shook my head, already feeling regret over my answer. "I can't."

She stepped closer, pleading. "Please. I need you inside me. I need to feel whole again." Her eyes dipped down to my groin, where my pants did nothing to hide my painful erection.

"Lina, I can't. I'd be too rough with you. I might hurt you. I'm too worked up to be gentle."

"Then don't," she said, reaching to unzip my fly. "I'm not a porcelain doll. I won't break."

My breath caught in my throat as her fingers crazed my cock through the thin fabric of my boxer briefs.

I was fully prepared to say no again when she continued.

"Please Angelo. Fuck me hard."

My belt clanked to the floor before I realized I'd even made a decision. I lifted Lina onto the counter behind her, then dropped to my knees, eating her pussy like I'd been starved for days.

Lina moaned and thrust her fingers into my hair.

I spent only a minute getting her wet before I stood. Gripping her butt cheeks, I tugged her to me, impaling her on my cock in one fell swoop. She cried out and I kept going, watching myself in the mirror as I pounded into her over and over like some sort of rabid animal.

Her nails dug into my shoulders as I felt her innermost muscles begin to tighten around me. Lina flailed back her head and screamed out my name as her orgasm hit.

Seeing her come only aroused me more. I'd always assumed she needed romance and foreplay, but I hadn't even kissed her

and she'd come so hard she would've knocked herself unconscious on the mirror if I hadn't snuck a hand out to protect her.

I lifted her up, pulling out of her and carrying her to the
bedroom. She nipped at my shoulder and I growled, dropping
her onto the bed before flipping her onto her stomach. I hoisted
her hips upward, reveling in the glorious vision of her beautiful
ass perched high in the air. Then I delved my tongue inside her,
lapping up the evidence of her pleasure.

When I slammed into her from behind, a sharp hiss escaped
her lips. I nearly asked if I'd hurt her, but then her hips moved,
meeting me thrust for thrust. I leaned over her, squeezing her
breasts then pinching her nipples in time with my movements.
Then I moved one hand to her hips, steadying us as I increased
the pace, and used my other hand to play with her clit. I didn't
expect her to come again, but right as the tension built to an
untenable level deep in my core, Lina exploded around me. Her
body thrashed wildly and I succumbed to the pleasure surging
through me, emptying myself deep inside her.

After, I collapsed on top of her, not even bothering to pull out.

"When did you say your birth control would start working?" I
asked once I'd caught my breath.

I heard her muffled swear against the bedding.

I slid off of her, grabbed a cloth from the bathroom, and
returned, dabbing delicately at her upper thighs. Lina didn't
move. I stretched out beside her, noting her eyes were closed, but
her grin told me she was awake.

"You came twice," I said. It wasn't an accusation, just more of a
surprised observation.

"So far," she said, grin widening as she opened her eyes.

I smiled, always up for a challenge.

Catalina

. . .

*D*espite both of us being completely exhausted, we made love a second time. And this time, it really was making love. I enjoyed it hard and fast with Angelo, but I also liked this slow and delicate version, almost like he was apologizing for hurting me earlier. Even though he hadn't.

After, I curled up on top of Angelo, my leg draped across his legs and my head on his chest. He tucked the covers over us and roped an arm over my waist, securing me in place. His breathing evened out, but I knew he wasn't asleep. He was probably replaying every moment from the evening, just like I was.

I realized I'd need some time to process everything he'd told me about Julia, along with everything I'd read. I knew I should be scared, at least on some level. Afterall, my husband had essentially admitted that he was, in fact, deeply entrenched in the mafia and that he'd had no choice but to brutally murder someone who had threatened to reveal his family's secrets.

But I also knew that I wasn't scared in the slightest of the man currently holding me tight.

"Lina," Angelo said, his deep voice shattering the silence of the night. "You should sleep."

"I can't."

He was quiet for a full minute before he spoke again. "Who told you about Julia?"

I hesitated, not wanting to get Dave in trouble, but then again, I trusted Angelo. He wouldn't hurt someone who had tried to protect me. So, I told him everything. I expected him to be surprised that someone in criminal justice knew about his family, but he wasn't. Instead, he was hung up on the fact that I spoke with men at work.

"That's why I didn't want you to work," he said.

I practically snorted at the ridiculousness. "Really? You're so insecure that you can't even let your woman talk to another man?"

His head pulled back so that he could've seen me, if the room weren't pitch black. "Did you just call me insecure?"

I breathed a laugh. "Yes. Yes I did."

"Lina, go to sleep before I demand a blow job to help reestablish my security."

I smiled at that, and somehow, I did fall asleep, but only briefly. And when I woke, I decided the blow job would probably make us both feel better about everything. But then that led to more sex, followed by another brief nap, followed by an insane makeout session that probably would've led to more sex except that neither of us had any energy left to commit.

By the time a deep sleep finally overtook me, I somehow felt closer to Angelo than I'd ever dreamed possible.

CHAPTER 19

Catalina

It was after ten when I finally rolled out of bed, yet it felt alarmingly early

"I'm so sleepy," I whined, stifling a yawn as I shuffled around the bed, pausing by Angelo's side.

"You should go back to sleep," Angelo said. "I don't have anything I can't delegate today. Let's spend the whole day in bed."

I nearly moaned at how tempting the idea was. "I have work though."

"Call in."

"And say what? I've never skipped a shift before. I can't exactly call in and tell them I spent the entire night fucking my husband and can barely walk let alone sit."

Angelo sat up, grabbing me by the waist and hoisting me back into bed. I straddled him, peering down at his sleepy face. "Yes, that's exactly what you should say."

I laughed, trying to imagine my boss's face if I actually told her any of that. She blushed just shelving romance novels and probably would have a cardiac arrest at the thought of real people engaging in sexual conduct.

Angelo reached over, snatching my phone off the nightstand. He unlocked it and toggled right to my contacts. Then, he picked up his own phone and began dialing.

"Don't you dare," I squealed, reaching for it.

Angelo flipped my onto my back, straddling my torso in a way that pinned my arms. I probably could've escaped if I'd tried harder, but I was distracted by his groin, inches from my face.

I heard the phone ringing and panicked, but then assured myself he wouldn't say anything. The call went to voice mail and Angelo peered down at me, at mischievous look in his eye.

"Yes, hi, my name is Angelo Conti. I wanted to let you know that my wife Catalina Conti will not be able to make it in to work today or tomorrow. I'm hoping she'll be able to rest so if you need to reach her for any reason, I'd appreciate you calling me at this number instead and I'll be sure she gets the message. Thanks," he said.

I sighed. "That sounded oddly mature for someone dangling his balls in my eyes."

Angelo flashed me a devilish grin, then pressed his cock between my lips. He wasn't fully hard yet, so as I swirled my tongue around the tip, his erection grew and knocked straight at the back of my throat. I gagged and turned my head to the side. Angelo chuckled and pulled back.

"No, I'm good now," I said, reaching for him.

"I need a shower," he said.

"I'll join you." I moved to get up, but Angelo placed one hand on my belly, easily holding me in place.

"No, you need sleep, Lina. Just stay here, get some rest. I'll shower, and if you still can't sleep, I'll bring you breakfast in bed. I'm not going anywhere, okay?"

I sighed, then nodded. I watched him trudge out of the room, and he returned with a glass of water for me. I took a few sips, and a moment later, I heard the shower start. I sighed and tried to think about everything I'd learned the night before. I still had the distinct feeling that I should be frightened but, if anything, it seemed even less scary in the light of day.

All I knew was that Angelo was a good man who had put his life on hold to take care of me. Maybe I was a shitty judge of character, but for now, I felt safe.

Angelo

After the longest shower of my life, I checked on Lina and found her sound asleep. Thank God for that at least. I needed to think, and I couldn't do that with her staring at me with those beautiful puppy dog eyes.

She seemed to believe every single thing I said.

And I hated that.

I actually hadn't lied to her, but I still hated that she trusted me. Lina's taste in men was so bad that she literally had to agree to an arranged marriage just so her ex-boyfriend wouldn't murder her. That is the kind of man she fell for, the kind who stalked and maybe tortured her.

So what did it say about me if she was falling for me?

Exactly.

Well, at least she had a type—psychos who hurt women. Yep, that was me. I hadn't meant to hurt Julia and I wouldn't mean to hurt Lina, but I didn't doubt that I would.

The only reason I'd even agreed to this stupid arrangement was because I'd viewed it as a business transaction. I was fantastic with those. I never fucked up business deals.

Personal relationships? That was a whole different ballgame. I couldn't get those right if my life depended on it. And now,

Lina would be the collateral damage of my next personal fuck-up.

The problem was that I was already in too deep. She knew too much for me to just walk away, and I wasn't sure I was strong enough to leave even if I wanted to. Even just in the short number of hours Lina and I were apart working, I missed her. Not just the sex, but *her*. I missed her adorable facial expressions, her sassy comebacks, and her shy smile. My fingers ached to touch her smooth skin, and my body yearned to feel her warmth next to mine.

Already, I couldn't live without her. But I needed to figure out a way to make sure that I wasn't the thing that killed her.

I grabbed some clean clothes and went to the guest room to dress silently. Then, I went to the patio to call Eddie and let him know I wouldn't be leaving the house today. I didn't give him all the details, but enough to let him know my dilemma. If anyone could help me figure out a solution, it would probably be Luca, but I wasn't quite humble enough to go to him for help. Yet.

After tackling all the business I could from the yard, I went back inside to clean up the dinner mess from the night before. Then I busied myself making lunch for when Lina awoke.

Catalina

I didn't wake until mid-afternoon, and my first priority then was bathing. When I finally emerged from our bedroom nearly an hour later, I found Angelo asleep on the couch. He looked like a giant with his feet sticking out over the end and his arms hanging off the side, but the sight was adorable nonetheless. From the looks of the house, he'd cleaned the entire place before passing out, which I guessed shouldn't have surprised me. Angelo was definitely a neat freak.

In the kitchen, there was a note on the fridge and a plate inside containing a sandwich and salad for me. I smiled and happily ate my lunch. I focused *not* on the fact that, less than twenty-four hours earlier, my husband admitted to murdering his last girlfriend, but on the fact that my husband was an amazing cook who willingly made me lunch before taking a nap. I was so grateful that I even loaded my dishes into the dishwasher.

Next, I made my way to the guest room. Earlier in the week, Angelo had re-packed the items I'd already unpacked. I would've been annoyed, except that he'd placed the cutest picture of my family next to my bed and my favorite one of me and my besties on the dresser. I couldn't stay mad when he was so thoughtful. Besides, I was starting to learn that as messy as I was, Angelo was just as tidy. The yin to my yang, so to speak.

I'd only made it through a single box when I heard footsteps behind me. I jumped dramatically, then realized it had to be Angelo. His large hands on my waist a moment later confirmed the guess.

"Sorry to startle you," he mumbled.

"It's okay. Thanks for lunch."

'It's almost dinner now."

"I didn't make anything, but we probably have leftovers," I said, not bothering to add that I just ate thanks to my late nap then long bath.

"We could order takeout. Are you hungry yet?"

"No." I hesitated. "Could we maybe talk?"

Angelo made a face. "I'm not sure I have it in me."

"Me either, but I have some questions."

"About?"

"Your work."

Now he really scowled in response.

I sat on the foot of the guest bed and waited for him to do the same. "I assume that your family's business is not completely within the parameters of the law, if the FBI is interested."

Angelo said nothing.

I sighed. "I don't need to know every detail, but I feel like I need more information to be able to stay safe."

He shook his head. "Keeping you safe is the reason I am not telling you any other details. The less you know, the safer you are."

I wasn't sure I agreed. "Can you at least explain what your involvement is?"

He pursed his lips, his eyes darting back and forth as if he were debating whether to answer. Finally, he said, "My father is the head of the family and the official boss of all businesses. Someday, I'm supposed to take over everything."

"So are you like the second in command now?"

"Not really. It's hard to explain, but that's just not how it works in our world. Dad's second in command will probably retire when he does. For now, I'm involved in all of the businesses, but I run the construction one and have a lot of involvement at the ports too. My background and education are in business, so I handle that side of things more than..." his voice trailed off.

"The crime part?" I supplied.

He frowned. "I was going to say the manual labor."

"Oh. Right. So you personally don't do any crime?"

Angelo said nothing.

"Or break any laws?"

More silence.

"Is that a no, or—"

"Lina, I'm not going to answer more questions. Trust me when I say you don't want to know the specifics. I'm not a good person. I'll tell you that much. I've done bad things before and I'll do bad things again. I'm a bad guy. You don't need the details keeping you up at night or messing with your conscience."

Angelo stood and started to the door, as if that were the end of the conversation. But when he reached the door, he paused long enough for me to ask one more question.

"And what about your conscience? Do the details keep you up at night?"

Angelo sighed heavily, but didn't turn back to face me as he answered. "Some more than others," he said, heading back to the kitchen to order dinner.

CHAPTER 20

Angelo

After a lazy day at home, we wound up spending most of the night making love again. We talked off and on throughout the day, and Lina would seem totally fine… but then she'd ask a question that would leave me wondering if she really was okay. It had to be a lot, learning that the guy you were forced into marrying was actually a murderer. She was probably handling it better than most would.

I felt terrible leaving her alone the next day, but I had no choice. I had some work that I couldn't possibly delegate. The best I could do was make it fast.

Lina pouted the second I crawled out of bed to get ready.

"I'm sorry," I said, for what had to be the hundredth time. "If anyone else could cover for me, I'd skip. I'll only be gone an hour. Two max."

"It's okay. I think I'll take a bath while you're gone. I have a book I've been meaning to read anyway."

"You read in the bath?"

She nodded as if that were the most obvious thing in the world.

I combed my hair, trimmed my beard, then started dressing right as Lina emerged from bed, rubbing her eyes. She stretched, then smiled.

"I can wait to leave until after you get naked," I offered.

That made her giggle.

"I'll even grab a drink and your book for you."

"I could probably get those things myself while you finish getting ready," she said.

"Any chance you'll still be naked when I get home?" I asked.

Her grin widened. "Two hours? Kind of a stretch, but I could probably make that happen as long as the hot water heater is up to the task.."

I tucked my shirt into my pants and had just draped a black tie over my shoulders when the doorbell rang. Lina and I both eyed each other.

"You expecting anyone?" I asked.

She shook her head, then started to reach for a tee shirt.

"I'll get it. You stay naked. It's probably just Eddie," I said, even though he'd literally never been early and I was positive we'd agreed that I was driving.

I peered through the peephole, where an average looking man stood on our front porch. He wore khaki pants and a polo shirt but his posture and demeanor were anything but casual. This guy was stressed.

I pressed the intercom button connected to the front door camera. "Can I help you?"

The man looked around, seeming even more alarmed. "I'm here to see Catalina."

"She's not available right now," I said, already pulling out my phone to cancel on Eddie. This guy didn't look like the sort of man who'd run with Carlos and his crew, but I wasn't taking any chances with Lina. She couldn't be alone if shady men were coming to the door.

"It's really important I see her," he said, eying the camera. "Or, um, if I could talk to her on the phone? She doesn't have to come outside."

I lowered my phone, my interest now piqued. "What's your name?"

"I'm Dave Williams."

I blew out a sigh. Of course he was Dave. Only a moron with a hero complex would show up at my home after telling my wife I was a dangerous killer. I shoved the phone into my pocket and opened the front door, stepping onto the porch before closing the door firmly behind me. Dave stepped backwards, nearly stumbling down the steps leading to the porch.

"Angelo Conti," I said, offering my hand. "Nice to meet you."

Dave tentatively shook my hand.

"I've heard a lot about you, Dave. And it seems you've heard a lot about me, too," I said.

Dave opened his mouth to speak just as the door opened behind me. Catalina had thrown on my tee shirt and from the looks of things, nothing else. She looked mouthwatering. I gazed back at Dave and decided he had reached the same conclusion.

"Babe," I said, mouthing the word "pants."

She scowled and lifted the tee shirt, revealing tiny shorts.

Dave's face flushed.

"Is everything okay?" Lina asked.

"Yeah, I just, um, well I went to see you at the library yesterday and that other librarian, the one that always wears her hair in a bun—"

"Faye," Lina supplied.

Dave nodded. "Yes, she said your husband called and said you'd be out for a few days. I was worried that something might have happened to you."

"Well, as you can see, she's fine," I said.

"You should finish getting ready," Lina said, turning to me and staring pointedly.

"Excuse us," I said to Dave, tugging Lina back into the house.

"Angelo, I don't want to make you late, but I think it would benefit us both for me to talk with Dave and straighten out some things."

"I'm not leaving you alone with him. He obviously wants to sleep with you."

She didn't dispute that, but instead rose to her toes and kissed my cheek. "Go. I won't let him in the house so you can watch us from the camera on the front porch like a creeper the whole time if you want. Okay?"

I relented, then remembered one last detail. "I take back what I said about the naked time. Do not get naked until I'm back. Or at least wait until the boy scout leaves."

Lina laughed, then opened the front door. "Can you stay and chat for a few minutes?" she asked Dave. "I'm going to make some coffee then I'll be right back out."

I finished with my tie and opened the front door to head out. I stopped and kissed my wife like we were about to make a baby. Then, I smirked at Dave.

"Lovely to meet you," I lied, heading to my car.

Catalina

I tugged my shorts so they covered more of my thighs, then made my way outside with the coffee. Dave stood on the edge of the porch, awkwardly shuffling his feet back and forth.

When he saw me, he flashed a polite smile. "Thanks. You didn't need to make me coffee."

I set both mugs on the end table between the two glider chairs and motioned for him to sit. "You were kind to come check on me, so it's the least I could do." I watched as Angelo's SUV zipped out of the driveway . "As you can see though, I'm good."

"Are you though? You don't look sick. And it is a little strange that Angelo was the one that called your work."

"I wanted to ditch work but I was uneasy about lying. I've never played hooky before, if you can believe it."

"Yeah, I can believe that. You seem like a rule-follower," Dave said, sniffing his coffee before sipping it, almost as though checking for poison. "That's why I didn't expect to see you with a guy like Angelo."

I shrugged. "That's what I wanted to talk to you about. I asked him about Julia after you showed me the police notes. He told me it was the truth. It's a horrible tragedy, but Angelo didn't have any good choices there. I've heard the stories about his family and I'm sure you must hear even more in your line of work. But you also have to realize that not everything you hear is true."

Dave set down his mug and stared at me, but I kept going.

"I think you're a good guy, and I'm sorry I didn't tell you sooner about the marriage. But, as you can see, you don't need to worry."

"Would you tell me if he were hurting you?"

"He's not. And he never will. I am positive of that." I rose to my feet, signaling the end of the conversation.

"Ok, well, take care. I can give you my number in case you ever need anything," he offered.

I almost agreed, then shook my head. "You know where to find me." I meant the library, but of course now he knew where my house was too. That was odd. "How did you get my address by the way?"

"I've got lots of friends on the police force. So, I snooped. Sorry. I promise I'm not normally a stalker. Your absence just triggered an alarm in my brain after what I'd told you that day, and—"

Dave and I both turned as there was a massive crash near the back of the house.

"What was that?" I asked, as if he'd know.

He peered in a window. "It almost sounded like a window broke."

I cringed, agreeing with his assessment. "Shit." I flung open the front door and dashed towards the back of the house. I had expected to see a rogue baseball or maybe even a bird.

Instead, I nearly slammed into two vaguely familiar Hispanic thugs.

I skidded to a stop, panic washing over me.

"Carlos wanted a chat," the first one said, pressing a gun to my side.

I screamed, at a total loss for what to do. I swiveled my head, hoping to find a weapon or escape route, and to my relief, I saw Dave had followed me into the house.

A moment later, the relief dissipated as a third guy pointed a gun at Dave's back.

The terror in his eyes told me he'd be of no use in my escape.

The guys forced us both into an old Ford Taurus. I at least got to ride in the back, wedged between two of my captors. Dave was stuck in the trunk. Panic swirled through me as I tried to think of a plan. My arms were tied securely behind my back, and not just with a belt. Whatever they'd used felt like rope or something else rough, and it was already biting into my skin even when I didn't move. I couldn't see the knot and didn't think I had any chance of untying it. And the binding was definitely too tight to slip my arms over my head or around my legs.

After my solo shopping adventure on the honeymoon, I knew that Angelo could track my phone. Unfortunately, my phone was still at the house. And there were definitely cameras on the porch, but the guys had dragged us out the back. Would Angelo have been able to see anything, besides me—and Dave—walking alone into the house?

I swallowed the lump quickly forming in my throat at the realization that poor Angelo probably thought I'd invited Dave inside after promising we'd stay on the porch. Surely, he couldn't have heard the commotion we heard, not from the camera anyway.

I turned to my captors. They were speaking in Spanish, but not saying anything of importance. They were discussing some girl they'd seen at a bar and debating who would win the game tonight. I cringed as a fresh wave of stale sweat wafted towards me from the guy to my left. As I shifted closer to my right, I gazed up at the driver. He had short, black hair and pudgy cheeks that made him look much younger than he was. I vaguely remembered Carlos calling him Baby Face, but that wasn't his name. I squeezed my eyes shut and concentrated.

Suddenly, it hit me.

"Martinez!" I called, leaning forward in my seat, trying to act casual. That wasn't his first name, but we'd always just referred to him by his surname. "How's your sister?" She'd just had a baby the last time I'd seen him. I couldn't remember if it was a boy or a girl though.

I saw his eyes narrow in the rearview mirror, and wondered if he was annoyed I recognized him, or annoyed I asked about his family. I thought that was what you were supposed to do though, humanize yourself, so your captors don't want to hurt you. I needed to remind these guys that I knew them. We used to be friends. Maybe we still were in their minds.

I shuddered at the thought.

"Still fat," he finally said. The guys sandwiching me in both laughed, jostling me as their oversized bodies shook.

"Hey now, didn't she just have a baby? Give her a break. I mean, what's your excuse?"

That last part was obviously a risk, but the guys all hooted a big "ohhhhh" like I'd really insulted him, even though they were clearly way more overweight.

"Are you a good uncle?" I pressed.

He hesitated. "I don't know. I'm not a baby person."

"I could give you some tips. I used to babysit all the time."

Before he could answer, his phone rang. He answered instantly, telling me it was Carlos. I could only hear one side of the conversation, but I translated it all as he went.

"Yeah man, we got her, but..." he paused, then sounded stressed when he continued. "No, she's fine, but it turns out she wasn't alone. He was still there. I don't know who we saw leaving earlier."

There was another pause, this one even shorter. "No, of course we didn't leave him. He's in the trunk. I thought you could decide what to do with him." Martinez rubbed his forehead. "Yeah, we searched them both. No phones, no weapons." He glanced out the window as if checking our location. I gazed up and did the same.

"We're ten minutes out," he said. He disconnected a minute later.

I chewed the inside of my lip, trying not to panic. I didn't recognize the area we were in, but I remembered Angelo saying he'd done some research on Carlos and where his gang operated out of, so hopefully Angelo knew. Well, and hopefully he could figure out that was who'd taken me. He was a smart guy, so surely he'd know that, right?

I exhaled slowly through my nose. I wished my heart would stop racing. My body's physical signs of panic were making it really hard for me to keep my brain calm and I needed to try to concentrate.

It sounded like the guys thought Dave was my husband. At least that had to be a good sign. They wouldn't be expecting anyone else to come rescue me if they thought they'd already nabbed Angelo. Of course, Dave would surely tell them his real identity from the start.

Before I could brainstorm any further, Martinez tossed a black bandana over the seat. "Blindfold her," he said.

I felt the tears welling in my eyes before the fabric even touched my face.

CHAPTER 21

Angelo

Every bone in my body ached when leaving Lina. Knowing that tool, Dave, was with her maybe should have made it better, but it didn't. And then I just felt like an asshole for being jealous when my primary concern should've been protecting her. So yeah, I was distracted and a jerk by the time I met up with Rico and Eddie.

I resisted the urge to check the cameras every five minutes. I didn't need to spy on Lina and Dave. I trusted her. Besides, the more I focused on work, the sooner I could get home. I stuck to my word and finished right around the two hour mark. I pulled in the driveway already picturing the sight of her glorious body partially submerged in a bubble bath, perfectly ripe for ravishing. I parked in the garage and went straight to the bathroom, not even slipping out of my shoes until I reached our bedroom.

The bedroom and bathroom, however, were empty.

Deflated, I sighed. Lina's phone sat on the edge of the bathtub, right where she'd placed it before I left for work, but the tub looked dry, almost as if she'd never started her bath. Surely she wasn't still on the porch with Dave? I made a beeline to the front door and peered out, finding two cups of coffee on the small table, but no Lina and no Dave.

"Lina?" I called, shutting the door behind me.

I pulled up the camera on my phone, rewinding to the moment I left and watching the front door footage in fast-forward. Almost instantly, my stomach clenched. My car was barely out of the driveway before Lina scurried into the house, Dave hot on her heels.

Nausea washed over me and I slumped against the front door. Had I seriously missed all the signs? Nothing in her behavior had made me think she was even remotely interested in Dave. I rewatched the moment they entered the house again, and confirmed it. She led the way, not him. He hadn't forced her, for sure.

Fuck. I actually thought I was going to be sick.

What other explanation could there be?

I wallowed in my self-pity for a full minute before snapping out of it. What exactly did I think happened, that Lina brought Dave into our home and fucked him there? That didn't sound like her. And if she was still here, why hadn't she answered? Were they hiding? Had they already finished their tryst and now she was simply trying to hide the evidence? That would explain why her phone was still in the bathroom.

I swiveled and peered out the front, realizing I hadn't thought to confirm his car was gone. Usually, I was hyper-aware of such details. Today though, I'd been so focused on getting home to Lina that it hadn't even occurred to me to note the presence of any cars in front of the house.

I wrinkled my nose. Dave's Honda Civic hadn't moved from its spot directly in front of my nextdoor neighbor's house. For a professor, the guy sure wasn't very smart. Did he seriously expect to get away with an affair, being this obvious?

I blew out a sigh and started towards the guest room. "Lina? Dave? Come out, come out, wherever you are."

I barely made it ten steps when I stopped dead in my tracks. Broken glass dusted the floor around the back door. My heart clutched in my chest as I lunged forward, confirming someone had broken in. I swore, calling out Lina's name again as I pulled up the camera footage, this time for the back door cameras.

Nausea swirled in my belly as I watched two Latino guys bust through my back door. A moment later, two more popped into view. Less than two minutes after that, the first guys rushed out of the house, carrying Lina. The coppery taste of blood filled my mouth as I watched them shove her into the back seat of a beige, mid-2010s Ford Taurus with a dented front left bumper. One of the men had his arm over her mouth, so I couldn't tell if it was taped shut, but her eyes were uncovered at least. I thought her arms were tied, but I couldn't be sure.

A minute later, the other two guys emerged with Dave. They chucked him into the truck with such callousness that I couldn't be sure he was still alive.

I swore again, then dialed Eddie and Rico. I grabbed an extra gun and my best knife while catching them up on everything I knew. Then, hopped into my car.

Without Lina's phone or purse on her, I couldn't track her location. But thanks to our research on Carlos, I had a few good guesses of where they might have taken her.

I couldn't see the plates on the car, but the description matched one that had been parked at a warehouse about a half hour away on the day Rico had followed Carlos and taken photos. That was where I was headed. Eddie would meet me there, too, along with a couple other guys he'd call. Rico would check out another possible spot with a few of our other guys.

I drove as fast as I could, determined not to think about what I'd do if Lina wasn't at the address when I arrived. Or worse yet, if she was there, but those scumbags had already done something to her.

Catalina

My terror rose through the roof the second everything went black. I tried to focus more on my other senses, but there was nothing distinct to hear or smell, and I certainly couldn't touch or taste anything. I planned to resist exiting the car, but the guys lifted me out like I was a doll. I screamed, more as a reflexive response to being hoisted high in the air with no ability to see where I was headed than as a planned move to attract attention for potential rescue. Still, it was probably the smartest thing I'd done all day.

A sharp sting of pain spread across my cheek as the back of a hand slapped me, abruptly stopping my screams.

"Damn it, Perez. He said don't touch her," a voice snapped through gritted teeth.

Perez, I repeated in my mind, both memorizing it for later and trying to determine if it rang a bell. A moment later, my butt landed on a hard slab of wood.

A chair. I started to shift, but my hands were yanked back, and I felt the rope being secured to the back of the chair with some additional binding. My heart raced. Somehow, I was even more helpless now than before.

Thinking fast, I said, "Untie me please. I need to use the bathroom."

My words echoed, leading me to think I must be inside a huge room. At first, there was no answer, but a moment later, I heard a familiar chuckle. My stomach churned and bile rose into my throat.

"Carlos," I whispered.

"Si, mamacita. What's up?"

I felt his hands stroke the side of my face then run through my hair. An involuntary shudder rolled through my body.

"I see the hair grew back," he cooed.

I didn't reply. I couldn't bring myself to speak when he was so close that I could feel the warmth of his rancid breath.

"What, no saucy comeback for once?" he asked.

I clenched my abs, garnering all of my inner strength. "I can't exactly return the compliment when I can't even see you," I said, my voice sounding slightly less shaky than it felt.

A moment later, he yanked the bandana off my eyes, ripping a few hairs with it. I blinked to adjust to the light and tried to take in as much of my surroundings as possible without fully taking my gaze off Carlos. For the most part, he looked the same as I remembered. He had boyish features and could easily pass for someone nearly a decade younger, especially when he was relaxed. He kept his thin, black hair trimmed short, and was usually generally clean-shaven. Today, I noticed some stubble.

"Thank you," I mumbled. "Can you untie my hands? This rope burns."

Carlos made a face as if he were considering my request, but then he shook his head. "Naa, you're scrappy. I don't need to mess with that." He turned to Martinez, who stood behind him. "This kitty has claws," he joked.

The mention of a kitten reminded me of Angelo. I squeezed my eyes shut, desperate to hold back the tears. I was unsuccessful, a fact which clearly amused Carlos. He'd always been a sadist.

He wiped his finger under my eye, grinning. "Tears of joy over the reunion?"

I turned my head to the side, taking in the surroundings. We appeared to be in an abandoned warehouse. A couple of armchairs sat in one corner, arranged around a TV. Several folding tables filled other parts of the warehouse. Stacks of bagged items covered the tables, but from where I sat, I couldn't identify the contents of the bags.

Carlos roughly shoved my face back to face him. "Eyes on me, mamacita."

I exhaled a shaky breath. "What do you even want with me Carlos? You could find someone way better than me, don't you think?"

He narrowed his eyes as if considering it.

"You know I'm married now, right?"

At that, he leaned back in his chair, kicking his feet in front of them and crossing them at the ankles. "So I hear. Tell me more about tu marido."

I kept strong. "I think you know all about him."

"What makes you think that?"

"You're a smart guy," I replied. I actually believed that. Carlos was also cruel, greedy, and narcissistic. But Carlos was no fool.

"Angelo Conti. Heir to the famed Connecticut branch of the Italian mafia. How'd you meet him?"

"Tinder," I said, keeping a blissfully straight face.

Carlos's laughter burst out of him so hard that spit landed on my cheek. He shook his head and grinned. "That's good. See, that right there is why I don't think I can find someone better. Well, or at least why I don't want to."

I shrugged. "Well, I'm married, so…"

Carlos leaned forward again, his new proximity sending prickles up my spine. "You know the thing with marriage though, that part about till death do us part?"

I tried to swallow the lump in my throat.

"I feel like the whole marriage is null and void once one party's dead," he continued.

"Carlos—"

He held up his hand, abruptly turning his head to the side like a dog who just heard some noise in the neighbor's yard.

He turned back to me a minute later and sighed. "I think my

next appointment arrived early. If you'll excuse me, I'll be back as soon as I can," he said.

Carlos tossed the bandana to Martinez. "Cover her eyes again just in case. And if she makes even a peep, tape her mouth shut."

I sucked in a breath, but stayed completely quiet. The idea of having anything covering my mouth terrified me even more than losing my vision again. I just needed to stay calm. This extra time was a blessing. Now I had time to think of a way out of this mess.

Angelo

I beat Eddie to the address he'd sent me. I stopped about two hundred yards away, but still easily spotted the Ford Taurus in front.

"It's here," I said, my voice sounding more like a growl.

"Damn it, Angelo, do not go in. Sit tight. Do a lap. I'll be there in…five minutes," Eddie promised.

I debated killing the engine, and therein also ending our call. I couldn't just sit here and do nothing while some monster tormented Lina. My Lina.

"Angelo, listen to me," Eddie continued through the speaker as if he could read my thoughts. "If you rush in there solo and fuck up the rescue, they still have Lina. If you wait three and a half more minutes, Antonio, Vinny and I will be there. Rico and Georgio have already turned around to come meet us too. Right now, Vinny is texting the other guys for backup. We can handle whatever is inside that warehouse, but only if you wait another three minutes."

I blew out a sigh. "I won't go in, but I'm going closer. I drove in from the back and didn't see any guys there. I can't tell from here if anyone is inside the car, and there might be someone in front. I'll look in a window and text how many inside."

"Angelo—" Eddie said, but I switched the car off, ended the call, and shoved the phone into my back pocket. I grabbed my SIG Sauer from the locked glove box and kept it securely in my hand even though I already had a Glock at my hip and another at my ankle. I'd never been a Boy Scout, but I sure liked to be prepared.

I tugged a ski mask over my face and shut the door to the SUV without latching it, therein avoiding making any noise. Then I jogged to the back of the building, constantly surveying my surroundings as I moved. I stopped at the furthest window of the warehouse, but was not surprised to find it painted black. The thing with shady people was that they tended to not make it easy for passersby to observe their criminal operations. I'd hoped we wouldn't have to go in blind, but it wasn't looking good.

Worse yet, there appeared to be a security camera ahead. I suspected we wouldn't find any cameras out front, since those gangsters had presumably just carried my wife from their car into the warehouse, but we'd need to double check later. I tapped out a quick text to Eddie, then returned to my car, right as he and Antonio pulled in with Vinny right behind him. They jumped out of their vehicles and we all approached the building.

Within a moment, we could see at least one man in front of the building. His back was to us, and he appeared to be smoking a cigarette. Antonio turned to me, silently seeking permission. I knew exactly what he was asking, and why. As the best shooter amongst us, Antonio could take this guy out with one shot. But if he did that, we'd have no chance of getting information from him about Lina's whereabouts if she wasn't inside this warehouse. And we might alert the other guys to our presence.

It was a risk we had to take. I was confident Lina was here. I could almost feel her presence. Besides, I'd seen them put her in that very car.

I nodded to Antonio, then held my breath. The rest of us froze while he crept closer. For an instant, I thought he might make it all the way to the guy, enabling a direct contact shot, which would be much quieter. But then the guy turned when Antonio was about fifteen feet away. Antonio fired a single shot, and the guy hit the ground.

Unfortunately, despite what the movies suggest, silencers don't make gunshots completely silent, so we no longer had the advantage of sneaking up undetected. I called Rico, who answered on the first ring, right as another guy ran out of the building, only to be shot by Antonio.

"Take out the camera in the front, then go in that way," I told Rico, shoving the phone back into my pocket then jogging towards the entrance with Eddie. Vinny had checked that the main compartment of the Taurus was empty, but just then, I heard a thumping coming from the trunk.

For the briefest of moments, I let myself hope that it was Lina, even though I'd seen them chuck Dave in there. I jogged to the car while Antonio and Vinny covered me, then held my breath as I swung open the trunk.

A wide-eyed Dave peered up at the barrel of my gun. I sighed and took a step back, lowering my mask for a moment. The guy started to move, and I shook my head, then shushed him.

"Do you know where they took Lina?" I asked, my voice barely a whisper.

"No, I couldn't—"

"Shh!"

He shut up.

I debated leaving him in the trunk, and honestly, that was probably the safest place for him, but I didn't want him to slow me down later, after I got Lina. I waved my SIG in the direction of my car. "Get in the black SUV, but don't make a peep and don't touch a thing. I'm going to get Lina."

The moron looked like he had questions, but I silenced him with a single glare, then hoisted him out of the trunk. His arms were tied behind his back, but I didn't think I had time to mess with the ropes while we stood there. I needed to go find Lina.

CHAPTER 22

Catalina

I'd been blindfolded and ignored for at least an hour, but had come up with exactly zero good escape ideas in that time. For the last fifteen minutes, I'd eavesdropped on Carlos chatting with one of his friends about some business crap. They were discussing whatever his meeting was about, but they had so many codewords for everything that I couldn't quite tell what they were selling or when. My best guess was drugs, but I couldn't be sure.

How had I been so oblivious to all this when Carlos and I had been dating? I'd known he wasn't a Dean's List goody-two shoes type of guy, but I'd truly never realized his friends and him were actually a gang. Or that his vague jobs were actually drug deals and gun heists. Although, given that I was currently tied up in an abandoned warehouse, I probably wasn't the smartest.

I decided to reiterate my request to use the bathroom. That still seemed like my best bet for possible escape plus, well, at this point I really did have to pee. And now that I could hear Carlos's voice and knew he was at least nearby, I figured he was more likely to be the one to help me to the bathroom. Not that I was eager to have Carlos see me pee, but it was less disturbing to think about than some random dude helping with my shorts.

But just as I garnered the confidence to say something, I heard what I could've sworn was a gunshot. My heart thudded erratically, and just as I was about to reassure myself that I'd misheard, there were two more. And a frenzy of activity inside the warehouse.

I couldn't help it. I screamed. I screamed so loud that my ears burned and my throat stung. A moment later, clammy hands covered my mouth.

"I warned you, mamacita," Carlos said. "Now we'll have to tape that pretty mouth shut."

Without even thinking, I chomped down on his fingers as hard as I could, only letting go when his free hand struck the side of my face so hard that my chair tilted to its side then froze mid-air. The ear he'd slapped was ringing and I could already feel my eyelid and cheekbone swelling.

I didn't want my mouth taped, but I'd already pissed him off. I had nothing to lose at this point. Well, except my life. I screamed again, only stopping this time because I heard another gunshot. This one was closer, and a second after I heard the blast, my chair toppled the rest of the way to the floor. With my arms tied, I had no way to brace myself against the fall. My elbow hit, then my head crashed into the concrete, bouncing twice before settling against the cold surface.

✦

Angelo

*T*he last thirty-seconds had passed in a blur, and now time seemed to freeze as I surveyed the scene in front of me. Eddie had signaled for me to wait, to let him and the others bust in first. But then I heard Lina scream, and the first thing I saw when I'd spotted her was that creep, Carlos, hitting her.

He'd tied her to a chair and blindfolded her, and now he was slapping her so hard that he knocked her chair onto its side. My stomach had lurched, and I rushed forward without thinking.

I killed him with two clean shots, much better than he deserved, in my opinion. I kicked him out of the way and crouched down by Lina and cradled her head in my hands, dropping my gun to the side. Rico and Mike came up beside me a moment later. Rico shoved my gun in the back of his pants and checked Carlos's pulse with a gloved hand.

I delicately lifted the bandana off Lina's eyes, but she didn't open them.

I started to hyperventilate. She'd been fine a minute ago. I'd heard her scream. What had changed? Had I shot her?

I began frantically passing my hands over her body searching for invisible injuries, but there was no blood, aside from a cut on her face.

"Lina," I said. "Lina!"

"She hit her head," Mike said. "She'll be fine."

"You're not a doctor," I snapped. I didn't miss the look he and Rico exchanged then, but I didn't care. I reached for my knife and began cutting her arms free. By the time I'd sawed through two sections of the rope, I was able to slip Lina's wrists out of the bindings.

"It's clear. We took out a camera in the office, plus the one in the front. Didn't see any others. Georgio grabbed about two kilos of smack. It's time to go."

I didn't move, aside from smoothing Lina's damp hair off her forehead. My brain was struggling to process what he'd just said. "Wait, what? Two kilograms?"

"Yeah. So the cops will think this was a rival gang."

"Oh." That made more sense, as we weren't typically in the

business of selling heroin. Drugs were profitable, but also led to a lot more violence and territory wars than imports and exports or money laundering. If my brain had been fully functioning, I would've instructed my guys to clean up the scene so there was no trace of us, so I supposed I should be proud that they didn't actually need me to tell them what to do.

"Do you have her?" Eddie said, tapping his foot with annoyance.

I stood, then crouched down to pick up Lina. Mike grabbed the bandana and ropes, then carried the chair to the other side of the warehouse, hiding any sign that they'd ever had a hostage.

Rico had pulled the Yukon closer, so we didn't have far to walk. Still, my arms were shaking as I carried Lina out, not because of her weight—she was lighter than most of the stuff I carried at work—but just the stress of it all. I started to load her into the back seat when I heard a shout from the other direction.

I turned just as Georgio raised his gun towards Dave. The moron was jogging towards us, hollering something.

Fuck.

"Don't shoot," I said.

"Is she okay?" Dave asked, slowly as he neared us, bracing his hands on his knees and panting like he ran significantly further than a couple hundred yards.

"Get in the car," I said. I scooted in, leaving the door open for him, cradling Lina in my arms. I lightly kissed the bruising on her wrists and pressed my lips to her forehead, lingering and uttering a silent prayer of healing.

Dave scooted in beside us, and Rico took off before Dave had even shut the door.

"Who is that?" Georgio asked from the passenger seat, eying Dave like a piece of gum on his shoe.

"Some friend of Lina's," I said, in between kisses on each of Lina's knuckles. "Carlos took him, too."

"Did someone call 911 yet?" Dave asked. "I couldn't find a phone in your car, and then I got out and looked around and—"

"Now can I shoot him?" Georgio asked.

I ignored him and called Adrian. Adrian Patras was the one man in my trusted circle who was not even remotely Italian. He'd come into my life years ago, as my younger sister's boyfriend. For years, I'd hated him. But then, he'd become a lawyer, and he'd demonstrated his willingness to assist with matters of questionable legality when he needed the money. Most recently, he'd helped get the charges dropped after everything with Julia.

But now, I wasn't calling him because of his legal expertise. Now, I needed his connections. After my sister had dumped him for Luca, he'd eventually started dating a doctor named Melissa Adams. Dr. Adams had proved enormously helpful in treating the random injuries guys like me tended to incur in the line of work... injuries that we couldn't typically address in the emergency room. Melissa had also helped my sister with two different head injuries.

Adrian answered quickly, as I knew he would.

"Catalina hit her head. She's unconscious. I need Melissa to meet us at the hospital if she's not already there," I said.

Adrian cleared his throat. "Catalina, your—"

"Wife, yes," I supplied. He hadn't been at the wedding, but he had met Lina briefly at the family dinner.

"Right. I'll call Melissa, but um, depending on what happened and how she looks, you might want an alibi putting you somewhere far away. If your wife comes in looking like a domestic violence victim, they won't hesitate to lock you up and ask questions later."

I swore under my breath. I hadn't even thought of that, but yeah, Lina looked like someone had tied her up and beaten her. Of course the cops would want to blame me after they failed to get any charges to stick for Julia's death.

Adrian hung up before I could thank him. That's how well trained he was. Finally.

I would've felt bad, asking him to contact Melissa when I knew they'd broken up months before, but I was desperate. I didn't want some crappy intern looking at Lina's head.

"What's wrong with her head?" Dave asked. "Did those guys hurt her?"

I was about to answer in the affirmative when I realized that was a lie. Sure, Carlos had slapped her, but when I'd decided to shoot him, Lina was fine. She was conscious and screaming. Carlos had caught her chair and stopped it from toppling to the ground. *He* kept her safe from a serious head injury.

What caused her head to crash into the concrete was me. When I shot Carlos, he lost his grip on the chair and Lina fell. I was the reason she was unconscious. I hurt Lina, not Carlos.

"That didn't sound like the cops on the phone," Dave continued, undeterred by my silence. "We should really call them."

Georgio's sigh filled the SUV.

I was about to reply, when Lina's eyelids fluttered. Relief so intense flooded my body that I thought I might pass out.

"Lina, baby, oh thank God. Hey, can you hear me?" I leaned a little closer, but tried to give her space.

Dave also leaned forward, and I shoved him back against the seat, hard.

Lina blinked, then licked at her cracked lips. "Angelo? Is that you?"

"Yes, it's me. You're safe now, okay? I've got you. You hit your head. We are going to get you checked out."

Lina's lips curled into a smile. "You found me."

"Of course I found you."

"You said you'd keep me safe and you did."

"That's my job," I said, but I didn't exactly agree with her assessment. I promised to keep her safe, and then I let her get kidnapped, traumatized, and god-knows what else. Then, I gave her a concussion.

My phone rang. It was Melissa. I answered.

"Hey Angelo, it's Dr. Adams. I talked to Adrian, and he said you were headed to the hospital. I'm not on duty now, but—"

"My wife was unconscious. You have to see her," I snapped.

"Geez. If you'd stop interrupting, I was going to say I could meet you at your place. Is she awake now?"

"Yes."

Melissa paused. "Look, if you think she needs emergency care, you should take her to the ER, but depending on what happened, you might want me to check her out privately first. Only if she's stable of course, but if there are going to be questions…"

"Won't she need a CT or something?"

"Not necessarily."

"Giada did."

Melissa sighed. "Your sister needed a CT the last time she hit her head because she had recently suffered a severe head injury with brain bleed that led to amnesia. Most concussions don't need CTs."

I glanced at Lina. Her cheek and eye were swollen, and it didn't take a genius to know she'd been hit. Her wrists also displayed the clear signs of having been restrained.

"Yeah, okay, meet us at my house."

I turned back to Lina, focusing on keeping her awake and distracted. I kissed her forehead, smoothed her hair off her face, and whispered into her ear. I felt a hundred pounds lighter when we pulled in the driveway and I saw Melissa was already there, but Dave immediately started protesting.

"No, we need to go to a hospital. The cops will want to document all of her injuries for the police report, and—"

"Shut up," I said. "Let me get Lina inside and talk to the doctor and then I'll deal with you."

Eddie rushed over to our car and helped Lina out, then

handed her back to me to carry inside. I took her to our bedroom and started to lay her on the bed.

"I've had to pee for over an hour," she said.

I bit back a smile and helped her to the bathroom. She insisted I leave her alone once she was actually on the toilet, so I waited outside until I heard her washing her hands.

"I could've carried you to the sink!" I said.

"I'm fine to walk, Angelo. I'm not even dizzy."

She washed her hands, then walked to the bed, leaning back against the headboard. My eyes focused on the welts around her wrists and I winced, thinking of her positioned on this same bed, but with my belt restraining her hands.

I was no better than Carlos.

"I'm Dr. Adams, but you call me Melissa," Melissa said, crouching down beside Lina. "I'm just going to do a couple of tests to rule out any serious brain injury and figure out if you need a CT or anything. Then we can clean up some of these other wounds."

I took that as my cue to go. "I'll be right back, baby," I promised Lina, pressing a kiss to her forehead. Then I grabbed Dave by the shirt and dragged him to the kitchen. I motioned for him to sit at the table.

"Dave, none of us are calling the cops today, and I'd advise you do the same," I said, once I was sure we were out of earshot of Lina.

"Why? Those guys kidnapped your wife. If you don't care enough about her to report the crime, that's on you. But they kidnapped me, too. I was locked in a fucking trunk for hours. It was terrifying. I don't know what kind of shit you do for fun, but I'm not letting them get away with this."

Rico rolled his eyes and sat on the other side of Dave.

"No one got away with anything, Dave. There were five guys at that warehouse today."

"Six," Rico corrected.

I cringed at how out-of-it I'd been to not even notice that minor detail. "Okay, six. Four guys who kidnapped you, the one who ordered it, and his bodyguard."

"They all can go to prison. We have more than enough evidence. I know the system, and—"

"They're all dead." I said.

Dave opened and closed his mouth several times without saying anything. A myriad of expressions crossed his face over the course of the next minute. Finally, he said, "I don't understand."

"Lina's ex-boyfriend Carlos was involved in a drug cartel. He was a bit possessive, and that's why he sent some people to kidnap her. I don't think they planned on you being here, but I assume they either would've left you in that trunk until you suffocated or starved, or they would've killed you."

Dave's face flushed, even though he had to have realized this.

"I don't know what they'd planned for Lina, and I don't actually want to think about it. It doesn't matter though, because the second they hurt my wife, they signed their own death warrants. Your criminal justice system doesn't accomplish what you think it does. Guys like Carlos have connections. Even if he were behind bars, he could hurt Lina, especially if he thought she helped put him behind bars."

Dave didn't disagree with this, so I continued.

"Now, Carlos and everyone else who saw Lina at that warehouse today is dead. Me and my guys wore masks and gloves, so no one saw us at all. Even if they had, it doesn't matter, since we destroyed the cameras. As far as the police are concerned, no kidnapping ever occurred today. The only thing that happened today was that some lowlife drug dealers got jumped by rival gangsters and ended up dead."

"The police will investigate six dead men," Dave insisted.

"They won't. They'll see six known criminals in a ransacked warehouse full of drug residue. They may do a sham investigation, but the truth is, no one will give a shit about any of it, and you know it."

Dave swallowed audibly. "What's to stop me from calling the cops?"

Rico rolled his eyes, but I stayed calm.

"A few things. For starters, your conscience. I could've left you in that trunk to die, but I didn't. I also could've shot you and no one would've ever known it wasn't Carlos. But again, I didn't. You're welcome." I paused.

"Second, you claim to like Lina, and letting her move on from this traumatic experience without the messy aftermath of some extensive investigation is going to be much better for her mental health."

I took a long drag from my bottled water before finishing my list of reasons.

"And last but not least, if anyone calls the cops about today, they're also going to find camera footage of you outside the warehouse today."

"Because I was kidnapped and dragged there."

I nodded. "But that wouldn't really explain why the cops would find some of the missing heroin in your apartment, or the sudden influx of cash in your bank account, would it?"

Dave's mouth formed a straight line. "You're going to frame me."

"None of us are going to do anything, Dave. If you choose to take this to the cops and frame yourself, that's on you. And as for the money, well, I'm not in the drug business. I think we've got about a hundred and fifty thousand wholesale worth of heroin, so—"

"Two hundred," Rico interrupted.

I nodded, appreciating his knowledge of the current valuation. "So, your share of that is pretty sizeable."

"I don't want a share of drug money."

I raised my hands and shrugged. "Me neither, but here we are.

We couldn't just leave the drugs, and we don't deal that sort of thing, so we'll just divvy it up and move on."

Dave opened his mouth to keep talking, but I stood, seeing Melissa hovering in the hallway.

"I need to get back to my wife. Rico here can answer any other questions you have." I hurried over to Melissa, but she looked calm. "How is she?" I asked. "Do we need to go to the hospital?"

"I don't think so. Her vision is fine, she's tracking objects okay, and her pupils are normal. She'd got a headache, but no nausea or vomiting. You need to keep an eye on her for the next twenty-four hours though. Call me if her headache gets worse, or if she starts vomiting or having trouble speaking."

I nodded.

"She doesn't need stitches or anything on her face. Ice should help with the swelling, but it'll probably look worse before it looks better."

"What about her wrists?"

"They'll be fine. Maybe some ointment to keep them moisturized." Melissa sighed. "Look, Adrian mentioned that he didn't think it would be good for your wife to be seen at a hospital or anywhere really with any sort of injuries that might be construed as domestic violence, and—"

"I did not do that to her!" I snapped.

"Jesus, Angelo. Chill. I was only going to say that as a doctor, if I saw a patient like Lina, my first assumption would be that this was a domestic violence situation. So it is probably best to keep her home until her face heals. The wrists might take a little longer, but she can cover those with a long shirt."

I nodded. "Alright. Thanks." I handed Melissa a thick roll of cash, then walked her to the door. Rico had finished chatting with Dave, and they were all leaving too. Aside from the glass guy Eddie had called who was fixing the windows around the back door while my cousin supervised, Lina and I were alone.

I watched Dave scuffle to his car. If I'd seen him on the street, I would've described him as nerdy or weak. But he'd actually held his own today. Dave had proven he had balls just by showing up to my house in the first place, and then by not pissing himself when chucked in the trunk of a car by drug dealers. He'd kept up the bravery by challenging me and my guys when we insisted on not involving the cops.

I definitely didn't like the guy, but I did respect him. And I had to wonder if Lina would be better off with him.

I padded down the hallway, keeping my steps light in case Lina was napping, then paused just outside the room where I could watch her. Her eyes were closed and her chest rose and fell evenly.

Yeah, I'd told Melissa I hadn't done this to her, but that was a lie. The concussion was directly on me, and the rest was my fault to. I'd promised to keep Lina safe and now she was lying in bed, bruised and battered, all because I failed yet again.

Lucky for her, now that Carlos was out of the picture once and for all, Catalina didn't need to be shackled to me anymore. Our arrangement was over. She could be free, and I wouldn't have another chance to hurt her.

I tiptoed back to the kitchen and called Adrian. Maybe it was still close enough to the wedding for an annulment.

CHAPTER 23

Catalina

I hadn't meant to fall asleep, but Melissa had given me some medicine that knocked me out. She said it would help me relax or help with the pain or something, not render me comatose, but the sun was setting by the time I woke again. My throat was so dry I could barely swallow, my lips burned, and my head throbbed.

"Angelo," I croaked, assuming he was right next to me.

He didn't answer, so I rolled over, grimacing as pain radiated down my face. I peered around the room.

I was alone. There was a glass of water on the nightstand, so I pushed up to sit, then sipped the water. When I drained the full glass, I slowly stood. I wasn't dizzy, so I walked to the bathroom. I desperately needed a shower, but I wanted to see Angelo first. As soon as I opened the bathroom door, he was there.

His eyes were filled with alarm, but he simply reached for my arm, as if to help me.

"I woke up and you were gone."

"Melissa said to let you rest. I didn't want to wake you. Are you hungry? Eddie dropped off some food."

As if on cue, my stomach growled.

"Go back to bed. I'll bring it to you," he said, practically forcing me down.

I glanced around the room. "Is my phone—"

Angelo reached into his pocket and pulled it out, handing it to me. "Sorry, I forgot I had it. You had left it by the bathtub this morning."

I accepted it but kept looking at him. Something was off. He seemed different. Distant.

"I called your parents, gave them the gist of it all. They know you're okay and that Carlos is gone."

"Thank you," I said. I waited for him to say something else, or maybe just to lavish me with kisses, but instead he backed away.

"Let me get you food. I'll be right back."

I watched him leave, then turned to my phone. My parents had texted, saying they were glad I was okay and asking me to call in the next couple of days when I felt up to it. Other than that, I just had a handful of unremarkable emails.

Angelo returned a minute later with a steaming bowl of soup and a sandwich. I'd hoped he'd stay with me, but he insisted on leaving to get me napkins, then ice for my head, then more water. By the time Angelo finally sat beside me, I was done with the soup, and he scurried off to the kitchen with the bowl.

"Why do I feel like you're avoiding me?" I asked.

"I'm sorry," he said.

I took a couple bites of the sandwich, then registered that I was already full. I set it back on the plate and turned to Angelo. "I might want more in a little bit, but I'd really like a bath now."

"I'll fill the tub." He disappeared before I could say another word.

Slowly, I made my way into the bathroom. I stripped naked, wincing at the proliferation of bruises along the side of my body.

I hadn't felt all of those, but I supposed I'd been distracted by the more pressing injuries.

"It's from when the chair fell over," Angelo said, watching me in the mirror, his eyes filled with more pain than I'd ever seen.

I turned to him, realizing for the first time how hard today must have been for him. I reached to put my arms around him and he stiffened. "I'm sorry," I said. "I hadn't even thought about how awful today must have been for you."

Angelo pulled back. "You don't have to apologize for anything. All of this was my fault, not yours."

His tone was so harsh that I wasn't sure how to reply.

"Let me help you in, then I'll get you more to drink," he said, his voice softer now.

I accepted his hand, and stepped into the tub. Angelo helped me lower myself into the water, and I winced as the heat stung my various cuts. Angelo turned away, as if he couldn't even stand to look at me. Then, he left to get my water.

As I adjusted to the temperature, the water soothed my aches and my anxiety. I was glad to wash the day away. I supposed a shower would've been more effective, but I didn't think I had it in me to stand upright long enough to wash my hair.

"Please join me," I said to Angelo when he dropped off my drink.

His handsome features wrinkled into a frown. "I don't want to hurt you."

"You won't."

"Lina, no."

I sighed. "I don't want to be alone."

Angelo sat on the floor beside the tub.

"That's not what I mean. Look, I know you had a terrible day too, but I've never been kidnapped before. Or blindfolded. I thought I was going to die and it was really awful and I just feel so alone right now."

I didn't mean to start sobbing, but I did. I was bawling so hard that the water was sloshing around like with were waves in the sea. I was so focused on my rant about how miserable my day had been that I didn't even notice Angelo had stripped naked until he nudged me forward and climbed into the tub behind me, pulling me back against his chest and wrapping his arms and legs around me.

He didn't say anything, and he didn't need to. Completely enclosed in his embrace, I wasn't alone anymore. I was safe.

We stayed in the tub until the water began to cool. And then Angelo added more hot water and helped me wash my hair. I dried off and braided my hair, then finished the sandwich in bed. I fell asleep with Angelo's arms wrapped around me.

Angelo

I spent the night memorizing every detail about Lina, from her tantalizing sweet smell to the soft, even way she breathed. I noted how her eyelids fluttered when she dreamed, and I watched the tiny twitches of her arms every so often. I even tried to cement to memory the warmth of her skin against mine, and the weight of her body draped against mine.

At one point, she rolled over and her hair draped across my face. I started to reach up to scoot the strands out of my eyes, then stopped. Someday in the very near future, I'd miss the feeling of her wayward strands tickling my cheeks.

I didn't mean to fall asleep, but at some point, I did. And the second I woke up, I panicked. I'd wasted hours I could've spent staring at my sweet Lina. That was time I could never get back.

I waited until she woke to head to the kitchen, and then I busied myself making her a breakfast worthy of a four-star restaurant. I wanted nothing more than to spend the entire day in bed with Lina, but I couldn't. The more I let myself fall for her, the harder it would be to cut ties. I needed to do the right thing. Melissa told me to watch Lina for twenty-four hours, so that was what I'd do. And then, I'd get out of her life.

I'd heard back from Adrian, and he had good news. While the rules for annulling a marriage in Connecticut were limited, there was an exception allowing annulment when the marriage was performed by someone who lacked the legal authority to perform the wedding. Adrian thought we could argue that exception applied, since no one in the U.S. would really check the credentials of our Italian officiant. His only concern was that we lost the spousal privilege if we weren't married, but I didn't envision anyone asking Lina to testify against me, anyway.

So, that only left the matter of whether we annulled or divorced. To me, it didn't really matter how we characterized anything. My life without Lina would suck regardless of how we labeled the relationship, and I didn't plan on attempting future relationships. But for her, the distinction might be significant. An annulment would make it as though she'd never really been married, whereas a divorce was, well, a divorce.

I just needed to keep my distance until evening so I didn't lose my nerve to actually let her go.

I waited until mid-afternoon to tell Lina that I had to leave. I knew I couldn't tell her the whole story in person. I'd never be able to look in those gorgeous emerald eyes and tell her I didn't actually want to be with her.

Catalina

I woke up still wrapped in Angelo's arms, but then he was distant all morning. He claimed he needed to work, then insisted on cooking me a feast for lunch, even though

I was still stuffed from breakfast. And then after lunch, he said I needed to rest.

"I don't need to rest. I've done nothing but rest," I said. "I need to get out."

Angelo appeared to consider that, then nodded. "How would you feel about visiting your parents for a while?"

I wrinkled my nose.

"Sleepover with Kristi or Madison?"

My lips parted in surprise at that suggestion. "Are you trying to get rid of me?"

He angled his head to the side as if that were a ridiculous notion, then busied himself tidying the already-spotless room. "Of course not, but I don't want you to be bored, either. The threat is gone. There is no reason for you to be stuck hanging around the house anymore. You can go out with friends or do whatever you like. You're a free woman."

"Oh. Right." I smoothed a hand through my hair. How had I not yet realized that?

Neither of us spoke for a moment, and then I had a follow-up question.

"So, am I okay to take public transportation again, or Uber?"

"Yeah, whatever you want." He hesitated, then continued. "And actually the timing for that is good, because I have to leave town for some urgent business. I was hoping I could postpone in light of everything that happened, but it doesn't look like I can."

"Oh," was all I could muster. "You're leaving me?"

Angelo's expression was unreadable. "Business trip," he repeated.

"When? And how long?"

"Should only be a couple days. Three or four nights max," he said, answering my second question first. "And I'm supposed to fly out tonight."

"What? No." Instantly, my pulse skyrocketed. I started hyperventilating at the mere thought of being alone all night. "I can't be alone," I said.

Angelo swiveled to me, pulling my face against his chest. "Shh, okay, don't worry. You'll be fine. I can postpone if I have to, buuuuut…" he paused after drawing out the word. "That's why I suggested the sleepover. Or I could have one of the guys come stay at the house with you."

I stiffened at the thought of Eddie or Rico sleeping in the guestroom. I'd reached the point where I was comfortable with them driving me places, comfortable hanging out with them even. But I'd probably feel more secure alone in the house overnight than with one of them babysitting me.

"I'll check if Kristi or Madison is free. Don't change your trip on my account," I said, heading back to the bathroom where I'd left my phone. I paused by the mirror, grimacing at my reflection. My eye looked downright normal, but the swelling in my cheek and lip was still noticeable. Hmm. That could be an issue.

I returned to the kitchen. I expected to find Angelo still cleaning, but instead, he was simply bracing himself on wall, breathing heavily. I watched him for a moment before asking, "Is everything okay?"

He jumped, then flashed the fakest smile I'd ever seen. "Yes. Fine. Are they free?"

Okay, weird. "I didn't text yet. How would I explain my face? They'll assume you beat me up and that's why I want to get away for a couple of nights."

"Tell them I've been gone for a few nights already and you're going crazy. Say you decided to buy some used bookshelves online and that yesterday, you tried to carry them up the stairs on your own and fell. Figure out some way to show them the time-stamped photo you sent me the day before, when your face wasn't bruised, to prove that part of the story."

I listened to all of that in awe. He'd barely paused before talking, and then it all made perfect sense. My friends knew I liked to read and that sounded exactly like something I'd need to do. And the details about the timing, well, that was just enough to get them not to ask for more. "Did you come up with that right now?"

Angelo shrugged. "I'm best at thinking on my feet."

"Clearly." I returned to the bedroom and texted my friends.

"So bored," I wrote. "Angelo has been gone for 3 days and just told me he'll be gone at least another 2 nites, maybe 3. Can we do a sleepover?"

Kristi replied instantly. "I'm in! Your place?"

I winced. "We could, but I'd rather not. I miss him too much here. Plus he's kind of a neat freak."

"Bahahahaha," came her knowing reply.

"I can host," Madison said.

We busied ourselves discussing who would bring what, then I set down my phone to go tell Angelo my plans.

CHAPTER 24

Angelo

Kissing Lina goodbye was the hardest thing I'd ever done. I knew I'd been distant all day and worse yet, I knew she'd noticed. But my goodbye was sincere. I told her I'd miss her, and I meant it. I kissed her like I'd need that kiss to last me a while—and I did.

I garnered every ounce of my willpower to walk out to my Escalade and drive away from my perfect life. I didn't have any business out of town. I just needed to get away so I could end things in the easiest way possible.

I drove straight to the shipyard and worked until I felt like my eyes would bleed. Then I texted Lina goodnight. As soon as she replied, I went to Eddie's, drank myself into a stupor, and passed out. The next day, I slept in, then gave the hangover several hours to work its way out of my system.

I'd been watching Lina's location through the tracker on her phone, so when I saw she'd entered a movie theater, I knew this was my opportunity. I waited a half hour to be sure the movie had started, then called. As predicted, she'd silenced her phone and my call went to voice mail. I took a deep breath, then left my message.

As someone who basically lied for a living, this call shouldn't have been so hard for me. But it was.

"Lina, it's Angelo. I was hoping to talk to you in person, but I guess this might make it easier for both of us. I wanted to tell you that I spoke with Adrian, and we can have the marriage annulled. It'll be like it never happened. Since there's no more threat to you, there's no reason for us to stick together. You can go back to your old life."

I paused, feeling my voice waiver. "I don't know what the situation is with your old apartment, so I can give you enough money to cover the rent on a new place for the first year, and um, of course if there's anything else you need, don't hesitate to ask, but that's all I can think of. Uhh, okay, I better head back into my meeting."

I disconnected the call and rushed to the toilet, emptying my stomach contents.

Four hours later, when I still hadn't heard a peep from Lina, I decided my instincts were right. She was better off without me. And maybe she actually realized that. Meanwhile, I could only think of one thing that might help take the edge off the pain I felt over the prospect of life without her—mindless sex with someone else.

I was too ashamed to even go to one of the clubs my own family ran, so I went to the next best spot. Luca's. My brother-in-law's family owned a handful of nightclubs and a couple of them also employed the types of dancers who offered lap dances in private rooms. Sure, I could go to a bar and meet a woman to have sex with the old-fashioned way, but that was too much work. I needed to feel without thinking at all.

I paused by the bouncer, unsure if he recognized me. "Is Luca here tonight?" I asked.

"Who's asking?"

"His brother-in-law, Angelo." I waved at the security camera above our heads, then started to the door. "I'll wait for him by the bar."

I stepped inside, and the barrage of sounds, bright lights, and smells accosted me. Suddenly, I realized I couldn't do this. I didn't want another girl, and it wouldn't help anything anyway. I turned back towards the exit right as a voice called my name.

It wasn't Luca, but his best friend, his second-in-command, and the dude who lived with him and my sister, Alessio.

"Luca's in Italy," he said, staring at me as if I was a complete moron. Which, obviously I was since I'd forgotten that fact. "Is everything okay?"

To his credit, Alessio actually looked concerned. But Alessio and I were not family, and whatever loyalties he owed my sister by virtue of her marriage to Luca did not extend to me.

"Marriage problems," I finally said. "I thought the girls would be a good distraction, but I'm probably better off just going to bed."

Alessio snorted. "Bed is always the safer bet, but not always the most fun. Good luck, man."

I went back to Eddie's to sulk in peace.

Catalina

The sleepover with Kristi and Madison had been a blast. We'd danced around her kitchen, painted our nails, and applied moisturizing face masks. We binged on tacos, mixed our own margaritas, and nibbled on M&Ms till our bellies hurt. Mostly though, we gossiped.

As it turned out, they didn't even notice my black eye until after I told them about my clumsy fall. Neither of them seemed to suspect anything about Angelo or otherwise out of the ordinary about it. They did, however, notice the marks around my wrists. I'd made a point to wear a long-sleeved shirt that fully covered my wrists, but then I'd rolled up my sleeves when we were blending the second batch of margaritas.

Instead of just asking about the marks, Kristi had said, "What sort of kinky shit is your new man into?" Her question had made me think about the night with the belt, and I'd instantly blushed.

Once my friends saw my cheeks go beet red, they assumed those marks were from wild sex and not a kidnapping, and I was happy to keep the topic focused on the many, many talents Angelo had. I didn't blab every detail of our exploits, but I did make sure to tell my friends his ability to bring me to climax multiple times in a row. Honestly, I felt like I owed them that information. I would hate for them to settle for any man who couldn't do the same for them, so they needed to know it was absolutely possible.

The next morning, we'd all slept in and then headed out for brunch, followed by shopping, and then a matinee. Angelo had called shortly after the movie started. I'd ignored the call like any decent human, then excused myself to the bathroom a few minutes later. I was going to just return the call, but he'd left a voice mail.

Stupidly, I was beaming ear-to-ear while listening to his voice mail. A voice mail in which he, apparently, dumped me.

I had to listen to the damn message four times to even understand what he was saying. The cold, businesslike tone of his voice contrasted sharply with the message, the gist of which seemed to be that our marriage was over now that Carlos was dead. Actually, Angelo was saying our marriage never really happened.

And he, for one, didn't sound the slightest bit sad about that.

I rushed out of the theater.

I texted my friends that I had food poisoning and was heading home. I needed to be alone. I took a cab, then ignored the familiar prick of fear as I unlocked the door to the house and let myself inside. I walked from room to room, checking for any sign of burglars even though I knew the threat was gone. Then I turned the alarm back on, crawled under the covers, and cried.

When I regained the ability to stop crying long enough to breathe I thought about calling Angelo. Maybe I'd misunderstood. Maybe we could discuss it.

But I didn't really see how. Angelo had made his opinion clear. To him, our marriage had always been a business transaction. A simple arrangement where he protected me from Carlos. Now that Carlos was out of the picture, Angelo's duties were complete. He was free to return to his previously-scheduled, normal life.

Sure, I'd assumed I meant more to him, but why had I thought that? Well, two reasons. First, because Angelo was so protective, and second, because of the sex. Both reasons were ridiculous. Angelo protected me because that was his part of the bargain. And he had sex with me because he's a guy and I made him promise not to have sex with anyone else. Enjoying sex with me did not mean he viewed our relationship as a real marriage.

Angelo had never once told me he loved me. He hadn't said he was falling in love with me, that he couldn't live without me, that he wanted to be with me forever, or anything else of that nature. He had told me I was gorgeous, sexy, funny, smart, and kind. He was also very complimentary about my bedroom skills. Why had I read more into his words? Why hadn't I just accepted what he told me at face value?

I couldn't even be mad at him or leaving me now. The guy was basically a saint. He'd essentially solved all my problems, and he'd given me the best sex of my life in the meantime. And now, he was offering to pay my rent until I sorted my shit out and got my life back on track. He'd told me from the start that he couldn't handle a relationship. It was not his fucking fault I'd gone and fallen for him.

I was an idiot.

I cried myself to sleep.

When I woke, I had over a dozen texts and voice mails. A flicker of excitement zipped through me. Surely, one of those had to be from Angelo. I scrolled through them all then screamed into my pillow, finding they were all from Kristi, Madison, or, oddly enough...Dave.

Dave had texted a few times the day before too, and I'd just ignored him. The way I saw it, our business was done. Kristi and Madison deserved an answer, though.

"Still queasy," I wrote. "Never eating eggs again." Then, just because they'd offered to come take care of me, I added, "Angelo coming home early to play doctor."

Even the thought of him playing doctor made my heart ache.

I let myself cry for a solid hour, then debated my options. I could stay in bed and wallow the rest of the day. I didn't have to work until the following morning, and I was completely alone, both in the house and in life in general.

Or, I could bite the bullet and meet Dave for coffee like he wanted. Surely, meeting up with Dave would get him off my back. Maybe it would even distract me from my current shitty life.

Before I could change my mind, I texted him that I'd meet him in an hour.

Not surprisingly, he beat me to the café. I spotted him at a discrete table in the corner and waved, then proceeded to the counter and ordered my coffee without removing my sunglasses.

"Let's sit outside," I said once my drink was ready.

"I think it's raining," he replied.

I shook my head and started to the door. Clouds had completely blocked any trace of sun, but no precipitation was falling. I plopped down at a table and sipped my latte, glad I'd dragged myself out of the house.

"You don't have to wear the glasses around me," Dave said. "I know why your eye is all bruised. Actually, your face looks pretty good."

"Thanks." My eyelid didn't look bad, either, in terms of bruising from Carlos. But both eyes were bright red and puffy thanks to the excess of crying I'd done over the last day. "So you wanted to talk about what happened?"

"Well, I wanted to make sure you were okay. And that you were on board with this crazy plan about not calling the cops. I mean, no matter what Angelo and those other guys did, you and I were victims of a crime, pure and simple. We didn't do anything wrong."

I sipped my coffee, buying time to come up with a response. It occurred to me that Dave could be recording me, trying to trap me into saying something that backed up his story. I didn't want to risk doing anything that would complicate things for the Contis, but I also wanted to offer Dave the reassurance he clearly needed. Afterall, he was just a nice guy that got swept up in a really traumatic situation all because of me.

"I'm so sorry about everything that happened the other day," I finally said. "You should've never come over. You were kind to check on me and you don't deserve to get roped into my drama."

Dave frowned, but I continued.

"And I agree with everything Angelo said to you. I stand by him one hundred percent. If you have questions, you should go see him at his office."

A flicker of annoyance crossed his face, then recognition. He set his phone on the table between us. "I'm not recording this, Lina."

I shrugged. Lots of people had multiple phones.

Dave sighed, then looked around us as if searching for someone. "Did you really come alone? That's surprising. Where's Angelo?"

"Work," I said, my abs clenching at the mention of his name.

"I figured him for the overprotective type," Dave continued. "He just lets you wander town alone?"

"I wouldn't call him overprotective," I said, emphasizing the prefix. "He was protective because he knew my ex was a psychopath." I exhaled a shaky breath. "I'm not sure if you saw in the news, but the police found the bodies of some drug dealers in a warehouse across town. Apparently some rival gang members shot them and stole the heroin or something. Anyway, their leader, Carlos Ortiz, he was my ex-boyfriend. I was young and naïve when we were dating and had no clue he was selling drugs or in a gang. When we broke up, he became kind of a stalker. Angelo knew that and he went out of his way to try to keep me safe from Carlos."

"I did see the news about that. Looks like the police arrested some guys from another gang and might charge them with the murders." Dave's tone was pointed, but I wasn't taking the bait.

"Wow. That was fast. I'm not going to pretend I'm sad Carlos is gone, but it seems like a great thing if this also gets a bunch of other drug dealers off the streets."

"Even if they're innocent?"

"Is anyone ever innocent?" I replied, just as cold, fat raindrops began pelting the table.

Dave grabbed my elbow and led me into the café, where we ducked into a table at the far corner. I could barely see through the dark sunglasses, so I hesitantly took them off. At first, I kept my eyes down, staring at my coffee. But the second I peered up, Dave noticed.

"Are you sure you're okay? You look like you've been crying."

"I have. A lot."

"About your ex?"

I almost nodded, but then I realized he meant Carlos. I swallowed hard, already feeling more tears well up in my eyes. With how much I'd cried since hearing Angelo's voice mail, my eyes shouldn't have even been able to produce more moisture, and yet, somehow they were.

I bit the inside of my cheeks, but then my whole body felt hot from the effort of trying to hold in the tears. I gave up trying and instead covered my face with my hands. Dave gave me a moment, then offered me a couple of napkins. I blew my nose on one and used another to wipe my eyes, then offered a smile so fake that I probably looked insane.

"If you want the whole truth, I think Angelo and I are done."

"Done? With what?"

I barely resisted the urge to smack the confusion right off Dave's face. Why was he making me spell it out? "I think our marriage is over. He called me yesterday and left me a voice mail explaining that he thinks we should get our marriage annulled."

Dave looked even more confused at that. "Why would he want to do that?"

He must have seen the murderous look in my eyes, because he clarified his question.

"Didn't you guys just get married? What changed?"

I wasn't sure that question was any better. "Obviously he doesn't want to be married to me," I said, now crying so much that Dave had to dash to the counter to grab another stack of napkins. "Apparently he only married me as a favor to my dad so he could keep me safe from Carlos. Now that Carlos is dead, Angelo wants nothing to do with me."

Dave frowned and shook his head. "Huh?"

I decided to just spell it out for him. "None of it was real. Well, for Angelo anyway."

"But I saw you guys together. That morning I came over when you were wearing his shirt and it really seemed like you'd just… I mean, and you had a honeymoon, right? Like, you can't tell me you weren't sleeping together."

I cringed at the notion of Dave thinking about me and

Angelo. "What does that have to do with anything? You don't have to be married to someone to sleep with them."

He rolled his eyes. "Well, you're saying it's all fake and that's just not the case."

"There's no rule in Connecticut that you can't get an annulment if you've already consummated the marriage," I said, in case that was his point. I'd know, because I'd spent way too long looking into it all. Not that any of it mattered. If Angelo wanted an annulment or a divorce or whatever, I wasn't going to fight him. I wanted him to want me, not to be legally stuck with me.

"So you were crying about Angelo because you didn't think it was fake?"

I was tempted to chuck my coffee in his face. How had I never before noticed how dense Dave could be? "Yes. I knew my dad hoped Angelo would keep me safe from Carlos but..." all my breath whooshed out of me as I thought about all the hopes and dreams I'd entertained about Angelo the past two weeks.

"I actually wanted to spend the rest of my life with him. I was completely obsessed with Angelo and just too blind or stupid to realize he didn't feel the same way."

Dave wrinkled his nose and shook his head. "No."

"What do you mean, no? You don't get to tell me how I feel. If I want to cry in a coffee shop because I've lost the love of my life, I can do that. You don't get to tell me no!"

Several patrons turned and stared. Apparently, my volume had gotten a bit too loud. I sunk into my seat and buried my face into my coffee cup, downing the last half sip.

"That wasn't what I meant, Lina. I'm saying I don't think any of this makes sense. I saw how Angelo was with you. You can't tell me he doesn't love you. I've never seen someone look as miserable as he did when he saw your injuries. The man was crying. And he kept kissing you. Like, not your lips, but all the little bruises on your arms and hands. It was weirdly sweet."

Having been unconscious at the time, I hadn't known any of

that. But I wasn't sure it changed anything. "Well, he doesn't love me, so…"

"But what makes you think that?"

"Because he said he wants an annulment." *Duh.*

Dave shook his head. "No. He loves you. I've never seen a man more in love than Angelo is with you. I don't even know why I'm saying all of this because, well, I've had a thing for you since I first saw you at the library ages ago. You are the most beautiful woman I've ever seen and your laugh is my favorite sound and I feel like we'd be perfect together, but over the last week, I've finally realized that between Carlos and Angelo, I am absolutely not your type."

He paused for a sardonic laugh. "And when I came to your house the other day, I was worried Angelo had done something to you, but then as soon as I saw you guys together I could see I'd gotten it so wrong."

Dave rubbed his brow, then continued. "I still think you're probably better off without Angelo. No matter how much you say he's a good guy, we both know what he does and the harm that can lead to for you. But you can't tell me that man doesn't love you."

As Dave spoke, it hit me. Dave had figured it out.

Angelo thought I'd be better off without him. He was leaving me because he did love me, not because he didn't.

I flew to my feet so fast that my chair flipped backwards. Again, everyone turned and stared, but I didn't care. I had a mission. Dave stood and I gave him a huge bear hug.

"You are a genius. Thank you," I said. "Let's do this again sometime."

Dave opened his mouth to say something, but I was already rushing out of the café. I didn't think Angelo would take my calls, but I really needed to know when he would be back in town. I wanted to talk with him in person.

So, I called Eddie.

CHAPTER 25

Angelo

I was sifting through a stack of supply orders at a wooden desk in the construction trailer when Eddie bust in. His sheepish expression told me he'd fucked up, but my first guess was that he'd done something bad with the club, and not with my personal life. I sighed, downed a large swig of my coffee, then motioned for him to talk.

He eyed the other guys in the trailer, which really made me uneasy. If the fuckup was bad enough that we needed privacy, I was going to need a lot more caffeine.

"Christ, Eddie," I mumbled, deciding it was easier to follow him outside the trailer than to ask the other guys to leave. "What did you do?" I asked once we were alone outside.

"Lina called and—"

"Why would she call you?"

"If you'd let me talk, I'd tell you. I assume she didn't think you'd answer. Anyway, she said she had some emergency and really needed to talk to you in person ASAP. She wanted to know how soon you'd be back in town and if I could ask you to come by the house first thing."

"Shit. Is she okay?"

He shrugged. "She sounded fine, but…"

I reached in my pocket for my keys, then jogged back inside the trailer to grab them and the other items I'd left in my desk drawer. Eddie hurried after me as I rushed to my SUV.

"She thinks you're out of town. How are you going to explain it if you get there in twenty minutes?"

"Don't know, don't care," I said, slamming the door and starting the engine. I sped home, relieved to see everything looked intact as I arrived. Of course, the last time something horrific had happened to her, the front of the house had looked fine, too.

I unlocked the garage door, punched in the alarm code, then poked my head inside the house. The place was a mess. Multiple pairs of shoes, stray tissues, a pillow, a hoodie, and several socks littered the hallway. I couldn't tell if the house had been ransacked or if Lina just hadn't bothered to clean up.

"Lina?" I called, poking my head around the corner.

I heard a sharp gasp, and there she stood, staring at me open-mouthed. Her hair was damp, presumably from the rain we'd had earlier, and the emerald cardigan she wore that matched her eyes perfectly was buttoned all askew.

"I thought you were out of town," she said after a solid minute of us both staring at each other. "I was going to pick up before you came back."

I followed her gaze around the living room, which was even scarier than the hall by the garage had been.

"I…I…" I stammered. "Are you okay? Eddie said there was some emergency."

"I was going to make dinner too. Or breakfast or cookies or something, depending on when you'd be back," she said, apparently following my lead on completely ignoring the other person's questions. "I thought Eddie was going to call me back and tell me when you'd return, and then I had this whole plan and…"

I still wasn't sure what to say.

Lina glanced down at her outfit and then rubbed her face. "I was also going to shower and do my hair, but um, okay. Here goes."

"Wait, here what goes? Are you okay?"

"I'm fine."

"Is your head—"

"It's good. No headaches or anything."

"I could call Melissa," I offered.

"Angelo, I'm fine," she snapped.

Tension filled my body. "Lina, why am I here? You got my voice mail, right?"

She rolled her eyes and choked out a laugh. "Oh yeah, I got your message. Asshole."

That was fair.

"Can we sit down at least?"

I hesitated. "I'd rather stand."

"Suit yourself." Lina sunk onto the couch across the room.

"Lina, I have a lot of work and—"

"You can spare five minutes. You owe me at least that, Angelo."

Her sharp tone caught me off guard, but I supposed she was right. I nodded, and braced myself for the lecture I deserved.

"So, like I said, I got your voice mail. You know, the one where you said we should get our marriage annulled and just pretend none of this ever happened."

"That's not exactly what I said. An annulment is just—"

"I know what an annulment is. And I know originally the point of our arrangement was to protect me from Carlos," she interrupted.

I had to look away when she said that. I couldn't stand to see her sweet, innocent face and think about how I'd failed her on my part of the deal. Literally all I had to do was keep Lina safe from one man, and I'd failed miserably. She still bore the signs of my failure on her face, wrists, and all down the side of her body.

"I understand that under that original agreement, it would make sense to end everything once Carlos was out of the picture and you'd fulfilled your part of the bargain," Lina continued. "But you can't tell me nothing changed."

I turned back to her, not sure what she meant.

"Somewhere along the way, you and I became friends, and then lovers. And I know you're not going to stand there and deny we had amazing chemistry in bed."

Lina paused, but she was right. I wasn't about to deny that fact.

"I also think it's possible for two people to have amazing sex and not necessarily be soul mates or even really in love," she continued. "And maybe I didn't make this clear to you, but that was not the case for me. I get that our relationship was supposed to be fake, but my feelings for you were real. They still are. I—"

"Lina," I interrupted. "Don't make this harder than it has to be. I get what you're saying, but it doesn't matter."

She flew to her feet, thrusting her tiny frame right up in my face so fast that I actually stumbled backwards a step.

"You don't get to tell me that my feelings don't matter. And you will listen to every word I have to say."

God, she was so fucking sexy when she was assertive like this. My dick jerked to attention, but I just nodded and dropped my eyes to the floor.

"I fell in love with you Angelo. And I don't know why I never told you, except that I didn't realize I had a deadline. The thing is, I could've sworn you felt the same about me, too."

I opened my mouth to speak, but she cut me off with a sharp look and a raised hand.

"When I listened to your voice mail the first oh, twenty times,

I thought you were saying you wanted to end things because you didn't love me. But then, earlier today, I had coffee with Dave and he helped me see that—"

"You had coffee with Dave?" My heart raced with instant jealousy.

Lina gritted her teeth and glared. "I had coffee with Dave and he helped me see that you were actually trying to end things because you love me."

"Dave said that?"

"Dave said you love me. I believe his exact words were that he'd never before seen a man look so in love," she said.

I felt my eyes widen. I actually couldn't believe Dave would say that, even if he did think it. "I thought Dave was interested in you."

"He is. Or he was, anyway. I don't know. Not the point. The point is that *you* love me. You're only trying to dump me because you think I'm better off without you. You're still convinced everything with Julia was your fault and now you're blaming yourself for the stuff with Carlos. You think if we stay together, I'll get hurt."

I stood there for a moment, completely silent. Then I dropped to the couch. My brain kept telling my mouth to say something, but offered no ideas. She'd hit the nail on the head, but I couldn't even confirm as much.

Lina stared at me for a moment, then she continued. "When I first met Dave, he was in the self-help section, looking up books on bereavement. His fiancée had died in a car accident, months before that day. He's like, as upstanding of a citizen as you can possibly get, and the woman closest to him died, really young, and in a super tragic way."

I grimaced at the grotesquely irrelevant story, but still said nothing.

"And did you know Kristi has four older brothers?"

I shook my head.

"The oldest one was married for five or six years. He's a pastor. You know, like a man of God. Anyway, when his wife was pregnant with their second baby, she was diagnosed with some aggressive form of breast cancer. They couldn't do chemo or anything while she was pregnant, and she ended up dying before the kid's first birthday."

"That's terrible," I said.

She nodded. "So tragic. Do you see what my point is?"

I shook my head. I had no fucking clue why she was telling me all this depressing shit.

"Angelo, people die. Men lose their partners in really sad and tragic ways even when they have boring, law-abiding or even godly jobs like professor or pastor. Husbands can't protect their wives from everything. It isn't your responsibility to make sure I live forever."

I thrust my head into my hands, no longer okay with Lina's penetrating stare. She didn't seem to get it, that this was different.

Lina dropped to her knees in front of me and put her arms on my lap, denying me the space I so desperately needed.

I pushed back and turned my head. "Lina, it's not the same. My job was to keep you safe from Carlos. I can't even look at you without seeing how badly I failed."

Her fingers pressed into my cheek, forcing my face towards hers. "Angelo, the fact that I'm here, that you can look at me, means you didn't fail. I'm alive. I'm okay. Carlos is gone, and I'm not. I talked to my parents, I went out with friends. I met some weird dude for coffee. My life is going on, and that's all thanks to you. How do you not see that?"

I inhaled and exhaled slowly. "Did you know I was the one who shot and killed Carlos?" She was blindfolded, so she couldn't have possibly known.

"Okay, so you see? You saved me."

I shook my head. "No. Because you were fine when I came in.

Your chair had started to topple over and Carlos caught it. I was the one that made him drop the chair. I was the one that gave you the concussion and all those bruises. You don't need saving from Carlos. You need protection from me." I stood abruptly, and she fell backwards as if demonstrating my point. I'd barely made it one step away when she reached out and yanked me back by my arm.

"No! You're wrong. You will never hurt me, and we both know that. You didn't cause my concussion, because you didn't kidnap me or tie me to the chair. Nor were you the one who slapped me so hard that the chair nearly fell over. All of that was Carlos and we both know it, so stop blaming yourself. The only thing you could possibly do to hurt me is walking away from this, because that will kill me."

I turned back to Lina. Her eyes had been red when I'd arrived, but now they filled with fresh tears. I'd never seen her look so sad or so desperate, and it physically pained me.

"Look me in the eyes Angelo. Tell me you don't love me," she said, gripping my other hand too so that I was fully facing her.

I said nothing, as she knew I would.

"God, Angelo. I just want to be with you. I've never met anyone else that makes me feel the way you do. I'm so happy with you, and I don't even want to imagine a life that I can't spend with you. I love you."

Lina roped her arms around my waist and pressed her face into my chest, hugging me so hard I could barely breathe. Or, maybe that wasn't why I was struggling to breathe. I couldn't remember the last time I'd had a rush of emotions this over-powering.

I pressed a kiss to the top of her head. "I love you too, Lina," I finally said.

Her arms went limp, then she peered up at me. "What does that mean?" she asked.

I shook my head. "I don't know."

I waited for her to fill in the blanks for me, to spell it all out again so I didn't have to, but she'd already done way more than her fair share of the work. I took a deep breath, and bared my fucking soul.

"You're right. I'm scared that I'll hurt you or that you'll get hurt because of what I do and who I am, and I honestly don't know how to deal with any of that," I began, mesmerized by her wide eyes gazing up at me through thick, damp lashes. "But I'm miserable when I think about a life without you, too."

Lina smiled, and suddenly, her face felt way too far from mine. I lifted her into my arms, and she wrapped her legs around my waist.

"Say that first part again," she said.

"I love you?"

She nodded. "Yes, that part. But don't make it like a question."

I couldn't help but chuckle, but then gazing into the eyes of the most gorgeous woman I'd ever seen, I suddenly felt serious again. "I love you Catalina Lucia Alvarado Conti. I love your passion for books and your laughter and your feistiness. I love your dancing and your shower-singing and your freakishly cold feet. I love your compassion and your courage. I maybe even love your messiness."

"You do not love that."

I laughed. "I sort of think I do. I'm not saying I'm ever going to stop picking up all the crap you leave all over the house, but I like all the little reminders of you. I can't take two steps without thinking of you."

Lina smiled again, and I couldn't help myself any longer. I licked my lips, then hovered them just above hers. She closed the gap between us and our mouths crashed together in a beautiful reunion. I'd somehow forgotten how amazing it was to kiss Lina. Every swipe of her tongue sent shivers down my spine and the way our lips moved together was like a synchronized dance.

I debated carrying her to the bedroom but decided that was

too far. Instead, I carried her back to the couch, angling myself sideways off the couch so I could keep kissing her while undressing her. I paused after tugging off her leggings, looking to see if any bruises lingered on her leg.

"Oh shit, I haven't shaved," Lina said, her voice breathy.

"I don't care," I said, dragging my tongue along her leg despite her protest. When I reached the apex of her thighs, I lapped at her through her silk panties, then reached to remove the garment so I could continue.

Lina thrashed against me, reaching for my belt buckle. "No. Inside me, now."

I was about to argue, then decided against it. If there was one thing Lina had proven today, it was that she knew what she wanted and was prepared to fight for it. I was no match for this woman.

I unfastened my belt and lowered my pants to my thighs when Lina reached for me again. I yanked one pant leg down past the knee so I'd have a little more mobility then shifted over her, kissing her on the mouth before thrusting into her.

"Oh, God yes, Angelo," she whimpered as I filled her fully.

I bit back a groan. How had I forgotten how good she felt wrapped around my cock? How good she sounded, moaning my praises? I was a fool for ever trying to pretend that a connection this perfect could be only physical. We began to move together, and I knew neither of us would last very long.

I pressed a kiss to her forehead, then lowered my lips to her ear. "I love you, Lina. Now be a good little kitten and let me hear you purr." Her innermost muscles clamped down tight around me and I had never felt more at home.

Hours later, after four orgasms for her and three for me, we'd managed to finish undressing, shower, and move to the bed.

"I can tell you're itching to go pick up the house," Lina said, snuggling closer to my chest.

I laughed. I'd almost managed to forget about the clutter she'd somehow scattered throughout every room during my brief absence. "It can wait," I said. But then I reached for my phone. "There is something that maybe can't wait though."

I typed out a text to Adrian. "Forget about the annulment. Find something official showing Signore Albertini had all the qualifications he needed. I don't want anyone questioning anything ever. Make sure Lina is stuck with me for good."

I angled the phone towards Lina. "Anything I should add?" I asked her.

"Maybe just that you're a moron for ever thinking otherwise?"

I smiled. "If I say that, Adrian will assume I've been hacked," I replied, sending the message.

Lina sighed and settled against me. "Will you say it one more time?"

She'd been asking all evening, so I knew exactly what she wanted.

"I love you, baby," I said.

Lina smiled, then yawned.

"You need a nap."

"I know. I don't think I've slept since you went on your nonexistent business trip." She gazed up at me, her emerald eyes sparkling. "If I fall asleep, do you swear you'll still be here when I wake up?"

"I swear on my life Lina, I will never leave you again." I kissed her forehead, then watched as she peacefully drifted off to sleep.

The End

ACKNOWLEDGMENTS

When I began writing the Mafiosa Princess series, I hated Angelo. It was easy for me to write him off as the villain of Giada's early years. Even once I decided I'd write a few spin-offs, it never occurred to me that I'd write an entire book with Angelo as the hero.

But as I gradually pushed Giada and Luca outside the boxes where I'd initially placed them as characters, I realized that every character had room for growth. And if there is one universal truth for dark romance, it's that the farther a character has fallen, the more satisfying the ultimate redemption arc will be.

That said, I hope you enjoyed Angelo's story. Either way, I'd really appreciate if you could drop a quick review about this book on whatever platform you use to buy or review books.

Writing often looks like a solitary act, but in reality, it involves cooperation from so many people—editors, cover designers, proofreaders, beta readers, reviewers, librarians, and of course, readers like you. My books never feel real until they're out in the world, being consumed by you, my loyal readers. So thank you for choosing **Oath in Ashes** as your latest read. I know your TBR is probably packed!

ABOUT THE AUTHOR

Liza Malloy writes contemporary romance and women's fiction. She's a sucker for bad boys, dimples, and muscles, and she can't resist a man in uniform. Liza loves creating worlds where her heroine discovers her own strength and finds her Happily Ever After. When Liza isn't reading or writing torrid love stories, she's a practicing attorney. Her other passions include gummy bears, jelly beans, and the occasional marathon. She lives in the Midwest with her four daughters and her own Prince Charming.

Visit her website at https://authorlizamalloy.wixsite.com/lizamalloy

Join her email list at http://eepurl.com/gnuROD

ALSO BY LIZA MALLOY

Sixty Days for Love

For Love and Italian

Forbidden Ink

The Brothers' Band

The Brothers' Band: The Next Track

Hollywood Endings

Hollywood Beginnings

Supporting Roles

Legacy: The Awakening

Legacy: The Revelation

Legacy: The Reckoning

Mafiosa Princess

Mafiosa Princess: Sacrifice

Mafiosa Princess: Honor

Mafiosa Princess: Trust

Mafiosa Princess: Omertà

Mafiosa Princess: Loyalty

Mafiosa Princess: Faith

Mafiosa Princess: Family

Mafiosa Princess: Redemption

Mafiosa Princess Beginnings

Mafiosa Princess Becoming the Prince

Her Mafia Valentine (A Short Story)

Love All- A Steamy Sports Romance